Juan the landless

Juan the landless

by
JUAN GOYTISOLO

Translated from the Spanish by Helen R. Lane

A RICHARD SEAVER BOOK

THE VIKING PRESS   NEW YORK

Juan Sin Tierra
© 1975: Juan Goytisolo
© 1975: Editorial Seix Barral, S.A., Provenza, 219-Barcelona
English language translation Copyright © Viking Penguin Inc., 1977
All rights reserved

A Richard Seaver Book / The Viking Press
First published in 1977 by The Viking Press
625 Madison Avenue, New York, N.Y. 10022

Published simultaneously in Canada by
Penguin Books Canada Limited

Printed in the United States of America
Set in Linotype Times Roman

LIBRARY OF CONGRESS CATALOGING IN PUBLICATION DATA
Goytisolo, Juan.
    Juan the landless.
    Translation of Juan sin tierra.
    "A Richard Seaver book."
    I. Title.
PZ4.G722Ju   [PQ6613.079]   863'.6'4   76-55024
ISBN 0-670-41004-7

The face drew farther and farther away from the ass.

OCTAVIO PAZ, *Conjunctions and Disjunctions*

I'm completely dead to decency.

T. E. LAWRENCE, *Letters*

The word rather than the fact, guerrilla fighting rather than classic warfare, incantatory affirmation rather than objectivity, and in general, the sign rather than the thing.

JACQUES BERQUE, *Les Arabes*

I

According to Hindustani gurus, in the superior phase of meditation the human body, purged of its appetites and desires, abandons itself with delight to an ethereal existence, freed from passions and vices, attentive only to the gentle flow of a time without end, as light-winged as those soaring little birds of passage seemingly obeying only the soft and melodious inspiration of an invisible breeze and musically absorbed in remote contemplation of the sea: sensory stimuli and sensual excitations no longer have any effect on it, and immersed in the beneficent languor of an eternal present, it loftily disdains the absurd slavery of lustful pleasures, pure, svelte, airy, weightless, with the delicate fluidity of those clouds which at eventide enhance the majesty of autumnal landscapes, far from the world's feverish, frantic hustle and bustle: rising above the tyranny of petty contingency and hence offering to the devout admiration of the vulgar the solemn and tranquil demeanor of the ascetic purified by his acts of penitence and his fasts, the smiling indifference of the Brahman martyr face to face with the preparations being made for his own death, the serene composure of the fakir gracefully reclining on his bed of nails: but the body that observes you from the corner of the table, from the bright-colored jacket of the hi-fi record, appears to be proclaiming violently, in a shriek almost, that never, absolutely never, will it attain, even in the improbable case that this might have been a deliberate goal that it had set itself, to the superior phase of transcendental meditation, the austere but ineffable pleasures of the beatific contemplative life: neither an anchorite nor a fakir nor a Brahman: merely a body: an extension of matter in space: an offspring of the earth, to earth forever united: instead of a tight, neat line, a carefully confined surface, a lissome slenderness, the provocative ostentation of curves and roundnesses, a plethora of flesh, baroque splendor, an opulent and fruitful, bountiful, fertile body, solidly rooted in the inferior world thanks to a pair of feet which, though left out of the artistic composition of the portrait, give one every reason to believe that they are the equal of the rest in grandeur, prodigality, and excess: naked feet, doubtless, seeking the direct, symbiotic contact that draws forth from the primordial substance the life-force, the powers of generation: for a rich sap nourishes this body and sustains it, generously helps it to thrive, invents fabulous convexities: the confining edge of the low-cut neckline can scarcely contain them and favors a vast unfurling of waves which, although concealed beneath the velvety suppleness of the fabric, nonetheless prove appetizing to the eyes of the judicious spectator: roiled, towering surfaces which, from the imposing chin line downward, descend with windmill-like fury to the frontal apotheosis: a double crest, a supreme sea swell that the fearful Antillean hurricane has catapulted to the dizzying heights of an incredible prominence: the fatal wave rising in awesome splendor moments before crashing down upon the disaster area and sweeping away with wrathful precision the habitations, chattel, towns, industries, crops of an area teeming with life, transforming it, in the wink of an eye, into a dreary and desolate quagmire, abandoned to the moans of the victims, the barking of dogs, the hovering of vultures, sacking by looters and the starving, and the eager though tardy zeal of well-intentioned international charity organizations: but the wave does not in fact advance toward the shore and break, and the photographer's snapshot calms it, arrests it, immobilizes it: the Maginot line of the corset suggests, rather, the hypothesis of two hills, oval in shape and with a swollen surface, the salient point of which maintains itself in improbable, precarious balance: cordilleras, water courses, ridges, passes, hills, gorges?: no, geometry will express it better: circles, disks, spheres, globes that invite the study and observation, the discriminating speculations of the expert land surveyor who dreams of possessing for himself all the splendor and grandeur of the spectacular hemicycle: and the wicked creature knows it and hence smiles arrogantly, with full, round, voracious parted lips: simultaneously stretching out her enormous arms with the rather impudent gesture of someone urging the stranger to penetrate the arcana of the earthly paradise: the carefully fingerwaved hair, the broad, smooth forehead, the bushy eyebrows, the wide flat nose, the large gleaming-white teeth, the agile pink tongue, the shiny dark skin: two gilt pendants dangle from her ear lobes and seem to tinkle softly as she joyously dances a rumba, frantically waggling her hips, exactly as advertised in the bilingual caption written across the record jacket: THE QUEEN OF RHYTHM, LA REINA DEL RITMO: a real body, doubtless, that respects no other law save that of sovereign enjoyment: haughtily indifferent to the experiences of self-liberation and meditation: a resolute partisan of a very precise hic et nunc: a here and now located below the folds and undulations of the printed cloth which she flourishes and lifts in the air amid a whirlwind of laughter, making it clear to anybody and everybody that she, the fat girl, aspires only to give pleasure and receive it, since life is delicious and ought to be drained to the last drop, without prudery or theories, with a crude but clear awareness that there is no other reality save the one which a person sees, savors, and touches, and that "there is no such thing as sweet tamarind or a virgin mulatto": her cyclopean bulk stands out against the blurred buildings of a sugar plantation, and turning away, in order to walk around behind her, you will venture into the plantation yard: the faded, tobacco-colored photographs that presided over the conclave of phantoms of your childhood are not at hand to guide your footsteps and probably they still adorn the walls of the old mansion, in the country whose name you do not care to remember: the moorings having been cut, the root having dried up, there is little material to aid your memory: scattered over the table, the plank that covers the brass basin of the sink, the shelves of a rickety, ridiculous open filing cabinet, the Seeco records of the explosive fat girl lend a fiery touch of color that relegates to the background the remaining supernumeraries of your memory: the paperback volume with a greenish cover that contains an explanatory numbered diagram illustrating the various parts of a typical sugar evaporator: the photocopy of a terrifying "Explanation of Christian Doctrine Suited to the Mental Capacities of Newly Imported Slaves": a few images, in short, of that time, not so long ago yet now forever dead and erased from history, in which rebellion let its hair grow long and shook, with a hurricane of hopes, the stunted existence of millions upon millions of human beings condemned for centuries to the ideological servitude consubstantial with your native tongue, dazzling all of you with the spectacle of its wild and violent beauty, before the age-old predisposition of the breed to suppress the living liberty of today in the name of the imaginary liberty of tomorrow subjected creative invention to the imperatives of production, sacrificed the country to the growing of sugar, and again crushed its sons like cane in the sugar mill, returning the Semper-Fidel Island to its detested and sempiternal status of one great sugar plantation: no other object in the room can guide your footsteps along the arduous path of your return to the gene, to the sin of your origin with which they have burdened you: and lost in the vast expanses of the plantation yard, with your back turned to the fat rumba dancer, you will again be obliged to call upon the intermittent, almost moribund flash of the long-ago snapshots as you glide along, like a shadow, past the cane mill and the drying shed, the storehouses and the purging room: following the sinuous meanders of memory, searching for the slave shacks on the plantation: long before your aborted birth, just a little more than a century ago, invisible and omnipresent now, but still prepared to become incarnate, and freed from the stigma of the color of your skin, to begin the cycle all over again

take a good look at them: you will find that you recognize their faces: the plantation boss has called them together in front of the master's mansion and the tolling of the bell summons the wretched stragglers coming in from the cane fields to a privileged, direct witnessing of the portentous occasion: the tropical sun beats down on their heads and they shield themselves from it as best they can, with colored handkerchiefs and crudely woven palm hats: standing in a group apart, the females fan themselves with feminine gestures, eternal coquettes despite the dust, the filth, and their threadbare work clothes: the black straw bosses and foot guards keep watch in the background with their whips and their dogs and the household slaves finish tidying up the dais decorated with tapestries and rugs, where in all probability, when the hour has struck, the pure and virtuous family will take its place: you will interrupt your train of thought for a few seconds in order to sketch in the décor: sofas, rocking chairs, hammocks, a grand piano for the girl with musical talent, pots of ferns, baskets of fruit, bouquets of flowers: the portrait in an oval frame of some imperious great-grandfather will preside over the festive occasion, a little mulatto with angel's wings will chase the flies away with a palm-leaf fan: the remaining details of the scene figure in the period-piece descriptions of novelists of the era such as Cecilia Valdés, and the insistent peal of the bell will free you of the obligation of dwelling at length upon them: a tray with refreshments, an exquisite book of poems, a Beethoven score, a bottle of West Indian rum?: the careful mounting of the scene by the stage director will focus the attention of the unworthy worthy spectators on the double empty throne, which, mounted on a damascened pedestal and protected from the sun by a graceful canopy, also obviously awaits the sovereign presence, which, like the monstrance amid the gold of the tabernacle, will immediately confer upon it its very reason for being and crown it with the august power of its radiant, magic splendor: a liturgical symbol that by its mere existence overpowers and fulminates, enslaves and awes: while serving at the same time as solace and relaxation for pontifical and regal buttocks, being fitted out in this case with a little satin cushion whose exquisite embroidery hides from the eyes of the suffering masses the secret of a double circular cavity, beneath which, shielded by the sides of the canopied throne, there awaits in respectful but impatient expectation the sublime and sublimatory artifact, the toilet bowl, the beloved son of puritan concealment, the dernier cri of the mighty English industrial revolution: purposely situated in such a way that the virtual occupants may contemplate, from the apogee and plenitude of their glory, the modest common sewer ditch, which, located within the compass of their visual powers though not their olfactory ones, stands ready to receive the bountiful contributions of some twenty individuals of both sexes especially chosen by the clever, foresighted, diligent plantation boss: lined up at intervals of precisely three feet, thus conforming to the standards of a rigid military discipline, offering as they squat in view of the fraternal assembly those round, jovial bodily parts which certain naturalist photographers were wont to capture on film for the enjoyment and the delectation of connoisseurs, in the act of rivaling, in a festive group, the rubicund, chubby cheeks of Aeolus: skillfully playing their varied panoply of wind instruments: flutes and fifes, flageolets, oboes, clarinets, saxophones: obediently following the conductor's baton of the anonymous taker of the snapshot with the expert conciseness of musicians interpreting an overture as the ladies heave sighs of admiration in the proscenium boxes and a devotee of the art of bel canto follows the score from his orchestra seat, lighting himself, with the prideful parsimony of a firefly, with a minuscule pocket flashlight: but the picture on the postcard, despite all its lyrical effusion, only partially expresses the effect of the scene that you are attempting to depict: the obscure but harmonious succession of blessed, yea thousand times blessed, behinds that contemplate you and the humble and resigned masses, as though seeking to photograph all of you while at the same time making fun of you in the same way in which you are all making fun of them, with the sudden spasm of someone who bursts into a roar of laughter and thus dissipates his prolonged tension in a brief and violent discharge: the mockery is mutual, and once the demonstration is over and done with, and the offering deposited, the joyful donors will proceed to eliminate the consequences of their impulsive euphoria with the simple gesture of someone passing his hand across his face in order to wipe away the traces of a smile: with a pail serving as a wash basin: beneath the reproachful gaze of the family, which will meanwhile have occupied the dais: great-grandfather Agustín and his spouse, the young master, the girls, a group of poor but respectable relatives, the house slaves, a fluttering swarm of nursemaids: young mistress Adelaida plays the violin and, with theatrical hyperbole, young master Jorge pounds on the piano in a fit of inspiration, young mistress Fermina goes over her French lesson, the chaplain recites his matins, the little mulatto boy tirelessly chases away the flies, totally absorbed in his role of an exquisite cherub: the plantation boss drinks rum distilled from sugar cane and will crack his whip above the heads of the blacks, for the demonstration is about to begin: the technicians of the company that has patented the invention endeavor to conceal their nervousness beneath a polished veneer of British unflappability, and holding each other's hands with all the pomp of monarchs about to be crowned, the great-grandfather and his spouse will ascend the steps leading to the throne amid a religious silence: the former dressed in white from head to foot, with a double-breasted suitcoat, a gold watch chain, and a lighted Havana cigar: the latter, looking exactly like the faded portrait that kept watch over your faltering childhood, steps down the long hallway of the gloomy mansion: or better still: dressed in the ceremonial uniform of the Virgin Patroness of the Peninsula on the occasion of accepting the ritual homage of the Captain General attendant upon the celebration of the Día de la Raza: a crown of diamonds, a sky-blue mantle bordered in ermine, and the royal scepter, which she aggressively clutches in her hand as though someone were endeavoring to wrest it from her grasp and she were trying to demonstrate to the world her bellicose, well-nigh vulgar will to maintain possession of it: with the haughty frown of that other illustrious sovereign who forever crushed stubborn heretical sects and vowed not to change her undergarments until the infidels ceased to profane with their presence the sacred soil of the fatherland: standing, solemn and hieratic, at the side of the imposing master of the plantation: enveloped, like him, in the cloud of delicate incense that seems to issue forth from the tip of his cigar: heady and pure, fragrant as balsam: in carefully contrived harmony intended to enhance the joint effort required for the demonstration: the immaterial, invisible, odorless, perfect emission which, thanks to the back slit of the trousers ingeniously contrived by the clever family tailor, falls straight down through the double cavity into the central repository, the deposit box, as immaculate and aseptic as that of a bank: and thus concealed from the envious gaze of those who must content themselves with shifting about, by the sweat of their brows, the golden coins stored therein, without ever thereby laying up treasure for themselves or enriching themselves: desurplusvalued darkies of the common open sewer, in direct contact with the raw material, the vile apotheosis, the visceral emanation of the plebs: the English technicians bustle about the invention, endeavoring to divine, by way of the tension or the signs of relief of the protagonists, the success or the failure of the prophylactic operation: fathers of the creature, when all is said and done, they will swiftly stride back and forth across the dais, with their delicate hands behind their backs and their foreheads beneath their red hair creased in worried frowns: anxious to reach the end of the test: awaiting the verdict of the physician who is performing the difficult and painful caesarian in the next room: as the plantation darkies hold their breath and the chaplain prays and the horde of house servants falls silent and stands rooted to the spot: the suspense portends a grandiose event, and little by little the great-grandmother will cease to frown and will nod her head in approval: with the ineffable happiness of one who sees her efforts crowned with success and feels her heart swell with tenderness at the sweetness of the recompense: she will then exchange a glance of affectionate complicity with her spouse, pull on the chain hidden to one side of the dais, and closing her eyes in mystical ecstasy, will murmur in a half whisper I have shat like a queen

and though no one will catch the mistress's words, a thousand fantastic rumors will immediately make the rounds of the sugar plantation and the darkies will continue to be uneasy and perplexed, scrutinizing in vain the movement of her lips, unable to understand, because of their intelligence of savages and their scant knowledge of technology and theology, the jubilation of those who have fathered the creature, the new steam engine, the glorious flush toilet, who are dancing for joy, throwing sweets to the children and congratulating each other with effusive embraces as the great-grandfather celebrates in silence this clear and luminous triumph of the sublimatory occultist technology that further separates the animal from the human, the slave from the sucrocrat, and hastening to show himself equal to the occasion by virtue of the sacrosanct powers conferred upon him by his holy office, the salaried chaplain of the plantation falls to his knees, intones the verses of the Magnificat, and with his eyes brimming with tears, joyously proclaims to the four winds that Rome has already pronounced judgment, and taking into account the number and quality of the proofs offered in evidence, the event which they have just witnessed must be considered (beyond the shadow of a doubt, with any contrary opinion to be regarded as a sign of heresy falling under the jurisdiction of ecclesiastical tribunals, followed by the surrender of the condemned criminal to the civil authorities for execution) to be an authentic and positive miracle

a miracle, yes, a miracle: or perhaps you shit-kicking, shit-eating niggers believe that the Son of God and the White Virgin and the saints and blessed in Heaven defecated during their life on earth in stinking open sewer ditches and wiped their abominable asshole eye with leaves and corncobs?: the idea would be ridiculous were it not also blasphemous: for just as the Eye of God radiates light and snow-white purity, so the bestial anus, the eye of the devil, emanates infection and fetor, filth and sin: their respective functions are absolutely exclusive and diametrically opposed: so the angelic Saint Thomas Aquinas tells us: what is corrupted in part is corruptible in toto, and such an eventuality would be regarded as odious, sacrilegious, even by the most stubborn heretics: this is clear, and indeed self-evident: neither the Redeemer nor the Virgin expelled fecal matter: should there be proponents of such a monstrous untruth, they would be incapable of advancing a single proof in its favor: it would be futile for them to search through the Gospels, the Acts of the Apostles, the texts of the Church Fathers: simple human reason tells us that visceral eliminations, be they solid or liquid, not to mention all the other corporeal eliminations such as hairs, sweat, fingernail parings, secretions of mucus, would necessarily partake, should they have actually existed, of the divine nature of the Son or the supernatural and privileged nature of the Mother, and thus endowed with an immutable and imperishable essence, they would have been lovingly preserved by pious souls as precious sacred relics: but since such relics have not been preserved and we find no mention whatsoever of them in the books of the Bible or in the Church Fathers or in the works of the saints, we must conclude, consensu omnium, nemine discrepante, that they never existed and that the Redeemer and the Virgin were not subject to the animal needs that afflict men and oblige them to squat down in shame in the act of returning to the earth, in such a base and filthy form, that which they have received from it in the form of savory morsels of food and refined, tonic, mellow drinks: for it is here that the evacuatory hypothesis manifests itself in all its malicious absurdity: it is common knowledge that there is one respect in which animals and humans are patently inferior to plants and trees: the fact that the superfluities of these latter are pleasurable and delightful whereas those of bipeds and quadrupeds are nauseating and abominable, and if those of plants and trees attract us and satisfy us with the aroma and savor of their fruits, tell me: who besides the devil would find the sordid and horrible product of animal and human entrails pleasing?: this is the quid of the subject: and who will dare argue that the Redeemer and the Virgin compare unfavorably to vegetable species?: a three-year-old child would indignantly reject such errant nonsense!: it is plain to see that one of you little smart-asses is going to ask me: didn't the Redeemer and the Virgin eat?: the Gospels teach us the contrary: so tell us then, father: what became of the food they consumed if they didn't evacuate it?: ah, ye of little faith!: that is precisely what I was leading up to: if the metabolism of the vegetable kingdom is different from that of animals and humans, what's so strange about the fact that the metabolism of the Son of God and his sublime Mother is also different?: while the eye of the devil secretes corruption and impurity, that of the Lord exhales fragrance and harmony: it suffices to compare the volume and form of your behinds with those of sacred statues and images to be aware at the very first glance of their differing function: in the one case, the tight, light, ethereal line of a delightfully superfluous, exquisitely ornamental organ: in the other, the insolent, brazen curve that proclaims its vile relationship with obscene matter: ah, if only one could see the gentle, smiling, pearly Eye that the Virgin conceals beneath her heaven-blue mantle covered with gold and precious jewels!: only the blessed enjoy such a privilege and the Godhead itself is recreated in its graceful beauty: the most ecstatic phrases of the mystics would be incapable of accurately describing such a miracle of perfection: a second, a brief fraction of a second would permit you to appreciate the difference: the abyss that separates its Delight from your wretchedness: the salacious anus, the black sewer into which you dump your manure, your ordure, your stinking turds: the demon expresses himself through it, and that is why you remain mired in the filth of defecation and shamelessly give yourselves over to the vice of sodomy: but not everyone is like that: fortunately there are still classes: and the Lord, in His infinite wisdom, has ordained that terrestrial creatures shall rise above the animal condition and its impure secretions, in accordance with and in proportion to their merits: some with their filthy and abominable eye gaping open above the miasmas of the public sewer: others, purifying themselves little by little in a neat, secluded toilet: until they attain the ideal state of the saints and the blessed in Paradise, whose residues, Saint Bernard tells us, are transformed into a sweet, refined liquid, like unto myrrh and frankincense and the essence of musk: God, through his Divine Mediatrix, elevates His creatures step by step to the fragrant superior state, and today, rewarding the services of this holy and devout family that gives food and shelter to countless slaves, He has permitted it to rise one step higher on the steep stairway that leads from stench to perfume, from quadruped to angel, and has proved it in the eyes of the world by means of a simple and edifying miracle: the act of expelling, with neither sound nor fury, in a noble and aseptic manner: like myself, you are witnesses of the fact: let us bless the name of the Lord and give thanks unto Him!

what sort of music is played in the Heavens?: Bach, Handel, Mozart, Beethoven?: sonatas, lieder, operas, symphonies?: the information at our disposal is scanty and quite unreliable, though the frolicsome and mischievous air about the cherubim reproduced in the colored illustrations of the devotional books of your childhood nourishes the suspicion, and, indeed, almost the certainty, of a certain inclination toward, perhaps even a weakness for, Italian music: those light, rather catchy tunes destined to suggest, on televised news programs, the dizzying cadence of a championship bicycle race: when the chorus and orchestra attack the execution of the theme with brio, following the lead of the first violin: modulating arpeggios and trills, tremolos and staccatos that also send the audience in the theatrical paradise into rapture: the top balcony of La Scala, the apogee of the musical theogony!: unless, with that obscure military vocation that impels them to seek out men in uniform as their companions and partners, some famous female warrior dressed in armor or the wife of the admiral of the flagship of the Spanish Armada insists on a popular potpourri of jotas and zarzuelas: but there is nothing to support such a supposition and you must confess your total ignorance: Rossini, a nineteenth-century composer of Spanish operettas, or Brahms: what's the difference?: in any event the Deo Gratias that the chaplain will intone will be a brief and jubilant antiphony: pleasing, doubtless, to the ear of the Creator: but incapable of stirring the heart of the explosive fat girl, ready to launch her attack from the garish jacket of the record: thrusting her immense, cetacean bust forward anxiously, quivering like a bowlful of jelly: a rival of that other camp divinity roaring like a wild beast as she lay draped across the solemn black expanses of a grand piano: crying out for the tasty fruit for which the father of us all was driven out of paradise: the eternal bright, shiny apple inviting one to sink one's teeth into its deceitful rosy blush: or better still the banana: the tropical pineapple: the suggestive pear: greedily parting her enormous lips: secreting saliva like Pavlov's dog: crying out for all of it: until she suddenly explodes like a terrifying volcano: torrents of lava, conflagrations, fumaroles: interminable howls of Aetnean orgasm that the orchestra prolongs with delirious intensity: and the example will spread with sibylline logic: without waiting for the Latin verses of the antiphony, the blacks wind colored handkerchiefs around their necks and waists and dance the rumba and the shuffle, motioning to the females to join them with fluttering palms, their thumbs resting on the bulging flies of their trousers, as though making fun of the women: the slave girls also rise to their feet, shaking and waggling their private parts and their behinds, and the plantation yard will turn into a dance floor, decorated as for a midsummer-night fiesta: she, the fat girl, stretches out her powerful arms, taking the plantation hands beneath her extraordinary guardianship, and thereupon the family and the household servants will desert the dais with the piano, the furniture, the throne, and the watercloset: the chaplain will begin to speak

we have taken the females away from you in order to guard you against the opportunity to commit sin and incidentally to increase your productivity, and with stubborn perversity, you have persisted in vice: your wickedness is too deeply rooted and doubtless is irremediable: nonetheless, how beautiful a spectacle it would have been to see innocent lily-white souls beneath the modest disguise of a dark and unworthy skin!: all of you hard-working and chaste, indifferent to indolent pleasures, with your minds resolutely turned toward God and the sublime sacrifice of His Son: for the good shepherd sees everything and supervises your behavior with the attentive zeal of a plantation boss: the Mistress of Heaven would have encouraged you with her prayers, and her overseers and household servants would celebrate your meekness and piety, your precious treasures of humility, resignation, and tenderness: though black, you had the possibility of being honest and upright: and in order to aid you in fulfilling your goals, we put bolts and padlocks on the females' shacks: precisely in order that they not incite you to fornicate, with the weakness common to women of their breed: endeavoring to ensure that you would not live with them in sinful carnal cohabitation that will condemn you to the eternal fires of hell: but your perfidious nature has contrived to escape our anxious concern, our care, our diligent efforts in your behalf: and behind our backs you have continued to procreate impudent and despicable offspring, of dark quality and tainted origins: without stopping to consider that being with child is a form of robbing the master, and never thinking of the expenses involved in looking after you hordes of blacks: the poor man, continually burdened with your problems!: and then you complain because Don Agustín isn't happy: how do you expect him to be if you behave the way you do?: committing one sin after another: because any place suits you: in the cane fields, alongside the cane mill, in the gullies, behind the dump: I know, people have told me: sticking your black cigars out of your pants, pointing them at the black girls the minute we turn our backs: and they show off what they've got too: they pretend to be urinating, they part their legs like compasses, they show you their privates!: but the other Plantation Boss is watching from on High, and even though he's gentle and kind, eventually he gets angry: it's not enough that you offend his sight with your dirty color, your flat noses, and your thick blubber lips: on top of that you blacken your souls with horrendous sins: the Father is lying in his hammock, in the manor house up in the Sky, and wants to know what the blacks on the plantation are doing, and he asks the White Virgin: what's happening with those blacks in Lequeitio, over by Cruces, the slaves of the Mendiola y Montalvo Company?: are they behaving themselves?: are they obedient?: are they fulfilling their quotas?: are they making amends for their faults through work?: and the Mistress, poor thing, what does she see?: precisely what you're doing this very moment: looking at the female that's spreading her legs and defecating, the black girl that's urinating with her buttocks in the air!: and you've undone your buttons too, and are proudly brandishing your sooty devil's cigars: and she sees how you're playing with them and stroking them and doing all sorts of dirty things: and the Father, lying there in the hammock, lights his Havana cigar and keeps on asking questions: are they respectful?: are they submissive?: are they humble?: are they good?: do they say their prayers every day?: do they offer examples of purity and virtue?: are they faithfully following the sacred precepts?: the White Virgin pretends not to hear and changes the subject: young Adelaida is playing the violin, she says: a waltz that's very popular right now: master Jorge is looking through his telescopes: Don Agustín is going over his account books: because she's watching you, and if she tells the Master what you're really doing, he'll fly into a demoniacal rage: because even though it's after dark and the bell has rung for rest and repose in your shacks, she sees you when you steal over to the warehouse and join the black girls and let them touch your devil's cigars: young Fermina is reciting a marvelous poem by Alphonse de Lamartine!, the Virgin says: one that begins Pourquoi gémis-tu sans cesse, ô mon âme?: the Master on High fans himself beneath the mosquito netting and takes a sip of West Indian rum, but he goes on thinking about you, the blacks of Lequeitio: have they cut the cane stalks for crushing?: have they cleaned the cane mill?: are they taking good care of the sugar boilers and the evaporating pans?: one question after the other, forgetting nothing: who is stirring the boiling vats?: who is keeping the fires going?: who is carrying the sugar molds to the crystallizing tables?: who is taking away the bagasse and spreading it out?: and the White Virgin silently weeps and covers her face with her hands because it is pitch dark now in Cruces and instead of sleeping and recovering your strength for the good of your souls and bodies, you are indulging in all sorts of orgies and Witches' Sabbaths: and the happy Father continues to ply her with questions: tell me, daughter, are those darkies reciting the Pater Noster, the Ave Maria, the Credo, the Articles of Faith, and the Works of Mercy?: do they know that slavery is a gift from Heaven and that idleness risks leading them into sin?: young Fermina is reciting J'ai cherché le Dieu que j'adore partout où l'instinct m'a conduit, the White Virgin says: Don Agustín is going over the weekly plantation accounts: young Cecilia is doing the sweetest embroidery!: the poor little thing would like to help you, to tell the Master of the Sugar Plantation on High that despite the fact that you are black, you sincerely try to be good: but what can she do?: the Boss Son is also watching and noting all your faults down in the Book: although the night is black as ink, you won't be able to blend with it completely: your sweat, your moans, and that slightly acrid smell that you give off betray you: what biting, what panting, what hugging, what squeezing, what moaning with pleasure!: not even beasts of the jungle or wild mountain animals are that wanton: they at least do not sin: they are absolute brutes lacking a soul, but you have one: weak, abject, and sick, but, when all is said and done, redeemable: and that is why you work from sunup to sundown: to save it: and instead of progressing and bettering your breed you crawl backward like crabs: the Virgin would like to close her eyes and cover her ears because the Master has now gotten up out of the hammock and is sharpening the edge of his Collins machete, and if he appears on the terrace and sees you, he will descend like a lightning bolt to punish you: so she pretends that her mind is on other things and repeats the verses from Lamartine and hums the waltz that young Adelaida has been playing: because what she sees in the warehouse would frighten the devil himself: it is not even normal copulation, the act of generation pardoned by canon law: the propagation of the species is a noble aim, even when the end product is miserable, wretched, dark offspring: what is happening in there cries out for Heaven's vengeance: you are savage rascals, possessed of a decadent nature and contra natura usantes!: you force the black girls to turn around, and seek out their hind parts, opening up corrupt tunnels in their infamous blackness: and even worse: demanding that they kneel down in front of you, thrusting your burned cane stalk toward their blubber lips and sticking it inside: so that they may savor its sweetness and drain the last drop of molasses from it: don't try to tell me that isn't so because there are witnesses: eyes bulging, quivering from head to foot, possessed, taking your pleasure like animals!: and the females, oh, Lord, the females!: what wrigglings, what rubbings, what caresses, what bursts of laughter, what fondlings!

the chaplain appears to be on the point of suffocating: he grows red in the face, he sweats, he pants, he froths at the mouth with rage: the description of the abominable vices of the warehouse brings to his lips a florid Latin phraseology destined to cast a thin veil of modesty, or perhaps a tenuous veneer of culture, over the crude and frightful reality of the acts committed: cunnilingus, fellatio, osculos ad mammas, coitus inter femora, immissio in anum!: the expressions issue forth from his throat with evident difficulty, and in order to explain them, he accompanies them with convulsive, epileptic gestures, with frenetic wavings of his arms

you will divide the imaginary scene into two parts: or better put: into two opposed blocs of words: on the one hand nouns, adjectives, verbs that denote whiteness, clarity, virtue; on the other hand, a lexicon of shadows, blackness, sin: dressed in a suit and a panama hat identical to those of the great-grandfather, the Master of the Sugar Plantation on High swings back and forth in the hammock, sharpens his splendid Collins machete, and smokes a Havana cigar behind the gauze curtain of his mosquito netting: the White Virgin attends to the minor but essential tasks in the Manor House, aware of her superiority but making no ostentatious outward display of it, with only a spotless white frock and dainty furbelows bedecking her svelte figure, with its pale skin and blond hair: little winged mulatto servant boys gracefully chase away the flies from the Mistress with sumptuous fans
Marita, my girl, don't you hear me?
yes, Papa
I don't know what's the matter with you today: you seem to be woolgathering
it's true: it must be the heat
I was asking you about the plantation at Lequeitio: what time is it there?
my watch says exactly ten thirty
has the bell rung for retreat and silence?
yes, Papa
and where are the slaves?
where do you think they are?: in their shacks, of course
are they already asleep?
I imagine so
perhaps you're wrong, the way you were the other time: go out and have a look around
the Mistress goes out onto the colonial veranda of the man-

sion and aims a pair of opera glasses at the warehouses of the sugar plant: despite the ink-black darkness she can make out dusky faces, shadowy hands, members dark as pitch, ebony bodies: everything is the color of jet, mourning, and coal: the panting breath of the copulating couples suggests a feast of wild beasts in the propitious blackness of a secret lair: making sure that the great-grandfather does not see her, she will address the chaplain in a whisper

what are they doing?

his mouth gapes open like that of a fish out of water, and he will raise his hands to his neck in an attempt to relieve the choking sensation he feels: his wrath has given way to discouragement and sorrow: he resembles an Ecce Homo

O my Father, let this cup pass from me

what cup?

never mind, it was only a quotation

I can't see anything: these opera glasses are getting more and more fuzzy

that's all to the good!

come on, tell me, I'm in a hurry

no, no, I can't

don't be such a bore!

my lips refuse to describe this sort of scene

come off it: don't be such a prude

I don't dare

do it for My sake

it's something horrible!

tell me in Latin then

the chaplain will cross himself several times: the horrendous visions of what is taking place in the warehouse appear to have addled his brain: making a violent effort to control himself, he will speak in a trembling voice, his words intermingled with intermittent jerky pauses

> membrum erectum in os feminae immissint!
> socios concumbentes tangere et masturbationem
> mutuam adsequi!

penis vehementis se erixet tum maxime cum crura
puerorum tetigent!
anus feminarum amant lambere!
sanguinis menstruationis devorant!
coitus a posterioris factitant!
eiaculatio praematura!
receptaculum seminis!

interruption, emptiness, silence: as when you stop writing:
the Mistress will take a vial of smelling salts out of her
corset, and you will oblige her to inhale deep breaths from it
so that she doesn't faint: the moans from the plantation
blacks are growing hoarser and hoarser, and filled with horror, she will try to cover her ears: the great-grandfather,
lying in his hammock, is beginning to show signs of
impatience
Marita!
I'm coming this instant!
the Mistress quickly assumes an expression of calm composure, and sprays her face with a perfume atomizer before
returning to the drawing room: with her usual benign and
kindly disposition toward the blacks, she will make up innocent little white lies
it's an absolutely heavenly night tonight!: it makes one feel
like sitting in the summerhouse in the garden and gazing at
the stars through Master Jorge's telescope
why did you stay out there so long? did you happen to meet
someone?
yes, Father Vosk
and what did he have to say to you?
that the slaves are resting
do you know whether they've recited their nightly prayers?
yes, I believe they have
and the acts of faith, hope, and charity?

they've recited them too

and the petitions to die a good Christian death?

yes, and the Pater Noster for the souls in purgatory and the prayer to the holy Guardian Angel

that's fine!: may they continue to do so!: I feel a sudden desire to visit their quarters and give their sleep my blessing

no, you'll catch cold!

didn't you say that it's a splendid night out?

a very strong wind has just come up

I'll bundle up well

no, don't get up yet, I want to recite you a poem

in anguish, she hastens to young Fermina's study and returns with a quarto volume, beautifully bound in leather

this Alphonse de Lamartine makes me giddy!: do you know his poem "Le Papillon"?

no

well wait, and I'll read it to you

Marita, my child, you know I don't understand French very well

it doesn't matter: I'll translate it for you as I go along

the Mistress of the Sugar-Plantation on High reads slowly, with the same careful and elegant diction as young Fermina when the latter recites poetry

> naître avec le printemps, mourir avec les roses
> sur l'aile du zéphyr nager dans un ciel pur
> balancé sur le sein des fleurs à peine écloses
> s'enivrer de parfums, de lumière et d'azur

the great-grandfather listens to her in rapture, and thanks to this pious stratagem, he will once more forget the pitch-black sinners of Lequeitio: obeying a discreet signal from Mistress Marita, the little mulatto servants will serve him his favorite punch, made of rum distilled in Massachusetts, water, sugar, and a few drops of lime juice

what a good French accent you have!

really? it's because this Lamartine fellow inspires me, you

know what I mean?: he's what you call a terrific poet: and what's more, there's a profoundly Christian meaning behind his verses: shall I read you another one, Papa?
however many you like, child, however many you like

you will go on without a pause, your gaze wandering over the sloping ceiling with the dormer window, the green tiles of the sink, the engravings, the newspaper clippings, the book with the illustration of the vacuum evaporator, the photocopies of the catechism intended for blacks written by a priest, Duque de Estrada, pressing down on the hateful whiteness of the writing paper with the ball-point pen that cost you a franc and a half, allowing the unhappy Father Vosk time to recover from the shock, shake the dust from his cassock and his priest's hat, clear his throat so as to be able to speak clearly once again, try out a few gentle smiles, and paternally stretch out his arms above the perverse blacks of the plantation

well then, my sons, why do you think that they took you out of the remote jungles of Africa if it wasn't to redeem you through work and show you the straight and narrow path of Christian salvation?: do not be alarmed by the hardships that it is your lot to endure: your body will be enslaved: but your soul will be free to fly upward to the heavenly mansion of the elect: that is why we send our gunboats and brigantines and oblige you to cross the salty waters of the ocean: in shackles and chains, in order that the devil will not tempt you to return to a savage and uncivilized life, to the evil idleness of the most brutish animals: protecting you against yourselves: so that one day you may sit at the right hand of God the Father, absorbed in the felicity and the rapture of a thousand sublime visions: with a soul as white as the purest grade of sugar: the Master of the Sugar Plantation on High will look upon you with a smiling countenance, and no one will scorn you because of your dark skin, your kinky hair, your flat nose, your thick bestial lips: up there your tribulations and miseries will come to an end once and for all: the White Virgin will seat you at her table and will share her own food with you: instead of sliding further and further down into tainted blackness and eternally suffering its hereditary defects, you will gradually advance and improve your spiritual lineage, and better the dark and noxious quality of your souls: the Master on High has taken pity on your lot and will rescue you from the sad obscurity in which you live by granting you the opportunity to lead a life of purification and penitence: what an intoxicating and comforting prospect!: slavery is the divine grace by virtue of which you will enter the Kingdom of Heaven with an exquisite, immaculate whiteness: the Son of God, like the plantation boss, zealously oversees your labor both by day and by night: and just like the plantation boss here below, who supervises the work of cutting, loading, and transporting, not overlooking the old women and the young mulattos who gather up the cane stalks that have fallen along the wayside, and then goes to the sugar plant and watches over the Fawcett refining machinery and keeps an eye on the slaves who take care of the sugar boilers and empty the ashes from the furnace, on those who put the sugar loaves out in the sun to dry, grade them, and wrap them, the Plantation Boss on High keeps a daily account of your activities: he forgets no one, he notes everything down: he too is like an expert foreman of a sugar factory: exactly like Messié La Fayé: have you not seen him in his bowler hat and frock-coat examining the boiling pots in the purging house?: only he knows the secrets of sugar, the proper variety of sugar cane, the correct degree of concentration, the quantity of quicklime needed for the cane juice: in the very same way the Master Foreman of the Sugar Factory on High knows the hidden places and the secret corners of the soul: the one who labors with a happy heart and the one who labors out of fear of the whip, the one who accepts hardships with resignation and the one who endures them with rebellion in his heart: whatever you do or say or think he notes down immediately: he goes to see the Father each and every day and shows him the records: on the plantation Don Agustín keeps account of the newborn, the sick, the dead, the runaways, the injured: the other Master also goes over the notebooks of the Plantation Boss and keeps watch on the blacks from on High: in the fields and in the sugar plant, in the cane mill and in the boiling rooms, in the sheds and in the drying room, in the filtering room and in the forges: he sees who drives the oxen, who cuts the wood, who brings in the cane, who takes away the bagasse: one day the world will end and it will be like the master's saint's day and the birthday of the young master and the girls: for just as Don Agustín punishes and pardons according to the advice of the plantation boss, God will condemn or save the souls of slaves according to the registers and account books: white ones to one side and black ones to the other: some to be packed and sent to Heaven, others to be cast into Hell or sent to the Purging House: the clean, purified, crystalline, and perfect soul of the obedient black, of the docile slave, is like white sugar, with its glistening grains, without dross or impurities of any sort: but no soul is like that: all of them have impurities, like pan sugar or the greenish sugar that comes out of the evaporators: and to be purified they must undergo a long and arduous process of purgation: first of all, the souls cook in the sugar boilers like the cane juice in the tren jamaiquino, passing from one boiler to another, so as to decant them, clarify them, allow them to acquire the proper degree of concentration: in each boiler the hot syrups thicken and evaporate, lose their coarseness and residues: you have all seen the scum that comes off the cane juice in the form of a yellowish foam, haven't you?: that is precisely the way that the soul is freed of its impurities and clarified day after day and year after year, thanks to the gentle yoke of work: and even so, my sons, when it leaves the filter, the mother liquor is still not good: it must be taken to the evaporator and stirred hard until it crystallizes: it is the same with the soul: we must also separate the syrup from the sugar, put the latter in the evaporating pans and purify it: patience and docility cause the green and impure syrups to drain away: little by little the sugar at the top grows lighter, but sheer good will and a good heart are not sufficient to do the job: isn't it true that one must also pour in a mixture of water and clay, so that the water will filter through the sugar loaf and carry away the syrup that adheres to the crystals?: well, that is precisely what the plantation boss does with you when he assigns you humble and thankless tasks: he does so in order that the dark color of your souls may be washed away and in order that you may turn a lighter color: and just as the purging of the sugar lasts thirty or forty days, the purging of the soul may last thirty or forty years: but what does this ridiculously short period of time matter in view of the immortal glory that the Eternal offers you!: therefore do not curse your fate or lose heart: all these tribulations are necessary for the complete whitening of your souls: one day they will be put out in the sun to air like a sugar loaf: then the Plantation Boss on High will come along with his machete and slice open the loaf with one stroke, from the dark tip at the top to the white layer at the bottom: and it will be like the day of the Last Judgment: the black souls will be lost forever, like the burnt sugar that is thrown away: the residues, full of filth and impurities, that no one would want to buy: the middle part of the loaf is the pale brown sugars that will have to be purged and boiled over again until there remains in their souls not even the slightest trace of sin: and the clear lumps at the base, the fine, superior white ones, are the slaves who have diligently and zealously performed all the tasks assigned them by the plantation boss: souls that are saved, Arctic expanses, eternal glaciers of Nordic whiteness!

you will undertake to describe an Alpine landscape: Megève, Saint-Moritz, Andermatt?: Chamonix, Closters, Saas Fee?: the Swiss Tourist Office offers you its precious aid with a rich assortment of illustrated folders and booklets: wooden chalets, Christmas-tree spruces, snow-covered slopes of a schizophrenic whiteness: you will look them over one by one, fascinated by the dazzling display laid out in front of you, until your attention is riveted on the colored photograph illustrating the delights of Davos: swift sleighs drawn by reindeer glide softly along the road and an inspired winter breeze raises a dancing whirlwind of snowflakes: the members of the eminent family will set up camp in the middle of this scene with equipment suited to the weather and the circumstances: ermine greatcoats, snow-white fur caps, muffs and gloves lined with white mink: great-grandfather Nicolas and the tsarina stand there motionless before the camera, pleased to be gazing upon the immaculate symbol of their power, the illusory but dazzling sugar harvest spread out before their eyes: tsarevitch Jorge absorbed in the contemplation of stormy mountain peaks through the lens of his telescope: the grand-duchess daughters stroking the back of a stag or making snowmen or sitting astride a wise and discerning Saint Bernard: everything is clean and white, irreproachable, pure: with none of the vices and indispositions visited by a tropical climate upon bodies that are even more delicate and ivory-like: stains, perspiration, heat, dust, insect bites: upon the apotheosis of their radiant, saccharine whiteness: generously offered to the enraptured gaze of the plantation blacks, who will contemplate the colored slide with you as the chaplain continues to consult the pages of his catechism and goes on with his persistent indoctrination of the recently imported blacks: as flat-nosed, alas, as they are pinheaded: pointing out to them the abysmal difference that separates the great-grandfather from a Congolese, the tsarevitch from a Carabalí, the ski slopes of Davos from the common sewer ditch of Lequeitio: mentioning in passing the path to perfection, but stressing the gravity of their sins and failings

you are to blame because you don't fulfill your quotas: there are many of you, but only one plantation boss: today one of you turns up missing, tomorrow another, one day one of you makes mischief, the next day another: the boss man has trials to put up with every day: one of you escapes and heads for the mountains, another of you squats down to take a rest while cutting cane, another of you fails to take proper care of the sugar loaves: as cunning and crafty as jungle savages: thinking up a thousand ways to get out of working: and he must keep an eye on everything: the cane mill, the boiling pots, the filter, the dryer: making sure that everything works the way it should, struggling day and night on account of your sly tricks and devilishness: X who falls asleep alongside the heating vat, Y who takes time out while he's pumping the sugar-cane juice, Z who chitchats behind the cane crusher: day after day: even on Sundays he is unable to rest: for he must watch to see if you are cleaning out the troughs, scraping out the boilers, taking away the bagasse, doing the purgation properly: Don Agustín holds him alone responsible, and if he gets angry at him he kicks him out: and you are of no help at all to him: that is why the Plantation Boss on High gets mad, and punishes you when you least expect it: and one day one of you hangs himself and goes straight to Hell or loses an arm in the Fawcett or cuts his foot with a machete or falls into the boiling vat and is fished out dead: and who does the master bawl out?: the blacks?: no indeed: the plantation boss!: he has to take care of everything: the machinery and the tools, the slaves, the animals, the rations: he is responsible for everything that happens on the plantation: he's the one who must put up with all the unpleasantnesses, annoyances, difficulties, tribulations, problems: and on top of everything else you continually complain: about the work shifts, the whiplash, the dogs, the lack of sleep: but bear one thing in mind: the little birds in the sky sleep less than you do and never complain: why should you want to sleep longer than they do?: look at how happy they are and how they sing for joy as dawn breaks: God helps the early riser and a wide-awake black is better than one lying abed snoring: the lion does not sleep and is king of the jungle: the hands of a clock move around the dial twenty-four hours a day and if you wind it up it never stops: the early bird gets the worm, and yet you keep talking about needing sleep!: the Master on High and the White Virgin never enjoy a moment's rest: forever looking down in the direction of Cruces, worrying about the Lequeitio plantation: they don't sleep five hours the way you do, or four or three or two or even one: standing guard duty, night and day, the whole week long!: nor do they grumble about the food: the fact that all there is to eat are sweet potatoes and bananas and bits of bones with no meat on them, all of it black and awful looking: take a look at the animals on the plantation: they don't ask for codfish and jerked beef, tripe, rice, fine dishes: they never throw ladles if their food is not to their liking: are you determined to be worse than they are?: and yet you want the boss man to put up with everything and still be kind and gentle: as if his patience had no limits, as if he hadn't already spoiled you too much!: bad bread, you say: just wait, and when you're hungry enough you'll think it's soft and made of the finest white flour: no one can have everything he wants: all that any of us can do is not covet what we don't have and joyously avail ourselves of those things that are offered to us: an abstemious belly that willingly accepts scarcity is the only genuine base of freedom: how wonderful it would be if, instead of grumbling and cursing your fate, you were to reflect on the profound words of Seneca in his epistles to Lucilius: in like fashion, I have endeavored to resign myself to all the onerous burdens and adversities that have befallen me, for I do not obey God: I accept, rather, what he grants unto me: I am His disciple out of my own free choice, not out of necessity: nothing comes to pass that finds me downcast and with a sullen visage: what sublime phrases from the lips of a pagan!: and you, redeemed by the baptismal waters and with the path to salvation clearly laid out for you thanks to a providential divine plan, nonetheless accept your fate unwillingly and obey reluctantly!: and worse still: you are insolent: you swagger and are cheeky and impudent, and address the plantation boss with crude and threatening gestures: and then you moan and groan if he puts you in shackles and whips the hide off you: you complain that he is wicked and punishes you severely for a mere trifle: as though you had not sorely tried him with your tricks and evil wiles!: he is too kind and gentle!: but every so often his patience is exhausted and he really lets you have it: and instead of repenting and begging his pardon, the minute he lets you go you start daubing the walls of the sheds and warehouses with your stripes and circles: plotting your acts of vengeance and evil witchcraft, so as to lure him into your cooking pot and bring him misfortunes, infirmities, and grave harm

to the kapok tree, to the kapok tree!: it is midnight, the hour of the devil, and the slaves steal out of their shacks and cross the sleeping plantation yard, under the protection of the chaotic and delirious geometry of the stars on high: the dogs lie poisoned alongside the watering trough and the night watchmen snore in their sentry boxes, in a stupor brought on by powders craftily dissolved by the sorcerers in their daily ration of rum: a tropical night, such as those celebrated in Caribbean songs, warm and sensual, a night that swoons, not on the sands of the ocean shore but on the narrow paths and the shortcuts which, beyond the bagasse-drying plots, lead to the hills and mountain fastnesses where the runaway slaves have taken refuge: helping them find their way through the baroque profusion of bindweeds and ferns, thanks to an esoteric alphabet, a secret, clandestine code: the sound of the wind, the buzzing of insects, the cry of birds weave a subtle web of complicity as the sucrocrat family takes its rest, naïvely entrusting itself to the talismanic protection of the Guardian Angel: but it will be to no avail, and the plantation blacks will have neutralized him too by luring him into indulging his appetite for brillatsavarinesque gastronomy: a chubby-cheeked little angel stuffed with meringue and other delicacies from the Capucin Gourmand, so that he has apparently sunk into the almost speleological depths of a deep sleep: not noticing, in any case, the furtive shadows gliding along beneath the tutelary tops of the trees and their creeping, serpentine foliage: until they reach the open spot cleared by wielders of machetes and woodsmen round about the tall, solitary kapok tree: invoking the occult powers of the stew pot, into which there have already gone four little heaps of dirt, chickweed, hunks of beef, the cigar butts of the master: the witch doctor recites his magic spells and litanies, and suddenly the devils will give their consent and the great-grandfather will be firmly trussed up: in the smaller stew pans are the hairs from the brushes and combs used by the great-grandmother and the girls and a toenail of master Jorge: one after the other, the members of the family will undergo the same fate: the drums will beat frantically and by virtue of the powerful incantations they will symbolically reappear on the podium in the perfection of their sovereign whiteness: the master, behind the nuptial veil of his mosquito netting, going over the account books, swaying gently back and forth in his hammock: the great-grandmother, in the act of performing her Marian devotions before the meal is served: young master Jorge, with his orbs and telescopes: the girls, absorbed in their embroidery, the violin lesson, and the reciting of the poems of that Lamartine fellow who is sucking at the White Virgin's brains: hidden spotlights in the branches of the kapok tree project beams of light down on them, and in accordance with the rules of classic cinematic practice, you will swiftly select the details of the scene: seeking, with the expertise of a graduate of the Institut des Hautes Etudes Cinématographiques, the ideal closeup, the meaningful, revealing touches: the tense fingers of the great-grandfather as he sharpens the machete, the marble-white hand of the tsarina as she extends her blessing upon the table, Jorgito's goyesque-bourbon expression, with his mouth gaping open, young Telesfora's pin cushion bristling with needles, the blushing cheeks of Fermina as she recites Lamartine, the stiff arm motions of Adelaida as she plays on the violin the romantic waltz entitled "Over the Waves": linking arms, they will come downstage to acknowledge the applause, and at this precise moment, with all the caution of someone setting a trap, the dragoman-sorcerer will bring about the ominous catastrophe: sickness, apoplexy, the plague, misfortunes, a fatal accident, war?: no, much worse!: streams of perspiration will begin to run down their foreheads, beads of sweat will break out on their temples, the exudation will slowly soak the men's shirt collars and the taffeta edgings of the women's dresses: dark, greasy spots will appear on the great-grandfather's jacket just below his armpits and the slight moisture trickling down the neckline of the tsarina's dress will little by little impregnate the white satin of her breasts: impossible to stop the perspiration!: it will be of no use to fan themselves, to go out on the balcony, to imbibe thirst-quenching drinks, to wipe their faces with a handkerchief: the glands in their mouths will in turn secrete an aqueous humor and the liquid will flow out of the corners of their lips and run down their chins: slaver, foam, saliva, phlegm will mingle with mucus and nasal fluids to form a single ductile, yellowish flow that no handkerchief factory in the world will be capable of wiping away: a Kleenex, who's got a Kleenex?, the girls will exclaim in chorus: but despite the fact that they have not yet reached the age of puberty, three bright-red spots will stain the immaculate whiteness of their skirts, at the very place where the gaze of the stolid sons of Sunnyspain customarily lingers: revealing to the dusky spectators that they have indisputably burst into vernal flower: and the bloody first fruits will generously wet the cloth and gradually present the symptoms of a delicious hemorrhage: the sudden, mysterious appearance of the nubile state, joyously celebrated in all climes and latitudes with splendid sacrifices and fiestas!: unable to bear this tantalesque torture, the most brazen blacks will rush up onto the stage: clinging to the trembling knees of these girls who are still virgins but no longer children, they will eagerly raise the latter's skirts and greedily place their thirsting lips on

in Latin, in Latin, the White Virgin will beg

but even though you will endeavor to please her and write sanguinis menstruationis lambent, it will be impossible for you to continue: your command of Latin verbs and declensions is too shaky: not everybody who would like to can be a Cicero, and despite your Hispano bachelor's diploma, your schooling has proved pitifully inadequate: you will therefore return to your native tongue, to the vulgar romance language of the common horde, and continue

a Mosaic fount, in which crude, churlish drinkers enjoy wetting their gullets as they explore with expert, agile motions the curves and hollows of the rock: in a single stroke, not letting go of the pen for an instant: as the three ex-children lift their eyes heavenward with the rapture and ecstasy of Madonnas: or like that little saint Marie Alacoque as she receives the Great Promise: here is the Heart that has so loved all men, that has left nothing undone, even unto exhausting itself and consuming itself in order to demonstrate its love for them!: with their smiles of angelic beatitude and their gaze riveted upon a thousand glorious visions: seeking atonement for the scorn and ingratitude of the world: prepared to bestow abundant and extraordinary blessings upon their true disciples: who are on their knees too, in avid and refreshing bliss: but the master and mistress of the plantation and the tsarevitch contemplate the scene with you and their eyes gleam in horror in their deep-set sockets: mon Dieu, quoi faire?: the power of the stew pots is really fantastic, and any attempt to resist is doomed to failure: overcome by their weighty burden of shame, they will turn on their heels and haughtily turn their backs on you, the sole consequence of which is to reveal to the stupefied audience the humiliating coloration of their posterior hemispheres: the nonsublimated, nonhidden, nonodorless, nonaseptic visceral explosion that no safe-deposit box, sanctuary, or water closet will succeed in conjuring away: resoundingly proclaiming the mot de Cambronne: their undeniable membership in the human species, their solidarity with the suffering, squatting humanity of the devotees of the sewer ditch: and although forewarned by the bursts of laughter, they will realize that disaster is at hand, that it is too late to take countermeasures: the plebeian viscosity continually extends its sphere of activity, infecting the men's trousers, contaminating the women's petticoats: in vain they will seize hold of the dangling bindweeds and repeat the magic gesture of pulling the chain: the divine waterspout will not descend: the technicians will have gone back to England: and amid the hilarious laughter of the plantation blacks they will continue to pour out the ignominious dark-colored matter until the moment that the stew pots lose their power, the spotlights dim, and suddenly a disorderly retreat takes place: the scattering of the slaves in all directions: someone has sent out the alarm and the plantation bell is sounding the call to arms: the nightwatchmen awaken and come running with their dogs at the urgent summons of the plantation boss: shouts, cries, barks, lights, whistles: the

ancestral hunting party is being organized: the illustrious
family is fast asleep: the chaplain will begin to speak

and then all of you run away
you reject the aid of our light
you scorn whiteness
you embrace the shadows of savagery
the primordial darkness attracts you
with the somber splendor of its feasts
wary nocturnal creatures
you seek protection and asylum
in dark abysses and caverns
in the original womb of caves
the night counsels you
secretly and cunningly
and you put your trust in it
like swift and elusive animals
with the alacrity and perspicacity of savages
you contrive to evade our vigilant efforts to save you
from life in the wilds and in harsh climes
the dense thickets shelter you
and hinder our plans to capture you
our patrols and armed posses
vainly pursue you
along paths beset with dangers
you perversely defend yourselves
by means of subtle tricks and traps
burying pointed stakes in our path
launching sharp wooden arrows
suddenly attacking with your spears
hidden in burrows and crags
you set up nets and palisades to catch the mares of our posses
lying in ambush in tangled thickets and marshes
you cast off your garments in order to prevent our dogs from
    smelling you out

you scale the steep mountainsides
with the help of stubborn runaways
and in your dens and lairs
you recreate the fierce, savage life of the horrible African
    jungle
deaf to our magnanimous offers of forgiveness
giving yourselves over once again to idolatry and vice
disdaining the splendid benefits of slavery
eternal redemption through the sweat of your brows
you know the consequences
the wrath of Heaven
divine punishment
just and implacable vengeance
do not cry out in lamentation therefore
if on discovering your secret hiding places
our men treat you harshly and cut off your ears and send
    them to the master
they are upright men
and their chastisements
delight the heart of the Plantation Boss on High and the most
    merciful White Virgin
and hence
when you resist
you oblige them to make use of their machetes as retribution
    for your insolence
let no one be deceived or call them cruel
if they decapitate your chiefs and exhibit their heads along
    the streets, the promenades, and the public squares
impaled on the point of a spear and covered with filthy flies
as an example to the unwary
and a warning to imprudent fools

            usually they tie them fast, placing the left leg of one
            and the right leg of another in the same pair of
            shackles and with a rope between these latter they

are able to walk very slowly: each group of four are tied together by means of a rope of twisted strands running around their necks: during the night they also put handcuffs on them and sometimes they tie their knees together with a light chain: other *slatees* cut a slab of wood some three feet wide and make a notch in one edge that serves to immobilize the ankle of the rebellious slave, which is then encircled by a strong iron ring

to ensure safety on board, it is necessary to put shackles and chains on them and shut them up in the hold at night and even in the daytime when there are storms: as many of them are listless and seasickness and grief make them abhor exercise, they force them to eat and to dance by wielding the whiplash in order that they may appear to be healthy when they are put on the block at the slave market: it is also necessary to take precautions against suicide attempts

those that are for sale are kept in a sort of large enclosure: the buyers scrutinize them carefully feel them over make them leap in the air and hop up and down and stretch their arms and legs: they force them to turn round about in every direction they examine their mouths and look them over from head to foot and put them to the test in a thousand ways until they are certain that they are strong and healthy

having been informed that there is a runaway slave boy hidden in the hills they go there armed with shotguns and followed by some twenty guards on foot: seeing this horde of people approaching the boy becomes terrified and picks up a rock with which to defend himself: he takes refuge in a cranny in the rock where they are unable to get at him: they go for firewood and pile it up at the other end of the crevice in the rock and set fire to it: it burns till it sears the boy's skin, forcing him to come out at a run and throw himself in a mud puddle: they order another black to drag him out but he resists furiously: they shoot at him several times with grape-shot and throw stones at him: they finally drag him out badly hurt and force him to kneel down: he makes signs, begging them for a drink of water: they refuse to give him any, and when the hole is dug they put him in it and cover him with dirt even though he is not yet dead

the head of the runaway tops the stake like an unusual pommel of a cane and the flies alight in clusters on the unusually wide-open eyes the nostrils the swollen lips the hollows left by the severed ears the clots of blood on the neck that slide down the rough surface of the wood

you will break off your reading of the documents: passages copied from books and photocopies are superimposed in your memory on the letter of the slave woman to your great-grandfather, reviving intact your hatred toward the race that gave birth to you: the original sin that relentlessly pursues you with its indelible stigma despite your long-standing, intrepid efforts to free yourself of it: the virgin page offers you matchless possibilities of redemption, together with the pleasure of profaning its whiteness: a simple stroke of the pen is enough: you will try your luck once more

choosing among all the other black women the fat girl on the record jacket, as sexy as a bitch in heat: hair carefully finger-waved, broad, smooth forehead, bushy eyebrows, wide flat nose, large gleaming-white teeth, agile pink tongue, shiny dark skin: two gilt pendants dangle from her ear lobes and seem to tinkle softly as she joyously dances a rumba, frantically waggling her hips, exactly as advertised in the bilingual caption written across the record jacket: modest, retiring, and well behaved now: diligently performing her household tasks, with her most chaste spouse close at hand: doubtless awaiting the highly unusual visit of the Dove: meanwhile laying out the diapers of the future child: of the forever blessed fruit of her womb: you yourself: in the dark, extremely modest cabin where her lawfully wedded husband engages in his humble but honest craft: with the natural, somewhat stylized elegance of those neat pilgrims of the *Mayflower* in the wax museum in Massachusetts: the two of them dressed in simple, tidy smocks: their feet shod in the plainest of sandals: their likenesses captured as the husband wields a plane and chisel, or the wife does delicate needlework: domestic animals complete with their benign presence the peaceful picture of uprightness, happiness, and industrious labor: they have been selected with particular care: a gentle, docile ox, a sweet-faced ewe, a plush donkey brought back to life, a meek little lamb: your future mother is humming a simple lullaby and the provident husbandman is building a manger for the propitious animals belonging to the household: nothing more?: oh, yes: the ever-vigilant protection of the holy Guardian Angel hovering over the cabin with its snow-white wings outspread: the other details are not shown in the colored print and you will add them yourself: two shining crowns, resembling the rings of Saturn, form a resplendent nimbus around their heads, in open, almost violent defiance of the law of terrestrial gravity, and another heavenly messenger, whose functions are not at all those of go-between, will instruct the sublime couple in the hidden aims underlying the divine plans: giving them graphic explanations, in the form of luminous smiles, of the mysteries of the Incarnation and the Trinity: have you noticed what happens when you stand in front of a mirror?: as you approach it, your image appears in it at the same time: and if you take such delight in gazing at it that you kiss yourself on the crystal-clear surface, your kiss that you give yourselves will leave an opaque circle on it: thus, in one and the same mirror three different things are conjoined: your person, your image, and the opaque circle left by the kiss: you are the cause of the image, and the opaque circle stems both from your person and from the image produced in the mirror: and just as a ray of sunlight that shines through a sky-blue glass remains as blue as the crystal through which it has passed, without its color being thereby destroyed or faded in the slightest, in like fashion Alvarito, on descending to this earth to redeem all the world's pariahs from sin, will pass through the body of his Mother, feeding on her flesh and blood, without thereby diminishing her immaculate and virginal purity: the light-winged catechist fades from view amid a quivering flutter of feathers, and your future mother will take up her exquisite embroideries once again and the heaven-blessed male of the household will go on with his construction of the manger foretold by prophecy: the message has cast a ray of light in the innate darkness of their minds and both will ponder for hours on end the profound and admirable arcana revealed by the words of the angel: she sews on and on as her spouse sets up the manger and makes the necessary preparations in his capacity as host in order to welcome the Dove: building downy, comfy nests lined with feathers: installing slender swinging perches, setting out little cups of canary seed, clean and commodious little drinking cups: not omitting a single thing likely to make it become attached to the place and feel at home therein: in particular a soft and fluffy eiderdown on which the visited mother may incubate, when the time has come, her illustrious and eagerly awaited egg: and she will peer out the window and carefully scrutinize the sky, endeavoring to make out, among the many birds that cleave the air above the plantation yard, the swift and light-winged visitor: the other black women also slyly keep watch, hidden behind venetian blinds and jalousies, skeptical of the announced visitation, but envious of her singular privilege

who that darky think she is anyhow, puttin' on airs like a queen, with them blubber lips of hers and that kinky hair and such black skin that even the Good Lord hisself couldn't make it no lighter: heaven only knows how come she done took it into her head that we'uns ain't as good as she is and she gwine steal a march on us and get ahead of us in this ole world by takin' up with a white he-goat like that one I swear to goshen she's not fitten even to use for coal to light a fire with I kin tell you straight out that if you was to meet up with her in the dark you couldn't even make out her face less'n you was carryin' a lighted lantern!

but she turns a deaf ear and will disdainfully pay no attention to the vicious gossip: absorbed in watching the sky: and now the solitary Columba will swoop gently down upon the cabin and fly about the imminent mother with a thousand tender and amorous cooings: it will successively balance back and forth on the swings, alight on the head of the ox, peck at the canary seed in the little cups, visit the drinking cup: interspersing its elegant movements with brief and innocent evacuations that the tidy and obliging patriarch will hasten to clean up: its wings will flutter weightlessly round about the eager maternal mouth and spread out protectively, dexterously concealing her countenance: a singular genesis, dance steps and acrobatic tricks that the skillful Dove executes with ineffable murmurs as the humble craftsman sheds tears of joy and rapturously celebrates the sublime mystery of your Incarnation!: repeatedly drying his eyes and then inevitably bursting into tears once again: thus failing to notice the sudden apparition, visible through the window opening, of the imperious figure of Changó

Changó?

yes, Changó, the grandson of Agayú and the son of Yemayá

and Orugán, the lord of thunder and lightning: worshiped
by the electrified plantation blacks, who fall on their knees
as he crosses the plantation yard and heads for the cabin,
invested with the powers and gifts attributed to him in the
books on pagan deities piled up under your table: Saint
Barbara as well: but a male through and through beneath
the petticoats: spoiling for a fight, brave, daring, breathing
fire: with bloody banner, nimble Moorish steed and flaming
sword: a false smile plays over the fierce lips and the leonine
mustache gleams brightly above the dark, weatherbeaten
face: resplendent, fiery, solar: with the flexible handlebars of
it like the tip of a whip or a lizard's tail: aimed at the greedy
eyes that gleam as they watch from ambush the busy family
and the scene resembling a popular sentimental lithograph:
the mother captivated by the magic spell of the Dove and the
diligent patriarch whose face is bathed in tears as he collects
the little offerings of the visitor in a soft linen cloth: your
massive, undeniable presence now fills the empty doorway
and the docile animals in the picture will look you straight in
the eye and manifest unmistakable signs of anxiety: moving
uneasily closer to the Christmas crèche, fascinated by the
wild beast leaping about between your legs, attracted by the
soft, sweet enticement of Yemayá: but the principal figures
of the mystery apparently notice nothing, and the bewildered
Dove flies from the swinging perch to your mother, from the
seed cups to the drinking cup, fluttering about everywhere,
busily engaged in performing its vigorous and abundant
evacuations: nonetheless its final hour has come, and a single
movement on your part will suffice to kill it with one blow
and reduce it to a minuscule heap of feathers: your fangs of
steel will crush its fragile bones and the innocent blood will
drip down your lips and enhance the sumptuous splendor of
your mustache: as soon as the pitiful little corpse is added to
your well-protected store of precious booty, you will dismiss
the towel boy and draw closer to Yemayá: neither demon-

strating the slightest repugnance for incest nor fleeing to the top of the palm tree: leisurely contemplating her sweat-drenched brow, her lowered eyelids, her trembling lips: she is still stupefied by the acrobatic virtuosity of the now-deceased Dove: but eager to face the sudden assault of the wild beast: of the dark-colored and dangerous animal that you are proudly displaying, standing at the ready at the height of your groin: turning around with ancestral wisdom and offering it her chubby posterior cheeks: the rapacious beast will spring forthwith, and although the entrance to the cave is extremely narrow, you will push ahead, your blood on fire, resolved that victory shall be yours: the forbidden maternal possession will take place in the strangest possible position: the plates of an illustrated edition of the Kamasutra inspire you with their musical variations on the theme: soloists and virtuosos, flutes, double basses, trios that appear to obey every possible rhythm, in accordance with the al-legros, adagios, graves, ma non troppos, or andantes indi-cated by some prodigious maestro: with that eternally va-cant, slightly nirvanic expression of workers subjected to the dizzying cadences of a Detroit factory run on the principles of Taylor's time-and-motion system: choosing the most com-plicated position, determined to excel their amazing gym-nastic feats: the lavish gifts of the god assure your triumph, and holding her aloft thanks to a subtle coordination of your knees and elbows, you will continue your bold incursions as your other self awaits within the proximate creation of its body: as yet still immaterial, but already intuiting the ap-proaching advent of Being and its dazzling future destiny: the dusky, violent animal is now firmly lodged within the den and you will joyously witness its assaults: its bellicose, im-petuous charges: watching it root about and bite and bare its cruel talons as the spellbound mother continues her esoteric duo with the almost totally digested visitor, taken in, doubt-less, by the slight rustle of feathers, which, having now withdrawn, you will artfully cause to flutter: simulating caresses, endearments, flattering billings and cooings, imitating with your fingernail the rubbing of a beak and with your lips a gentle beating of wings: my love, my darling, my royal sovereign, my Dove, is that You?: and you, answering: yes, my black beauty, yes, it is I, your Turtledove, the best of the Three, the blessed patron of the Dove Breeders Association: and the expressions of rapture and ecstasy forthcoming from the object of this visitation will gradually rise in pitch until they reach Himalayan paroxysms: her primitive warble, like unto the song of the hoopoe, will little by little become the cry, half a shout, half a bleat, with which Tyrolese hikers with feathers in their hats greet one another in the mountains of their country, and will culminate in the stentorian roar that according to legend Sir Edmund Hillary and his faithful Sherpa, Tensing, let out at the instant that they stepped out on the roof of the world, up on the eternally snow-covered heights: and having settled down in the pitch blackness of the abominable cave, you will await with existential impatience the slow, abundant, juicy spasms that will miraculously engender your body: thanks to your wise decision to let the beast loose and allow it to graze in that nearby shady grove which all the Christian flock may legitimately visit on propitious days in order to ensure the divinely decreed propagation of the species: obliging it to tarry for a few seconds in this dull abode and there give up the ghost out of ennui and melancholy: but the gene makes its way upstream against the current and will arrive at its appointed destination with mathematical exactitude: reaching the maternal ovum, which, fecundated by it, will finally confer existence upon you and constitute the starting point of your hazardous journey: nine months to go yet!: time to mature and grow in the soft spherical egg: uncertain as yet as to precisely what color you will be, consumed with anxiety, scarcely able to wait to look in the mirror and see: the dreamy-eyed mother is also waiting, her entire heart and soul absorbed in hemming the Child's diapers: the other black women's tongues continue to wag: they are practically dying with jealousy, for the news of your imminent arrival has already spread far and wide and worshipers are flocking in from every direction with their humble offerings: a little basket of fruit, a cup of Maggi chicken bouillon, a can of condensed milk, a half dozen eggs: and your mother will thank them with a smile and continue her labors without interruption: the signs of the visit are beginning to be apparent: the print dress is getting tighter and tighter, and she will decide to make herself another one, motivated neither by prudery nor a desire to show off: avoiding both the shapeless folds dictated by puritan concealment and the barefaced impudence of your females who appear to delight in defying community standards of decency, fairly bursting the seams of their dresses, dropsically puffed up with false pride and vanity: falling into neither of these extremes thanks to some old but still useful patterns from *Elle* and *Le Jardin des Modes* that are a model of gracefulness, modesty, and economy: she will actively go about her maternal tasks, not knowing that your worshipers are planning to surprise her with a fabulous gift: the latest-model Singer sewing machine, with its corresponding written guarantee, bought on the installment plan, thanks to a credit card: everything is now arranged!: the announced epiphany is approaching, and the slaves assemble in the plantation yard, eagerly awaiting news of what is happening in the cabin: the horoscopes of the most expert astrologers unanimously agree on the hour of your birth and you must concentrate with all your might in order not to louse up your exit: with all the nervous tension of the funambulist who executes his dance on his tightrope or the acrobat who undertakes his death-defying triple somersault: you will suddenly leap out!: and it will not be necessary even to open your eyes or hasten to take a look at yourself in the mirror: you've been screwed!: a paleface, a

young lord and master, a motherfucking white: jeered at in chorus by all the indignant assembled blacks: cut off forever from the pariahs and the halfbreeds of this world: neither Unigenital nor a Messiah nor a Redeemer
who, you?

       don't make me laugh!

             with your defect?

II

1

When the harsh voices of the country that you despise offend your ears, you are overcome with astonishment: what more is expected of you?: have you not paid your debt in full?: exile has turned you into a completely different being, who has nothing to do with the one your fellow countrymen once knew: their law is no longer your law: their justice is no longer your justice: no one awaits you in Ithaca: as anonymous as any passing stranger, you will visit your own dwelling and dogs will bark at your heels: your hooded jellab, as tattered as a scarecrow's costume, will be taken for the usual beggar's rags, and you will gladly accept the offering of a few small coins: disgust, pity, disdain will be the earnest of your triumph: you are the king of your own realm and your sovereignty extends to the farthest reaches of the desert: clad in the tatterdemalion garments of the fauna that gave birth to you, feeding yourself on their leftover scraps, you will make camp in their garbage dumps and refuse heaps as you carefully sharpen the razor with which one day you will render your own brand of justice: yours is the freedom of the pariah, and you will not turn back
you will avidly embrace your magnificent anomaly

2

from among all the beggars in the marketplace, you will choose the most abject: the African harka demands of you a total, unconditional surrender, and you have decided to assume, down to its ultimate, delirious consequences, your devouring, promethean passion: handsomeness, youth, and harmony are permissible attributes enhancing even lawful and licit love, and you will ruthlessly rid yourself of them in order to embrace the most vile and ominous attributes of the illegal brotherhood of the body: old age, filth, misery, wretchedness suck you up in a violent whirlwind, with the irresistible force of an attack of vertigo: urine, grime, wounds, pus will be the daily nourishment that you will consume in lonely pride: Ebeh has perhaps not yet reached the age of thirty, yet the afflictions and infirmities characteristic of extreme poverty have already marked his person with the indelible signs of decrepitude: his shaved skull is an open sore, suppurating crusts and pustules appear amid the locks of an unshaven grayish beard: congenital syphilis has deprived him at an early age of his powers of sight and eaten away his nostrils and the cartilage of his nose, and his tattered garments barely cover the old scars and wounds that extend from his neck to the instep of his feet: when you approach him, he will feel your face inch by inch with his rapacious claws before causing his toothless mouth to gape open in a broad smile and eagerly encircling your breast with the sovereign imperiousness of a falcon: shifting sand dunes will blur the tormented trace of your caresses, and your enfolding embrace as you take each other in your arms will little by little take on the undulating configuration of the desert: a duel of birds of prey that tear each other's flesh to bits, enveloped in the sudden frenzy of their stroking wings!: with the steel of their curved beaks and razor-sharp talons sunk into the throbbing entrails, amid the romancircuslike shouts of the crowd: also thirsting for blood as the hand-to-hand combat reaches its paroxysm and applies to the furies of passion its crude and stern remedy: although in this case provoking instead the combined disgust and pity of the gaudily attired group of tourists circumspectly witnessing the scene from the boxes and benches: Frenchmen straight out of the pages of "Madame Express," silent-majority Yankee families, garrulous, gesticulating Italians, a few stolid sons of Sunnyspain: all of them having just disembarked from the jumbo jet with their collection of photographic-cinematic equipment and the usual accouterments of the planet of the apes symbolically described in the resplendent poem of Ben Xelún: and also on their guard against the traps and dangers of this suspect country and the proverbial duplicity of its dusky and evil inhabitants

be on your guard against ARABS

they are all thieves and they stink

they are capable of plucking your brains out

charcoal-broiling them and offering them to you on terracotta slabs

your fierce embrace attracts their virtuously reproving gaze and in their eyes is a perfect example of the abysses of contemptuous mockery, filth, and sin of the frightful Arab race: with mingled horror and compassion, they will lean over you with their cameras, and after capturing for the future mondocanesque museum of their memories this barbarous copulation, they will endeavor to mitigate your degradation and your vices with a magnanimous rain of coins

oh, comme c'est dégoûtant

take a look

I can't, it's so horrible

ils s'enfilent entre eux en public!

tíos guarros!

si a meno fossero giovani

l'Arabo è vecchio e spaventoso

tu crois qu'ils comprennent le français?

essaye de leur parler

Monsieur, vous n'avez pas honte?

fusilarlos, sí señor, fusilarlos

ah, los buenos tiempos!

it turns my stomach

io credevo che soltanto i ragazzi
oh, snap it!
please, don't move
try again
gentuza, eso es lo que son!
excusez-moi, Monsieur, je suis sociologue et je mène une enquête sur
disgraziati!
honey, we're so happy together
guarda, carina, che porcaccione!
qu'est-ce que vous pensez du mariage? n'avez-vous pas la nostalgic d'une famille?
el matrimonio, sí señor!
la pareja, el hogar, los niños
à quel âge vous êtes-vous rendu compte que
I'm getting sick
una fotografia ancora
une thèse sur les déviations psychologiques et sexuelles de
te das cuenta de nuestra suerte de haber nacido normales?
cuando pienso que habría podido ser como ellos
calla, chato, que se me pone la carne de gallina
avez-vous reçu une éducation quelconque?
oh!
what's the matter?
regarde, ils jouissent!
un momentino, per carità
look toward the camera
andiamo, è troppo orrido
nos van a estropear la luna de miel
no te preocupes, cielo, ahora mismo vamos al cuarto y fabricaremos un nene
sí, hazme un niño rubito!
when the babelic crowd disperses, one last inquisitive couple will take a closeup in color of the twin corpora delicti: the two of them are good-looking, harmonious, and young, and they will exchange a happy, conspiratorial smile that will

show off to good advantage the sovereign perfection of their teeth

3

in the middle of the nuptial bed and its resplendent coverlet, you will attentively contemplate your implacable enemy
the smiling
vernal
Fecund
Reproductive Couple
all nations, whatever their ideologies or credos, nourish and foster its myth: churches and governments, without exception, extol it, the various communications media exploit it to serve promotional and propagandistic ends: the Couple's image fills the wide screen in movie houses, it is obsessively repeated on countless pages in daily papers, it pops up along superhighways and subway corridors, it is multiplied to a dizzying degree in the cyclopean eye of the boob tube: the perfumed, snow-white purity of toothpaste emphasizes their natural harmony, face creams and electric razors contribute to their well-being, the mentholated aroma of cigarettes stimulates and intoxicates them, electric household appliances strengthen the solidity of their conjugal ties, marvelous, instant-acting detergents ensure them radiant happiness: airlines and tourist agencies place them in a vast, suggestive panorama of picturesque landscapes, monuments, and beaches: lying stretched out face upward, their sheer presence enhances the tempting décor of some paradisaical island: a transparent blue sea, feathery, languid coconut palms, fine, soft sand, Polynesian cabañas in the form of a Vietnamese hat, a native boatman or two with gauguinesque leis draped about their necks: an absolutely delicious "in"

drink delightfully refreshes their gullets, soothing suntan lotion softens their skin tanned to a tawny gold, andré-kostelanetzesque transistor music lulls them to sleep, dreaming of happiness: the symmetrical disposition of their bodies favors their mutual rapture behind the two protective lenses of spectacularly outsize dark glasses: snapped by the camera in front of a group of imposing ruins, dressed in diaphanous pierrecardinesque, clubmediterranean outfits that they wear with careful carelessness, they are the very picture of unclouded bliss, within the reach of everyone's pocketbook: unisex shirts and pullovers, pants in ingenious color combinations, the chronometric aid of the Swiss-watch industry, the latest miraculous camera produced by the fertile powers of invention of the Japanese: third-world natives wander by in the distance on camels or burros and disappear amid palms or olive trees, behind dusky hills or honey-colored dunes: thus everything, absolutely everything, contributes to their extraordinary splendor and adds subtle and delicate touches to their exemplary beauty: lipsticks, Kleenex, deodorants: Coca-Cola, ice-cold beer, whisky on the rocks: refrigerators, tape recorders, cars: travel, psychiatric treatment, credit cards: health clubs, diets, rest cures: and instead of growing old and fading away, getting sick or dying by accident, the Couple thrives and is rejuvenated, continually perfects itself, and full of self-admiration, seeks the means of perpetuating itself in accordance with the canons of the sacramental ritual: the selection of models is vast and guarantees the grandeur and magnificence of the ceremony: the bride is enchanting in her white satin wedding dress and her tulle illusion veil fastened down by a simple and original ornament: escorted by her father, she will arrive at the church in a picturesque coach drawn by two superb stallions, and once the moving ceremony is over, she will repair with her impeccably dressed husband to the celebrated restaurant where a cordon-bleu chef has prepared a rich and elegant wedding feast: and in front of the display windows of the Galerías Preciados in Madrid, the Samaritaine in Paris, Macy's or Bloomingdale's in New York, the dense, motley crowd that invades the asphaltjungle sidewalks amid the shoving and pushing characteristic of the rush hour will stop to stare with envious eyes at the luxurious model of a king-size bed destined to ensure the happy couple a long life in a happy home blessed with love, prosperity, and good fortune: an extra-firm, lace-tied mattress that assures proper support and lasting comfort: cash or credit terms: complete with matching balanced foundation boxsprings: don't doubt it for a moment!: its construction provides a wonderful night's rest: turn your dreams into a reality!: this week only at savings that are terrific: make up your minds, for heaven's sake!: this quilted, extra-firm favorite is for you!: the gaping bystanders jostle one another on the other side of the display window, and elbowing your way through the crowd, you too will examine, with your nose pressed against the glass, the other furnishings of the sensational bedroom: a luxurious three-piece leather suite, a six-branched chandelier, two night tables, each with its own bed lamp, an exquisite dressing table, a chest of drawers with an enormous bouquet of tuberoses and white lilies on top of it: a reproduction of Murillo's Virgin adds an elegant touch to the whole, and forming a pair with it, an image of the Redeemer, possessed of eyes that follow the person who contemplates it with a mute, heartbreaking gaze full of sadness and pain, presiding over the scene from above the nuptial bed itself: the Couple has just now arrived: the groom, in a top hat and morning coat, is carrying the bride in his arms, and her bashful blush, though attenuated by the delicate tulle of her veil, softly colors her cheeks: he will then solemnly deposit her in the middle of the eiderdown comforter, where the heaven-blessed act of procreation will take place, ad majorem Dei gloriam: the sighs of the protagonists emphasize the transcendent importance of the act, and with innocent modesty they will turn their backs to each other as they commence to undress: on either side of the regal bed, they will lay out on the corresponding chair the symbolic garments that cover and adorn them: the emotion that overcomes them is evident, and despite the brechtian alienation effect of the glass of the display window, it will communicate itself to the spectators crowded round about you and will strike you too like a bolt of lightning: all mystic visionaries have universally celebrated the miracle of generation, and what about you, you miserable wretch?: unproductive loves, base pleasures, infamous copulations, and never mind the rest!: the moment has come to regenerate yourself and harmoniously pluck the strings of the lyre!: the most luminous adjectives of your native tongue flock to your pen in a tumultuous throng and will convert you into a new, nobelable bard of patrimaternity!: your readers will heave sighs of relief, the critics will applaud you, classroom texts will proudly present your profound human sentiments for the respectful admiration of future generations!: the aura of historic responsibility overwhelms you, and you will gaze round about you in search of guidance and inspiration: various anthologies of poetry generously offer you their muses, and you will open one of them that you have chosen by chance: Some pray to marry the one they love, My prayer will somewhat vary, I humbly pray to Heaven above, That I love the one I marry: your enthusiastic reading fills you with rapture, and the flutelike voice of Vosk will spur you on: come on, my boy, just follow the rhythm, you'll see how easy it is!: but the Couple is now completely undressed and the glorious events taking place in the nuptial bed command your attention: seated on one corner of the bed, beneath the combined protection of the Madonna and the Redeemer, the spouses will read aloud a selection of papal encyclicals dealing with the sacrament of marriage and its aims before consulting the illustrated edition of *Sane Sex Life and Sane Sex Living,* which today's newlyweds are permitted to read, thanks to the aggiornamented blessing of the Grand Magus: in order to ensure harmonious conjugal relations which, without neglecting the aim of procreation, allow future parents a mild and moderate corporeal satisfaction: the illustrations in color offer a most generous sampler of positions that will ensure fecundation, and the Couple will study them with open minds but understandable circumspection: at once joyful, trembling, and uneasy: already foreseeing the minuscule and slight penetration that will start the gene on its well-known journey and put an end, after nine long months, to their atavistic anxieties: positions number three, sixteen, and twenty-four appear to be relatively easy, and they will make up their minds to follow the instructions for them with methodical precision: squatting down in front of each other, they will perform various gymnastico-respiratory exercises with the aim of relieving their nervous tension and facilitating the proper relaxation of their tissues: the wealth of experience set before them by the manual ought rightfully to permit them an exemplary conjugation of the verb *to make love,* and the impatient eyes of the crowd will be riveted upon the angle at which there converge, in chiaroscuro, the bridegroom's thighs, awaiting the indisputable signs of a change of state: not yet manifest, it would seem, by virtue perhaps of that powerful self-possession characteristic of those who exercise strict control over their bodies thanks to the iron discipline of yoga: serene and to all appearances self-assured, he will continue for one whole hour the inspiratory-expiratory movements that make the muscles more flexible and favor the proper afflux of blood at the crucial and most opportune moment: yet despite his growing signs of fatigue and the incipient nervousness of the bride, the expected tumular flux will not be forthcoming: no prophesied dilation is visible at the vertex of the groin, and the childish face of the bridegroom will little by little express a curious mixture of distress and shame: the manual, the encyclicals, gymnastics, and yoga do not suffice: in vain he will engage in further breathing exercises, scrutinize the colored illustrations in the book, read over carefully, phrase by phrase, the doctrines propounded by Church councils: the view of his thighs will continue to be ignominiously unobstructed, and as the present indicative founders and the hope of the future retreats in the distance, the amatory conjugation will proceed in the melancholy conditional tenses and slowly and pathetically slip into the imperfect subjunctive

if I had	you would have
if you had	I would have
if we had	perhaps we would have
if we could have	we never could have

the passive voice and the compound tenses have no place in the nuptial paradigm, and lacking a nihil obstat, you will be obliged to discard them: the tribulations of the Couple become more and more pitiful, and they will repeat gerunds and imperatives to no avail; irregular, perhaps defective, the Word refuses to rise up: and as the two of them sob out in chorus the irremediable past participle, the look of confusion and dismay on their countenances leaves a deep impression on the audience on the sidewalk and will little by little affect the great masses of the entire city: the exorcisms of your poetic anthology prove utterly powerless, and you will dejectedly throw it into the nearest sewer: for a few moments you will feel totally lost and will wander about aimlessly, with bowed head, amid the untamed fauna of Manhattan: but fate is still watching over you, and on lifting your eyes heavenward as you wait for the traffic light to change, you will be the fortunate witness of a sudden and resplendent Apparition

4

modern information theory and the spectacular progress of cybernetics helps us to situate her preferences: countries with an archaic and tribal economic system, based primarily on farming and cattle raising: barren plains and wastelands burning in the sun above the summer low-water mark or swept by chill winter winds: semibarbarous, pastoral communities, with an extremely high birth rate and a level of education whose average is close to zero: with a penchant for steep crags and gorges that allow her to show off with grace and elegance her talents as a weightless gymnast: the solitary tree, the bare fields, the crystalline spring that give rise to folktales and popular beliefs, to the singing of the antiphon: the damp hidden caves created by the geological action of subterranean waters, an ideal décor for her prognostications and levitations: it pleases her to break a path through the clouds and float among wisps and puffs of cotton, compete with the sun that is consumed with envy and force it to withdraw with bowed head, choose the brightest stars and adorn her ears with them: she is fond of making surprise appearances, preferably to youngsters: she chooses those who have had no book learning and know nothing of radar and the pill: she is lavish with little courtesies and smiles, she promises help and favors, she prophesies revolutions and foretells earthquakes, she voices capricious desires: her mantle and her crown rival those of the most magnificent princess dolls, and when she speaks, she uses the language of the country, in a piping, crystal-clear voice, a modern version, according to cinephiles, of the unforgettable Shirley Temple

5

but you are neither a youngster, nor illiterate, nor a shepherd, and the miraculous apparition calling to you from the spire of the Empire State Building is the glorious King Kong: recently freed from the chains of ludicrous exhibition on Broadway, he has climbed up to the sharp tip of the skyscraper and occupies his playful moments of leisure by grabbing with his paws the helicopters winging toward the roof of the Pan Am Building: the unwary pilots do not realize, fools that they are, that his presence is not a novel advertisement sponsored by the tourist industry in these difficult days of the dollar crisis, but rather a sudden, splendid reality: having discharged their load of passengers, the aircraft come crashing down like dragonflies amid the swarming hordes on the sidewalks, and your faunlike mentor rejoices at the panic and confusion that he has caused: the damsels he has carried off by force tremble with inexpressible happiness on his huge hairy palm, and the anthropomorph will contemplate them ecstatically and delicately brush the tip of his lingual dart along their thighs: seeking out their exquisite periodic nectar, like those greedy bear cubs, expert searchers for honey, that poke their snouts in beehives, paying no heed to the insects' wrath or their painful sting: as the damsels moan and sigh and melt inside with pleasure at the contact of the enslaving humid fire: dreamily, they will contemplate the fabulous dimensions of his attributes, muttering between their teeth the maxim erroneously ascribed to Saint Augustine: that marvelously beautiful credo quia absurdum against which Saint Bonaventure rebelled with such petty-mindedness: unable to make up their minds to reject, as did the curious character of the legend, this dizzying, utterly mad idea: lost, like the latter, in a state of contemplation that will continue for hours and hours before they finally regretfully decide to renounce madness: but the epic feat tempts them nonetheless, and the damsels will loudly curse the bitterness of a ludicrous fate that deprives them of this superior form of knowledge: biblical, total, immediate: impossible, impossible: all the vaseline in the world will not suffice to bring about the miracle: covered with shame, the hapless bridegrooms witness the astonishing exhibition of his physical endowments, and wounded pride, dejection, and envy gradually cast a pall over their faces: in any event, their inferiority with respect to your mentor is irremediable, and the damsels also note this and with lofty disdain give themselves over to otiose and humiliating comparisons: unlike the extraordinarily well-balanced heroine of the film, capable of passing with neither anger nor dismay from the arms of her illustrious abductor to those of a most unpretentious and pitiful fiancé, the panoramic revelation offered them there on the heights will traumatize them for the rest of their days, eliminating all possibility of a hypothetical return to normality: the gnosis has been too powerful: henceforth, the tenuous process of reasoning, the boring chain of syllogisms will appear odious to them: the concrete materialism of King Kong will follow them wherever they go with the clear evidence of its forceful arguments: and the honeymoon trip to Paris, on the advice of the best doctors, will further aggravate their mental state: the Eiffel Tower, the obelisk of the Place de la Concorde will keep alive the memory of the piercing vision, and instead of forgetting and resigning themselves to their fate, they will reject with scorn and loathing the dull, petty pleasures of marital scholastics: beneath the Arc de Triomphe, they will dream of the opening outward indispensable to praxis: of the sudden and brutal incursion of Teutonic philosophy, so similar to that other one, closer in time, incarnated in the siegfriedian monster and his superior preparedness with respect to artillery, which gave to the monument its reason for being during the virile debacle of the year 1940: identifying there on the spot with the symbolic emblem of their unconditional surrender to the victorious orangutan: forever imprinted on their retinas in the fullness of his convincing powers of persuasion: eternally prepared to take the dialectical, qualitative leap: with King Kong, your lord and master, who aims at the very center of their feminine selfhood with the pure rigor of his admirable categorical imperative

6

you will follow their example and glorify the amorous potency of the simian: putting your pen at the service of his magnificent disproportion, exalting his physical endowments with all the resources of verbal treachery: by way of the subtle, poisoned subversion of sacrosanct linguistic values: sacrificing the referent to the truth of written discourse and thereby accepting the consequences of your delirious deviation: your splendid loneliness of a long-distance runner: the insolent defiance of the order of the real: you will allow the Couple to reproduce amid courteous yawns and conceive and give birth to a loathsome child: the flaccid and useless offspring of some sloppily sentimental lullaby: will he be a tiny baby? with curly hair maybe?: the words of the song do not matter: his various anobucconasal orifices will give forth stinking secretions that little by little will pollute the model family atmosphere and necessitate the sonorous intervention of ambulances and fire-department companies equipped with disinfecting devices and gas masks: tepid procreative love irremediably bores you to death and you will extol, without remorse or scruples, solitary and empty pleasure, vile, abnormal, illicit pleasure: inspired by the splendid majesty of King Kong, you will celebrate from this time forward the unspeakable, the aberrant, the heinous: bringing out into the diaphanous light of day the monsters that terrify petty minds amid the sleep of reason: vile copulation, seminal dissipation that unites hapless bodies, turning their conjugation into a prodigal and exalting common consumption!: dreaming of the crepuscular vortex of a dead universe, where the crude, rough love that the simian proposes to you portends all manner of crimes to enhance and stimulate its imperious ferocity

7

in the subsoil of Manhattan today, along the labyrinthine network of sewers and tunnels lying below the surface of the island, a collectivity no less interesting and complex than that subjected to the computerized studies of sociologists has installed itself, lives, and attempts to propagate itself amid the dense shadows of its stygian lagoon: crocodiles, alligators, lizards, iguanas infest, in increasing numbers, these nauseating cloacae, and adapting itself to the unusual conditions of this environment, this collectivity slowly metamorphoses as a result of its somber nocturnal existence: new amphibious species, possessed of a monstrous voracity, multiply secretly and without arousing the slightest alarm beneath the feet of the uninformed and unsuspecting city: crawling, writhing creatures, shunning the light, feed upon their fetid waste products and await the occasion to abandon their parasitical life and vengefully emerge into the light of day: letting yourself down by means of little rusty ladders, making your way through a labyrinth of slimy, oozing passages, you will witness the spasms of their cold copulation and the oviparous hatching of their offspring: like the eye of the Cyclops, your inspiration gleams brightly by night and the desire to be like them nestles, insatiable, in your most secret heart of hearts: long, lithe, with a body covered with steel-hard scales, a huge mouth equipped with sharp fangs, webbed hind feet, a tail that is flat and particularly suited for swimming: abandoning your illusory role of lord and master of Creation (an erect posture, the power of articulated speech, an intelligent and impressionable soul) for the implacable rigor of this accursed fauna: darkness and filth will be your chosen lair as well, and one day, by way of the sewer drains and the entire water supply and sanitary system of the city, you will make your way, along with this fauna, to the very tops of the skyscrapers and take part in the invasion of housing projects and apartment buildings via the pipes of the sinks, toilets, and bathtubs: cunning, darting heads will shoot up out of the toilet bowls just as the hominid is about to to rest his strictly sequestered backside on the seat, and this surprise will cause him to recoil in terror, like the unwary hiker who lifts a stone with his walking stick and discovers underneath it a nest of vipers: but these reptiles are your friends, and your profound familiarity with them affords you satisfactions incomparably superior to those of the sempiternal casuistry (artistic, social, or moral) of the biped species: the descent on the animal scale will be an ascent for you: you bear on your forehead the mark of Cain, and even though, a heretic among other heretics, you do not share in the glories and the communal rites of its passionate liturgy, out of respect for the old men in turbans who display their suasive arts in Moroccan tourist folders, you will nonetheless exalt with your words the clandestine, night-wandering confraternity of snake charmers

8

when night puts an end to the prudent, reasonable productive activities of the bustling city, the worshipers of the beast

emerge from their habitual diurnal lethargy and after casting a wary glance along the deserted sidewalks, furtively
glide through shadowy, solitary zones, paying no attention
to the crepuscular flood of propaganda put out by the adversaries of ophidians

BE CAREFUL: THEY ARE EXTREMELY DANGEROUS

THEY ATTACK THEIR PREY WITH THEIR POISONOUS FANGS

THEIR BITE IS ALWAYS SERIOUS AND FREQUENTLY FATAL

THEY SOMETIMES STRANGLE THEIR VICTIMS IN THEIR COILS

THEY MAY BE AS MUCH AS FORTY-FIVE FEET LONG

this conventional wisdom, promulgated by paterfamilias,
makes no impression on them, and zigzagging across sinister corners in order to put any possible pursuers off their
track, they will explore the dark, damp places where the
hated and feared animal habitually conceals itself: caverns
with scaling, moss-covered walls, where the subterranean
action of water creates gullies, cascades, and stalactites,
dimly illuminated by a feeble bulb, of the sort that customarily
sheds its sickly light in dungeons and cells in the basements
of police stations: there, under the cover of, and more or less
with the complicity of, the dark shadows, they patiently
await the sudden apparition so as to fall on their knees and
pay it the usual homage of prayers of supplication: savoring
its powerful virtue with the solemn mien of those who close
their eyes in ecstasy as the necromancer deposits the pure
white talisman on their tongues: also kneeling, if not on the
ground, on a crude, humble prie-Dieu: immersed in the
beatitude of their sublime but incommunicable experience:
and not forgetting afterward the customary acts of thanks-
giving: the attitudes of profound desire, self-surrender, and
humility that manuals of piety recommend: but the frenzy
of the night urges them on, and abandoning the secret, secluded crypt, they will continue, with tireless zeal, on their
perilous pilgrimage: through dark and boggy zones that
lend themselves to their absorbing clandestine activity: not
to mention the natural ruggedness of the haunts where the

cunning, crafty, and cruel animal instinctively conceals itself: guiding themselves, with the aid of a mysterious sixth sense, along narrow paths and shortcuts until they reach the verdant hedge that serves it as a nest and conceals their reverent genuflection from the eyes of the world: orders, threats, imprecations fail to dissuade them from continuing their search, and intent upon their rustic devotions, they scorn with joyous temerity the danger that lies close at hand: their hunting parties take no notice of the rigors of the weather, the rules and regulations forbidding flushing game at night in public parks, the hysterical wail of the sirens of patrol cars: inquisitorial flashlights pierce the night above their heads, and the sound of heavy footfalls magnifies and enhances the risks of their sacramental liturgy: the fulfillment of the rites of exorcism will finally lead them to low-lying, swampy regions, and concealing yourself from their gaze, you will furtively take your place among them, amid the nasty creeping vegetation: descending through the many superimposed strata along which myriads of wandering shades roam, clad in ghostly togas, their silhouettes dimly outlined by feeble little lanterns and blurred by clouds of steam: from the healing pool of Bethesda to the tenebrous ergastula which ordinarily are one of the haunts favoring the robust disposition of the sovereign beast: the treacherous, tenacious ophidian, whose hiss the consummate hunter detects by keeping his ear expertly cocked: yes, it is there, and everything would suggest that it is awaiting the arrival of the unwary huntsman in order to paralyze him by means of the venom of its voracious mouth or the subtle asphyxia of its amorous embrace: petty-minded prudence inclines him to flee, but his passion for hunting asserts itself and lulls his fears of a fatal encounter: his passion is a superior form of warfare and he will throw all caution to the winds: single-mindedly, tirelessly, he will again domesticate the reptile with the masterful resources of his ritual wisdom and will search out the remaining hiding places in the cavern, eager to test to the limit the possibilities of his ministry, like those souls thirsting for perfection who scrupulously prolong the recital of their prayers long after the rites of the cult are ended: the adoration will continue throughout the night, and on the following day, when twilight falls, the Spartan cycle will begin all over again

9

you will subject geography to the imperatives and demands of your passion: from the narrow alleyways of Riad Ez-Zitún to the environs of the Gare du Nord, you will set in place the elements of the décor that in the future will serve as a background for your hosts: the sibylline snake charmer of the square of Djemá-el-Fná summons tourists and natives by beating rhythmically on his drum, and you will join the ring of spectators around him, endeavoring with the greatest of difficulty to conceal your emotion: you have slowly cast off the habits and principles that you were taught when you were a child: you no longer fit in them: like a serpent that sheds its skin, you have abandoned them along the roadside and gone on: your body has acquired the flexibility that allows you to crawl like an ophidian, and the mere sight of your former species arouses in your consciousness sumptuous images of verbal violence: your contact with this fauna will be that of the knife: the piercing scream of the girl staggering across the lobby of the train station creates round about her a sacred space inaccessible to those curious bystanders who do not share her delirium, and following her example, you will base your own invulnerability on a sudden defiance of their logic: the future of their world does not matter in the slightest to you, and no humanitarian considerations will corrupt your conscience: do not trust yourself: it is not enough to throw overboard your name, face, family, customs, homeland: the rigorous self-discipline must continue: every single word of your native tongue also sets a trap for you: from this moment forward you will learn to think by fighting against your own language

10

you will descend into the crypt once again: the inexorable rage you feel against the flock to which you once belonged and the pleasure of witnessing the humiliating mockery to which it will be subjected will warm your heart as you weave in and out of the stream of people heading down the dark corridor toward the nonrevolutionary, non-gold-covered little shrines: waddling along, furiously fanning themselves because of the heat, or pulling up the lapels of their fur coats as they shiver in misery from the cold, exchanging information in a hysterical tone of voice, powdering their faces, combing their hair, emitting giggles, piping trills, sighs, the members of the confraternity wander over to their hieratic sentinels, anxiously searching for their prince: their extreme state of agitation is the obvious response to the no less extreme repression of their tribe: a centrifugal force stronger than the law of universal gravitation has propelled them, like stray meteorites, into this remote, subterranean basilica: fallout from some terrible explosion, scattered by the winds to every corner of the compass, gathered together here by a trick of fate!: the flute solo magnetizes them and they dedicate their devotions to it: take a good look at them: their temerity knows no bounds: their antiphonies, communions, supplications are supplanted by the feverish rhythm of those who know that they have been sentenced to be executed at dawn and imbibe life in tiny little sips: more than four centuries of disgrace and affronts, prison, torture, the stake (ever since the rabid, rancorous decree of

a frigid queen and the autos-da-fé of her grotesque progeny) have gone into the creation of the endemic tension
that distinguishes them from the other activists of the confraternity: corpses whose death sentence in Hitler's ghetto
was commuted (faggots, a sackcloth sambenito, a gag, a
white scapular, a dunce cap of flames), their frenzied provo-
cation extends to the farthest corners of the earth: a centuries-old atavism impels them to indulge in melodramatic
histrionics and hyperbole, as when they arrogantly invent
out of whole cloth the character of the sad royal prisoner of
Tordesillas, the victim of love dreamed up by a film director
and played to the hilt by the actress whose name headed the
list of screen credits: concealing with extravagant gestures
the imperturbable immobility of her king: the handsome
Flemish flamingo, with pure white feathers on its breast and
blood-red ones on its back, shown in the colored illustrations
of the usual schoolroom textbooks: a warm-blooded, verte-
brate biped, possessed of a heart with auricles and ventricles,
a good swimmer, and either nidiphilous or nidifugous:
leaning with his back to the wall, like other members of his
species, with visible, deliberate scorn: clearly discernible
nasal orifices, bright piercing little eyes, a perhaps toothless
mouth, a cigarette dangling from his beak: wings folded,
long-shanked, he appears to be perched on one foot as he
draws the other one up from time to time and indolently
rests the sole of it on the chinks and cracks in the wall: and
with the silent assent of the palace guards and courtiers,
the nonboreal Aurora who plays the part of Juana la Loca
multiplies her demential gestures, enveloped in an aura of
admiration and pity for her tragicosplendid fate: her eyes
glisten roguishly beneath the thin black veil, her thick
makeup dissolves and runs down the corners of her lips in
ridiculous trickles: pointing her index finger at them, she
will murmur over and over, a thousand times, that the king is
not dead, he has merely fallen asleep: with that most peculiar diction shared by the starry horde of her imitators,

which, having fled the rigors of the country, now flourishes, a thousand leagues away, in remote and humble surroundings: history is eminently just at times: and Isabella the Catholic mother will witness, horror-stricken, the cruel spectacle: the vengeance of the execrated sodomite brother and his vilified friends: the scene is repeated daily, with no chronicler and no bard, and the absolute power of your antlike craftsmanship dazzles you: the ghostly soliloquy of mad women will avenge the memory of the king: brusquely, with a simple stroke of your pen, you will cancel out centuries of infamy

11

MAIS DIEU CREA LES ARABES
all of you exist
those are his exact words in the Koran
the best people ever to have lived in humanity's midst, you ordain what is just, prohibit what is unjust, and believe in me
these are the precise words to be found in the pages of the Book lent you by a comrade, after one of your usual meetings, along one of the asphalt-paved boulevards with an incomparable view in the City of Light that becomes less luminous with every passing day
and the love that you will find in their company will be as burning and as sterile as the desert plains: far from moist, moss-covered caverns that shelter the nocturnal activity of the underground water: everything is clean here: supple, muscular bodies, whose sinuous articulations are mindful of the smooth convexity of the distant sand dunes: when haze blurs their rounded forms and the searing breath of the simoon finishes its work of shading, imparting a sudden animal palpitation to the tawny landscape: curves and more curves superposed in surging waves, a promiscuous com-

munity that resiliently couples without becoming shapeless, simultaneous tensions and embraces in the warm and supple texture: serpentine irradiations that run over the undulating skin and delicately sculpt its contours with masterful sobriety: without feminine artifices or adornments: coppices, orchards, shady groves, delightful smiling meadows: nothing but muscles and stone: wasted away, corroded, eroded by the continual action of the wind: with no seminal rain to fecundate it: dry, so dry!: greenery is a sign of great effort and a reward: the solitary trunk of the palm tree indicates the invisible presence of the well, but you will not drink from it: the satiety common to the simple in heart fills you with loathing: the vigorous growth of the tree subverts its superannuated laws and with illegitimate pride you will slowly quench your thirst: its bitter sap is enough for you: what does it matter if dogs bark at your heels?: the caravan passes: the desert beckons to you once again, as vast and stubborn as your desire, and you will penetrate the dense configuration of its implacable copper-colored breast: mountainous arms will wall off the line of the horizon, mercifully isolating you from the fertile and hostile world: striding step by step across the sheath of its smooth abdomen, you will reach the next oasis thanks to the subtle instinct of the Meharis: Anselm Turmeda, Father Foucauld, Lawrence of Arabia?: amid those of your kind at last, immersed in their teeming human broth, scarcely recognizable beneath your grayish beard and the dust and filth of your clothes: dark glasses protect you and hide your piercing gaze from the curious glances of others: your eyes have lost the soft gentleness of adolescence and the maniacal fixed stare of their gleaming pupils as they search the immediate surroundings for prey will disturb the repose of any Nazarene who imprudently dares to take a peek at them: the traitor who wanders deliriously about the marketplaces of Africa is the negation of the order that governs his world and he will cautiously point an accusing index finger: this ungainly silhouette is deceptive: a severe prophylaxis is called for: unspeakable? a turncoat? a renegade? a sodomite? a pervert?: worse, much worse: he is a sower of winds: and as the saying goes

12

he who sows the wind shall reap the whirlwind

uttered a thousand times by circumspect and cautious throats, the warning will not reach fugitives of your kind, whom the centrifugal, forbidden passion has driven to these stony and barren purlieus

the baritones of the old order thunder in vain from the lecterns and pulpits of their committees, institutes, and churches, and armed with the precise dart of the word, you will jeeringly take aim at the great ugly mask of their pompous respectability and the curved and inflated profile of their dropsical self-importance

you will counter their spirit of authority and hierarchy, based on prohibitions and laws, with the egalitarian and generic subversion of the aroused, naked body

the phallus, that is correct, the phallus

the strong erect stem carrying sap to the calyx!

laughter will serve all of you as a snare

with its fierce, corrosive aid, you will deflate their fatuous balls and balloons and expose their petty, ridiculous fear to the realities of the world

one by one

you will snatch off their wretched, grotesque masks

bird in hand

but not scorning the hundred that fly away

you will oblige them to strip naked too and subject them to the cruel mockery of your vengeful discourse

hearken unto our words

the traps of your reason will fail to catch us
morality
religion
society
patriotism
family
are mere threatening sounds whose ringing reverberations
    will leave us indifferent
do not count on us
we believe in a world without borders
wandering Jews
heirs of Juan the Landless
we shall encamp there where instinct leads us
the Mohammedan brotherhood attracts us and within it we
    shall find refuge
give up your monotonous refrain
the familiar, age-old threat of shameful disasters and calami-
    ties
after us the deluge?
LET US SOW WHIRLWINDS!

III

not like today

when pent-up rage overflows sordidly in the secret precincts of hidden underground cellars and the basements of police stations, the physical humiliation of the hated-and-feared creature (the unconscious object of their envy and perhaps of their hidden desire), the stubborn rain of blows, anguish venting its fury on its own specter (failing, however, to thus exorcise it), the victim's stifled screams and the joyous panting breath of the uniformed Proboscidea (urging one another on with vigorous vocal emissions), the shouts of sale race dégueulasse pouilleux ordure saloperie (uttered in the language of Villon and Descartes), the fruitless attempt to answer (and perhaps a clumsy attempt to escape), the sudden decision on the part of the lead dog of the pack to unholster his revolver (claiming legitimate self-defense), the usual shout of halt (repeated three times, in accordance with regulations), the detonation of the bullets, the confusion, the screams, the panic of the mastodons, the feverish agreement of the witnesses, the successive different versions of events, the orotund statements to the press, the contradictions that leap to the eye, the accursed questions to which there is no answer, the stubborn, embarrassed silence
on a grand scale in those days
when the foul pack of hounds of the Allergie Française openly took the law into their own hands on the streets (door-to-door searches without warrants, mass arrests, discriminatory curfew regulations), and dozens and dozens of handcuffed corpses (with a bullet hole in their temples or

the bruises of strangulation) appeared, floating in the gentle current of the river so beautifully celebrated by poets, passing beneath those same bridges evoked by chansonniers to the soft, melancholy accompaniment of accordions and guitars (as meanwhile the city's municipal council voted the necessary funds for feeding the doves and whitewashing public buildings and monuments, and children filled the marvelous city gardens and parks with their gentle, musical chirpings) at that very point in time at which your irremediable hatred toward your own marks of identity (race profession class family homeland) was growing, in direct proportion to your magnetic attraction toward pariahs, and all the violence wreaked in the name of the civilizing flock of the faithful (to which you at least outwardly still belonged) widened the yawning abyss that had opened up between you and it, and the feeling of treachery and aversion nestling like an eagle within your bosom grew stronger and stronger, on contemplating with solidary pride the sudden threat they represented as they came up in compact groups out of the subway entrances, herded along with kicks and the blows of rifle butts into the black depths of police vans, and when there proved to be an insufficient number of the latter, standing there with their hands behind their necks on the broad expanses of pavement of this Place de l'Etoile that had suddenly become a star of David that revived the humiliations of the ghetto that lay less than a quarter of a century in the past

supposedly a thing of the past, but now suddenly existing once again

not in the subtle labyrinth of tunnels and narrow passageways perhaps conceived by a sickly mole in Prague in his delirious fits of insomnia

(the doleful creak of the gates leading to the subway platforms as they close automatically, the advertising slogan NICO-LAS FINES BOUTEILLES dementedly repeated over and over again along the stairways, maps of the bus lines, safety warnings that no one reads, ads for DU BO DU BON DUBONNET glimpsed in the sudden swift sweep of light from the subway trains, alluring inducements addressed to a prosperous consumer society, displaying a rich assortment of models of cars, group tourist excursions, toilet paper so soft that its touch is almost a caress, marvelous cheeses, sublime elixirs, exquisitely feminine or paternal articles of underclothing, benign institutions offering bank loans on easy terms, all of them shown against a background of souvenir postcard landscapes, blissful married couples, and sexy chicks, even when the fertile inventiveness of an aborted May strewed the walls with mocking, cynical, comic, fierce, insolent, dubious, joyous inscriptions, introducing a corrosive, blighting germ into the familiar polychrome bliss, followed by a predictable reflux of sacrosanct values, more favorable to the malicious, tortuous rancors of the, alas, not always silent majority, to the moral eructations of the unpolluted solid middle-class citizen, to the pale, eurocratic, and scarcely furtive hand which, above all suspicion, gives expression, with pencil, spray paint, or lipstick, to the somber images that haunt his dreams

MORT AUX BOUGNOULS

RATONS = SYPHILIS

UNE FEMME QUI COUCHE AVEC UN ARABE EST PIRE QU'UNE PUTAIN)

no, not there, outside, outside

when the summer blood-letting (exudation?) has rid the urban arteries of their manufactured toxins and the bloated city is recovering its original nubile silhouette for a few weeks: an August reducing treatment that is conducive to the free contemplation of its body without deposits of fat or varicose veins and lures the lonely foreigner left in the rear guard into undertaking a new and exiting journey: not to the haunts usually frequented by the omnipresent multitude on the move: the anonymous, featureless face of the hydra with countless heads: the décor, rather, of an old film dating from the thirties for lovers who kiss each other at the entrance to the subway: old men sitting on public benches, leisurely stollers, a harmless Salvation Army street band: perhaps a quiet game of pétanque: the thick cloud of vapor traces spirals above the deserted streets, and abandoned by its own offspring, suddenly the city belongs to you and the wogs

(far from the gregarious sun worshipers, the family house trailers jammed one alongside the other in camp grounds, the skins whose fake tan comes out of a bottle, the lizards lying stretched out at the edges of swimming pools: the resigned progeny-producing common herd, the cars driven along as though they were light tanks)

slowly, you will head toward the sewer ditch being installed by the department of public works which, like the hail of murderous machine-gun fire from a plane, has disemboweled the paved surface of the sidewalk and revealed the earth hidden below, scattering it along a line parallel to the wooden walkway provided for pedestrians along which you will venture as the humble artificers toil at your feet with their picks and shovels and the chatter of the pneumatic drill in the background pierces your ears with the muted impact of machine-gun bullets: desurplusvalued darkies of the common sewer, in direct contact with crude raw material, the vile apotheosis, the visceral emanations of the plebs?: long before your aborted birth in the bosom of the pure and virtuous family, with the imperious gesture of the plantation boss, as in the happy days of your great-grandfather's lifetime?: a cruel and unwelcome nightmare that stubbornly pursues you with its indelible stigma despite all your bold, long-standing efforts to free yourself of it: the virgin sheet of paper again offers you splendid possibilities of redemption, along with the joy of profaning its whiteness:

a simple stroke of the pen suffices: you will recreate their bodies
moved by the violent passion that they inspire in you, without conjuring away their three-dimensional concreteness with a sober linear description or destroying their sovereign reality through the illusory process of naming them: imprinting their physical existence upon the paper thanks to a luxurious proliferation of signs, the exuberant accumulation of figures of speech: making use of all the tricks of rhetoric: similes, synecdoche, metonymy, metaphor: stretching the muscles of the phrase to the limit, becoming entangled in it in an implicatory carnal embrace, engaging in hand-to-hand combat with slippery, elusive words: closely interweaving tough, knotty vine shoots, a process that you will keep watch on out of the corner of your eye with the same willing submissiveness with which the complement escorts the verb!: from above the trunk, past the fleshy flowering of their lips to the luxuriant, hircine foliage of the Babylonian hanging gardens: tightly clutching the ball-point pen, forcing its seminal fluid out of it, holding it erect above the blank page: with brusque, syncopated movements: a genesic plenitude between your hands: their heads poke out of the excavation at the level of your shoes, and your gaze lingers upon them, yielding to their animal magnetism: the smog of the city does not dim their splendor: their work clothes do not disguise their radiance of sons of the desert: bodies enveloped in the rigor and firmness of their beliefs, clinging stubbornly to their instinctive will to live as to a clear and incontrovertible axiom, you will allow their presence to force itself upon you with the blinding clarity of an aphorism: absorbing little by little their nomad spirit, their warm and beneficent solar essence: you too as independent and free as a Bedouin chief: master of the air, the winds, the light, the vast desert expanses, the enormous emptiness: overhead, the subtle colorless sky, and beneath your feet,

the trackless sand, like a glistening glacier

the camels moving at a swift trot cast their shadows on the ground as you and your men advance across the barren plains of Jordan, carefully following the railway line: the laurels of your victory in Aqaba still fresh upon your brow, your person imbued, in the eyes of the harka, with a charismatic power, enhanced by the signs that the enemy is close at hand: possessed of the same fervor as your men, expressing yourself in their harsh dialect, resolved to imitate their mental foundation and take on the Arab skin like a chameleon: your prowess as an expert at blowing up Ottoman locomotives is already legendary, and you will give the signal for the attack with a slight pressure of your index finger on the trigger of your revolver: the bright flare will mount into the sky and burst above the scattered convoy, the horsemen will leap upon the valuable booty, the chargers will whinny as though they had already caught a whiff of the rich feast that will be forthcoming: the slaughter will be carried out with the implacable precision of a ceremonial rite: soldiers and passengers will be stripped of their possessions and their bodies fall victim to the cruel rapacity of vultures: climbing up on the top of the boxcars, standing on planks resembling those of the walkway of the public-works project, you will begin to execute a nimble dance step, watching out of the corner of your eye your own moving silhouette, as in a Chinese shadow play: elegant gestures surrounded by a halo of tutelary messianism that will inflame the passions of your legion to the point of a delirious outpouring of words!: responding to their huzzahs and shouts of victory with a bold flourish of your revolver as you leap from the roof of one boxcar to another in the full regalia of your disguise: clad in white from head to foot, concealed beneath the billowing tulle veil of a bride at the altar, with the inspired lily-white candor of the sharp-witted magus of the Vatican: waving from the lofty heights of your boxcar balcony to the assembled horde of the faithful, reassembling their scattered forces with your magnetic powers, spurring them on to further and more fruitful ventures: dancing back and forth across the boards with the air of a prima donna, a pontifex, and a transvestite: the derailments follow one upon the other with a stepped-up rhythm, and the treacherous gunshot wound inflicted upon you by a straggler in the rear guard of the enemy will confer upon you a spectacular blood baptism: bright red stains will sully the immaculate whiteness of your garments with their impure viscosity, but your perilous career as a star performer will not end here: a prophet of the age-old dream of freedom, in the service of imperial British expansion?: or a juandeorduñesque victim of love in the luxorious caverns of Tordesillas?: becoming another quick-change artist like the celebrated Frégoli, you will continue your swift metamorphosis, leaping from one film to another without thereby abandoning for a single instant the pro-creative rut of the written word: with the silent assent of the palace guards and courtiers you will multiply the demential gestures, enveloped in the aura of your tragicosplendid fate: your eyes glisten roguishly beneath the thin black veil, the thick makeup dissolves and runs down the corners of your lips in ridiculous trickles: raising your pointing index finger in their direction, you will murmur over and over, a thousand times, that the king is not dead, he has merely fallen asleep: not in the cavernous subsoil of the movie house rocked by the tremors of the nearby elevated: on the boards that cover the framework of the boxcars and suddenly are extended so that they run alongside the sewer trench being excavated, thus solicitously offering pedestrians a convenient walkway: far from the cruel and captious plains of Jordan: in the heat of a summer day in Paris that beams its burning rays down upon the enslaved laborers of the public-works project clutching their work tools as, having recovered from your (optical) illusions and the tricks your eyes have played on you, you continue onward like the thin trace of your ball-point pen along the deserted streets of the city: like El-Orens before his secret mission in Deráa, with a snow-white turban atop his head, floating along in his billowing gandurah: your eagerness for nomad experiences in the farthermost corners of Islam will naturally lead you to reconnoiter the enemy's own camp: along the nearby rue d'Aboukir, in search of the minarets of Istanbul, to the tune of the "Turkish March"

hairottomaniacs

In the Plaza of Sultan Ahmed, to be more precise: reject-
ing the phallic invitation of the Obelisk of Theodosius and
the serpentine column, amid the little gardens that stretch
from the Blue Mosque to the basilica, heading toward
the latter and turning off to the right, in the direction of the
Kiosk of the Fountain and the prospect overlooking the
Bosporus: a group of Japanese businessmen aim their cameras like machine guns at the outer walls of the Seraglio,
and fleeing their anachronistic presence, you will go out
onto the Esplanade of the Janissaries and rest for a few
moments with them in the tutelary shade of the great plane
tree: your status as a renegade is conducive to friendship
with their leader, and together you will plan executions and
punishments, exquisite betrayals, and mass-produced tortures: the block of stone drips with blood following the
tiresome executions: a head lies improbably on the ground,
a mournful mask, all ready to adorn the keystone of the
arched gate of Bab-i-Hümayun: when the taciturn executioner plunges his gnarled arms into the holy font, the water
slowly takes on a reddish tinge: the haughty gatekeepers
yawn: the chamberlain nods: as usual, the renegades await
the reward for their services and among their number you
will spy, with a shout of joy, the ancient, centuries-old
author of the *Offering of a Learned Man:* the visionary Ibn
Turmeda in person, come from his distant and delightful
retreat to offer witness of his apostasy, accompanied by his
son Mohammed: their venerable beards rival those of the
sage patriarchs, and their eyes, like those of a falconer, observe the gregarious hordes of tourists flocking through the

Orta Kapu, sheltered beneath the broody hen's wing of an officious shepherd: a dragoman with a diploma, a polyglot who, after taking their tickets, will guide them to the sultan's reception rooms and the showcases full of priceless treasures, unless, obeying secret orders, he conducts them through the Gate of the Dead and announces to them, in a soft voice, their fall from grace and their fortuitous execution (the jail rules make no distinction between prisoners and visitors: once the threshold of the penal institution has been crossed, strangers must endure the rigors of the regulations governing prison life, mingled indiscriminately with the convicts and wearing the same uniforms that they do: the regulations provide for the occasional reversal of their respective roles, and even in the most favorable circumstances the visitor runs the risk of being forgotten in some lonely jail cell or, through some error or other, providing sustenance for the executioner's voracious ax)

you will fall in step with them, pay five lire for your admittance ticket, and scornfully turn down those who offer their services as guides or interpreters: armed, protected, well-nigh invulnerable, thanks to your ostentatious, aggressive exhibition of your copy of the *Guide Bleu:* safe now, walking along the paths and gardens of the Square of the Divan, refusing the bald invitation of the arrow that indicates the usual itinerary leading to the collection of Chinese porcelain and Ottoman copper, china from Vienna, pink Sèvres vases in the ·style of Louis-Philippe: heading instead straight through the Gate of Felicity, crossing the inner patio and the state reception halls, walking along the edge of the Kiosk of the Circumcision, the little pond full of goldfish: vain and self-absorbed, fat and round, like overfed courtiers of the ancien régime or zombies of the pseudo-revolution moving along in procession: till finally you reach the lookout point alongside the Bagdad Kiosk, which embraces the entire radiant panorama of Beyoglü and the Golden Horn, the Karaköy Bridge and the tower of Galata boats of all shapes and sizes, shuttling continuously from one bank to another, en route for the Bosporus or the shores of the Sea of Marmara

mournful sirens, arpeggios, farewells

piercing levantine voices, the earsplittingly loud pulse of the city!

seagulls cleave the soft air, hover above the Byzantine cupolas, wheel, descend, rise, hover motionless, pivot round again: you will join them and brush with the tip of your flying carpet the golden minarets of the mosques, and in one great swoop you will reach the column of Constantine and alight on the oneiric Tower of Bayaceto: the roofless Great Bazaar offers the spectacle of its human hustle and bustle, of the cancerous proliferation of merchandise: monotonous ancestral craftwork that still is unaware of the laws of supply and demand and obsessively repeats the same operation (the zero, the draw well, the circular waltz) ad nauseam: an infinity of identical objects that pile up and overflow along the edges of the side streets and the main arteries, interfere with the flow of traffic, and seek in vain to attract the attention of the passerby: when the loudspeakers of Suleiman the Magnificent broadcast the prayers of the muezzins, the birds take wing, circle, and fly off in every direction of the compass in a swift and deafening whirlwind: it is the hour of ablutions in the portico of Nurvosmaniye Cami and you will mingle with the crowd floating down the slope: a vast labyrinth of stairways, passageways, and patios that lead (mislead) one toward the main post office and the Egyptian Bazaar, the Karaköy Bridge, and the wharfs: warehouses and shops, street stalls, shouts and cries, vendors hawking their wares, countless mules, bicycles, three-wheeled motorcycles, bells ringing, horns blowing: the heterogenousness of the Warsaw ghetto, full of sound and fury, nourished by its own delirious frenzy: guttural voices, acoustic assaults, a dizzying squandering of gestures: a circus-like fauna, common in this peo-

ple of primitive and rustic shepherds, as yet scarcely indus-
trialized: a blind man dependent upon the inspired caution
of his cane, a family of six miraculously sitting astride a
single donkey, a Buster Keaton bicyclist balancing a rococo
pastel-colored meringue on top of his head: an old man
walks along bent double beneath the weight of a huge mir-
rored wardrobe chest and an impatient truck harasses him,
its horn repeating over and over, to the point of paroxysm,
the menacing opening bars of "The Bridge over the River
Kwai": someone barks out, with dogged conviction, the
merits and indulgences offered by a vast assortment of
combs: another recites a solemn, regal monologue above
the open, inverted parasol containing his collection of neck-
ties: two angry vendors gesticulate furiously and begin to
insult each other by means of obscene signs as their in-
comprehensible phrases die a violent death, victims of the
fearful din of passing traffic: a dense throng of pedestrians
blocks every possible exit and one's gaze founders in an overwhelming, unending nightmare of dolls and plastic sandals
take to your heels, make your escape!
your weightless carpet will levitate above the heads of the
wonderstruck crowd, rapidly gain altitude, trace helicoidal
spirals over the Byzantine walls and the red-and-white marble of the palace of Constantine Porphyrogenitus
four thousand feet below and at a distance of some seven
centuries, the natives of the city are engaged in subtle polem-
ics in the forum, a public debate having to do with the
abstract-concrete question of the sex of angels
(a knotty and difficult subject with few equals before the
enlightening intervention of Cinecittà and the swift and
fruitful visit of the blond celestial messenger to the bored,
somnolent family belonging to the haute bourgeoisie of
Milan: those arguing in favor of the sexual nature of angels
had reason on their side: the resplendent fly of Terence Stamp
and the fits of ecstasy of those so visited permit not the
slightest shadow of a doubt in this respect)

the Byzantian debate mobilizes the energies of all parties, and the icon of the Virgin endeavors in vain to ward off the danger in the most exposed section of the wall: the janissaries have already begun their attack, there is no time to lose: the mercenaries are fighting desperately at the Gate of Edirnéh Kapusi!: a band of archers from Sunnyspain is participating in the titanic (NATO-anic?) defense, readily identifiable by their ostentatious uniforms and the calm dignity of their words: an immobile, codified, peninsular mode of speech, an accumulation of proverbs and worn-out commonplaces, a vast pantheon of idiomatic secular excrement! clichés spring irrepressibly to their lips, and you will cleverly and perfidiously mix them up

in the country of the kind, the mind-man is king, one of them says

what's sauce for the noose is sauce for the pander, another says

necessity is the brother of all evil intentions, a third says

their obscure and unintelligible orders sow confusion in their ranks and hasten the baroque disaster: the Asian hordes will pour into the moribund capital of the empire and no power on earth can stop them: everything will go to hell in a handbasket!

(no, you are spouting delirious nonsense, and the Alexandrian poet knows it

the town where you have wasted your days continues to exist and you are condemned to living in it

> you will wander endlessly down its back streets
>
> old age will overtake you in its suburbs
>
> your hair will turn white beneath its rooftops

you will await the barbarians in vain)

flying above the cupolas and the turrets of the minarets of Islamized Byzantium, you will finally reach the Karaköy

Bridge and its harmonious, carefully attuned chaos: the stream of vehicles in the middle of the road, and on the sidewalks, the dense crowd, dark-skinned and impenetrable: hundreds, thousands of Turks with a feline gaze and bushy eyebrows, with the inevitable European-style flat caps imported wholesale by Ataturk atop their heads: their women are walking alongside them, the majority of them pregnant, and their offspring apprehensively gaze at the moving silhouettes of the boats slowly loosing their moorings and gently gliding away from the wharves: toward Usküdar, the Bosporus, the Sea of Marmara: or still farther in the distance, once past Ovid's Hellespont, making for the islands celebrated in Homer's verses, to Cavafy's nocturnal Iskandiria: as meanwhile, in the cafés on the floating dock, the habitués ceremoniously smoke their hookahs, connected to the tubes and water bowls, thus bearing a curious resemblance to amiable centaurs or incurable asthmatics: obliged, following doctor's orders, to resort to some complicated system of artificial respiration: impatient travelers besiege the pots in which fishermen are frying breaded mullet and bream, and the easily recognizable hashish vendor, with his disguise straight out of Carné-Prévert, whispers mysterious words in the ear of a virginal, scandalized, red-headed English tourist: suggestive oneiric monetary propositions, which the nebulous heir of Kipling will pretend not to hear, picking up his pace every time that the apprentice of Jean Gabin falls in step with him, unbuttons his shapeless jacket, and shows him, as quick as a wink of the eye, the dark, tempting, clumsily-rolled little cylinders: at fifty, a hundred, two hundred lire apiece: a sliding scale, a vast range of prices, within reach of every class of society! or else proposes to him an instructive, edifying visit to the hospitable academies of the Alageyik Sokak: pointing toward the dark, exotic little street modestly concealed behind the respectable building housing the Ottoman Bank:

hello, mister, young girl to fuck?: the beardless tourist hesitates: his childish, vaguely fishlike face gradually turns the same bright red color as his hair and his Victorian blue eyes reflect his predictable downfall: he will yield to temptation, yes, he will surrender: the pimp is already dragging him along by the arm, with obscene familiarity, and the odd couple will disappear in the bustle of the crowd, heading for the highest and most sinful quarter of the city: meanwhile you continue your stroll along the quai, the object of the solicitude of bootblacks and street hawkers, until you reach the soft-drink stand, where a splendid group of satraps are doubtless awaiting the departure of the boat to the islands, in full and solemn possession of their magnificent grandeur: their radiant garments gleam as though generating their own light and their abundant, resplendent stars trace a diurnal constellation unknown to astronomers: baritone gondoliers of your precarious, revocable pact of Atlantis, pompous and self-assured beneath the beneficent protection of a light, graceful nuclear umbrella!: the ostentatious dignity that they embody apparently forbids them to converse, and, metamorphosed into flinty statues, they stare fixedly at the closed horizon like sentinels, solemn and imperturbable: curious bystanders participate, like yourself, in the deliberations, and after violent argument, they will agree to award the prize to the hieratic Colonel Vosk: your ex-compatriot will greet this decision with a modest smile, shake a number of outstretched hands, and then his own hand will again come to rest amid the beribboned medals and decorations on his chest, like the paradigmatic hidalgo portrayed by El Greco

well, well, he says: so we're fellow countrymen!: will you believe me if I tell you that you are the first one I've come across in this marvelous corner of the globe?

the colonel bares gleaming gold-capped teeth beneath his thin, horizontal hairline mustache, and on spying your copy of the *Herald Tribune,* he will respectfully give voice to his anxious concerns as to the alarming state of health of the modern emulator of Doña Inés de Castro

reigning after death! a superlative performance! I saw the film and was absolutely carried away: seated there on the throne, as though she were still alive!: receiving the homage of the courtiers! what an admirable example of continuity!

Vosk will then recite a few verses of the famous drama: then, withdrawing from the group of military officers, he will lead you by way of the steep gangway to the first-class salon of the boat

the physical death or capitis diminutio of a great man is a mere happenstance of no consequence, he says: the body subsists, in a cataleptic or mummified state, and that's what counts: his authority remains intact, men of distinction offer him their respects, the common people revere him: everything goes on exactly as before!

exactly as before?

that's correct: exactly as before: the corpse is present, magnificent and invulnerable, and the entire country behaves as though he had not died, in order to avoid causing him displeasure in the hypothetical case of his resurrection: a really exceptional degree of political maturity! you share my opinion, do you not?

who, me? well, that would remain to be seen: as a matter of fact

yes, yes, you share my opinion! I know it, I intuit it, I sense it, I feel it: you think exactly as I do: we're twin souls: what an extraordinary thing, meeting you like this!

his gloved hand reaches out to touch yours and deposits in it a golden disk with the appropriate ribbon and a fuzzy, indecipherable inscription in Latin

here, a small gift for you

I'm very grateful to you, but

my dear friend there are no buts about it, it's yours: keep

it, I won't hear otherwise: a modest memento of our meeting: purely symbolic: the normal thing between two veteran warriors like ourselves, don't you think?: we live in isolation here and your opinion interests me: yesterday I received a whole bundle of newspapers from home: the mail is always terribly slow: two weeks or more!: that's why I asked you for the latest news: learning that confounded English language is absolutely beyond me and I'm not up on what's happening: though I know of course about the big Beatles scandal. What do they have to say about it in the *Herald?*
what scandal? you stammer
what, you haven't heard?
you answer no, you haven't heard a word about it
even though it's all over the papers?
no, you haven't heard a word
but it's made all the headlines!
no, you haven't heard a word, not a word
it's the one thing everybody's talking about!
no, you haven't heard a word, not a word!
incredible, he murmurs: really incredible!
his hand makes a vague gesture, as though to take back the gift, but it stops midway as he changes his mind
all right, I forgive you: it's the first time, after all: let's hope it doesn't happen again!
you humbly assure him it won't, no, it won't happen again
well then, to go on with what I was saying: one of the Beatles, the most brazen one of the lot, had a photograph of himself taken in the nude, with his Japanese mistress, who was stark naked too! and she told the reporters that she was expecting his baby: we aren't married, she told them, but it doesn't matter: I love him: and the two of them kissed each other square on the mouth!
there is a long pause
what scandalous behavior!
the colonel looks at you with bulging eyes, and after making

certain that no one is eavesdropping, he confidentially draws his armchair closer to yours

listen: this country: what do you think of this country?

prudently, you will reply that as a matter of fact, there is a great deal, a very great deal to be said about this country

yes indeed, he says: you're certainly right on that score!

right?

yes, absolutely right!

I'm absolutely right you say?

absolutely, totally right! you've discovered its secret!

its secret?

yes, its secret! the key to its national character!: its principle motive force!: its epicenter!

zealously holding the word back in his mouth, it finally tumbles out

sex! sex wherever you turn!: neither my wife nor I dares go out on the streets!

no?

no!: neither in the daytime nor at night: I swear: at no hour of the day or night!: on any of the streets!

not a single one?

not one, my dear sir, not one!: sex in the movie houses!: sex in the theaters!: sex in the ballrooms!: and in the magazines!: and on the sidewalks!: and in the newspapers!: and in the shop windows!: it's the same all over!: sex, nothing but sex!

all over?

yes, all over!: on television!: in the bookstores!: in the public parks!: in the art galleries!: last week, in fact, we were obliged to go to the opening of an art show and do you know what we saw?

no, what?

sex!: in the first room!: sex!: in the second!: all sex!: nothing but sex!

nothing else?

nothing!: to the point that when we got to the third room, my wife, poor thing, took me aside and said to me: if all the rest is like what we've just seen, I've had enough: if you feel you have to stay with the other guests, go ahead, but I'm going back home

did she go back home?

we both went back home!

you went back home?

indeed we did!: we simply up and left the vernissage! the sex of the vernissage!: the engravings!: the oil paintings!: the watercolors!: the gouaches!: nothing but sex!: we went straight home

Colonel Vosk's face turns beet red as he speaks and the purple veins at his temples appear to be about to burst: will they burst?: why not?: everything is possible on the written page!: when the boat anchors in the port at Heybeli, he will gravely bid you good-bye and, along with the other baritones, will stride, calm and collected, holding himself ramrod-straight, in the direction of the gloomy buildings of the Naval Academy

the mail boat will continue on its rounds from island to island and you will disembark at the dock in Büyük Ada: the passengers hurriedly take off in all directions like insects threatened with imminent destruction: you will do likewise and immediately reach the town square: shall you go to the right? to the left?: you choose to go to the left: past the combination bar and ice-cream parlor, the shop full of tourist souvenirs: reaching an esplanade of much vaster dimensions where a symposium of starving cats are performing their concert of mournful meows under the toscaninian baton of a splendid tiger-striped specimen: a tomcat, with the insolent arrogance of a bully: the bored coachmen are yawning in the driver's seats of the barouches, and without hesitation you will choose the one with the most vulgar face: setting off at a gallop!: up the winding corniche of the island, past autumnal spas that are fast asleep, in and out between dilapidated Turkish villas: Moorish vacation houses of the vainglorious bourgeoisie of the old empire, with lookout towers and cupolas, pretentious balconies serving no useful purpose, outlandish summerhouses: the megalomania of businessmen and bankers summed up in a collection of cheap colored postcards: Italian-troubadour gardens, inspired by D'Annunzio's overblown muse: discolored, crepuscular wooden palaces: ancient bath cabins wearing a disguise of painted prisoner's stripes: faster, faster!: the fierce coachman beats his animal with his whip, its hoofs give off sparks, the creaking of the wheels barely drowns out the sound of its heavy, panting breathing: the road zigzags like a snake, narrows to a steep path, climbs up the pleasant hill, runs along the edge of the ruins of a Coptic monastery: galloping on and on!: the animal shows signs of suffocation and exhaustion and the coachman curses in his native tongue, overcome with inexplicable fury: the cruel torments that he is inflicting make his eyes gleam and his limbs suddenly take on unusual, extraordinary dimensions: gigantic, enormous, tossing about as though caught up in a hurricane!: his shaved skull becomes a devastated plain, his twitching eyebrows spread out like leafy tropical ferns!: he keeps growing and growing: his ears, his arms, his belly, his attributes!: his stentorian voice echoes like thunder, a veritable earthquake of laughter causes his mountainous shoulders to shake: galloping, still galloping onward!: he is drunk on wine doubtless: the drooping tips of his handlebar mustache are dragging on the ground, twining about some unwary Isadora and strangling her!: the corpses are left behind, covered with dust and ants, with their black tongues sticking out: old men and old women for the most part, along with several pregnant women: and the mad ride goes right on!: along dizzying paths that end abruptly, taking shortcuts through the air when necessary: from the top the view is splendid and foreshortens the diffuse panorama of the islands: the Byzantine prisons of Sivri, the residence of Sir Henry Bulwer on Yassi: but why go on?: your description would be arbitrary: let the curious reader consult a Baedeker or any other guidebook: the bookstores of the planet are full to overflowing with them: and if the reader does not happen to have one at hand and his budget does not permit him such luxuries, too bad for him: he'll have to do without!

the vista from that vantage point does not inspire you: you will return to Beyoglü

to the chaos, to the hustle and bustle, to the thick broth of Beyoglü

to the Karaköy Bridge, by way of the subterranean passage that leads to the Great Stairway, and up the hill to the tower of Galata, then turning to the right, before reaching the latter, along a narrow alleyway lined with tiny cafés, eventually arriving at the border station of Alageyik Sokak, guarded, as usual, by a majestic Pluto poking at his gums with a toothpick, encapsulated in his tiny customs booth: visitors flock through the gates of the zoo and a loudspeaker broadcasts, mezza voce, the readily identifiable strains of the mass-mediatized *Concerto de Aranjuez:* a musical offering that lifts your spirits and fills you with pride as you descend the first flight of stairs and attempt to elbow your way through the crowds of curious onlookers bunched up together in front of the cages: Turks in European-style caps, with feline eyes and very bushy eyebrows, contemplating in rapturous silence the extremely varied collection of four-handed fauna: gorillas, chimpanzees, apes, orangutans that are smoking, reading, conversing, eating, knitting: or remain seated, doing nothing, their arms crossed, their legs apart, haughtily mocking the envious, miserable, less well endowed hominids: when they smile, some of them show a completely developed set of teeth, and the rustic Anatolian shepherd succumbs to their charms and allows himself to be caught by the tail; others of them restlessly scratch themselves with their agile prehensile extremities: the most patient of them sit waiting on grimy sofas or put the teakettle on to boil: from the limit prudently marked off by the bars of the cage, you will concentrate your attention on an enormous, dimly discernible specimen that snores, yawns, and perhaps belches, these actions being indulgently pardoned by the half shadow: its hairy breasts bulge out over the retaining wall of its neckline and its magnificent biceps swell as the creature reaches up to adjust the gold rings dangling from its ear lobes: there is no doubt about it: it is King Kong's rival!: boldly entering the cage, you will offer it a handful of peanuts: the trusting orangutan confidently reaches its hand out, and turning its momentary preoccupation to your advantage, you will take it by surprise: you will bring your lips up to its teats, knead them with your fingers, and absorb the thick liquid that spurts out in powerful bursts, bitter and scalding as a geyser: when, once aware of your lightning misdeed, the creature will attempt to react, it will be too late: your stout, inflexible virtue is already sounding the depths between its legs, close to the hircine lair and its secret anfractuosities: a splendid reincarnation of Changó, you will possess the immaculate Common Mother in a most peculiar position: paying no attention to her ear-splitting virginfemale shrieks, ripping open her doll's tunic and taking her from behind: locked in violent hand-to-hand combat, the two of you will finally roll over onto the cot: the abundant quantity and the quality of her geyser surpass that of the best Galician wet nurses, and as you savor it and swallow it, you will feel yourself becoming as invulnerable as Sir Galahad: Queen Kong will furiously squeeze your adorable, virile spheres, to no avail: the Holy Grail protects you, and now you may proceed to play games: she will claw you / you will claw her; she will bite you / you will bite her: delighting in the gentle, painless touch of her fangs on your precious privates as you tear her unclean ones apart and rip out handfuls of her hair: mortally wounded, the swollen teats will deflate like two fantastic balloons: their strength drains away unrestrainedly by way of the geyser, and assured now of your victory, you will increase your martial pressure on her inferior redoubt: little by little, the prehensile extremities of the Visited One release their stranglehold: her eyes rimmed with mascara stare glassily, and to put an end to your punishment of her, you will furiously bash in her teeth: your foreign presence fills the black hollow of the grotto, the moss-covered stalactites receive the burning seminal stream!: Queen Kong straddles the liliputian bidet and you carefully gather up the scattered fragments of her jawbone and make a rosary of them in order to commemorate your hard-won victory over the four-handed hominids of the place

walking upstairs again, amid the shadowy gorillas of the zoo
swift, light as a feather, cunning
unconquered
elbowing your way through the crowd
far from the herr-ottomans, erotomaniacs, hairottomanics
down the stairs
along the steep panoramic slope of Beyoglü
avoiding the dense traffic by taking the subterranean pedestrian passageway
heading toward the Karaköy Bridge
through the glistening Bosporan fish market, with its succession of open-air stalls
toward the floating dock
amid passengers who take the boat by storm, sailing with them in orderly zigzags back and forth across the Golden Horn, beneath the Byzantine walls falling to ruins and the red-and-white marble of the palace of Constantine Porphyrogenitus
the sun is still casting its warm glow on the turrets of the minarets and the cupolas of Istanbul, the shores of the Bosporus, and the Sea of Marmara: young Adelaida is seated

at the piano, playing with great feeling Beethoven's winged march, and an enormous exhaustion, that of a god who has failed, overcomes you

lord and master of things and of words, weary of Turkey and the Turks, on this first day of summer of 1973, the year 1351 after the Hegira according to the Mohammedan calendar, you will suddenly destroy all of them, you will cease to write

the
eighth
pillar of
wisdom

You will take advantage of the splendid prerogatives of your disguise: traversing the bare, orphan Anatolian plain: on the road to Damascus and the naked humiliation of Deráa: on horseback, on the eve of an almost Pauline revelation, awaiting the stentorian divine imprecation that will find your bones touching the earth and convert you into a blind proselyte of the honeyed opium of humanity?: or of the cathartic, fierce rebellion so minutely described in your well-worn copy of the *Seven Pillars?*: clad in the protective garb of your Arab friends: hidden, defended, invulnerable beneath the comfortable folds of the billowing gandourah, and your lanky, unkempt hair concealed beneath the showy kufie: erasing insofar as possible the traces of your previous paltry existence: having finally rid yourself of your irksome English personality thanks to the clever use of a highly colloquial Arabic: following the centuries-old invasion route, through the ancient, desolate crucible of three major religions, waiting for the moment that will enable you to pass beyond the limits of your narrow, petty destiny and make a place for yourself in the vast Bedouin universe in the vertigo and heat of action: savoring, in the company of your beloved Dahoum, the slow breath of the desert that appears to have been born somewhere beyond the distant shores of the Euphrates: the journey is arduous and the day a long one, and you will make camp before nightfall just outside Qalaat Simáan: alongside the abandoned ruins of the basilica that overlooks the dead cities of Upper Syria, a decrepit witness of offerings and pilgrimages: in the central octagon, with cruciform transepts, built in the same spot as the massive, towering column: identifying yourself with that stubborn Stylite who, disdaining worldly glory, retired to inaccessible heights in search of superior perfection: there resisting, for a period of twenty-seven years, the enticements of a smiling and ambiguous devil possessed of the powers and graces of human coquetry: resting a single foot on the platform atop the pillar, with the solemn, pompous air of a diurnal bird, a few scant inches away from the treacherous, guileful tempter: paying no heed to the lethal promises of his smile, the fresh and juicy solicitation of the impudent, outsize tongue: with arms extended like a cross and lips absorbed in the recitation of a prayer: but the remoteness and solitude of this summit offer you secret compensations and your seeming madness has its justifications: the diameter and the height of the shaft of the column, the polished cylindrical surface that serves you as a support would by themselves suffice to fulfill the most extravagant dreams of happiness of King Kong's devoted flock: add to this the ecstasies and raptures of the lofty vision, and the penitence will be transformed into a blessed garden of delights: not a hermit, a sybarite rather: chaste and virtuous in appearance only: in reality given over to the pleasures of the secret, nocturnal worship of the attributes of your cruel lord and master

sexual roots of political power: or political roots of sexual power: in any event the exercise of absolute dominion over unfeeling and inconsequential bodies, overt or tacit accomplices of an arbitrary, boundless will: the scornful manipulation of beings shorn of every vestige of humanity, whose cries of tighten-the-screws, long-live-chains enhance the illusion of a ceremony dramatizing the renunciation of their own destiny: their humble acceptance of their status as objects: the pleasure of yielding themselves up to a vast desert, as barren and desolate as a gleaming glacier: to plunge crudely amongst crude men satisfies your secret appetites and brands your attempt to free the peoples subjected to the Ottoman yoke with an obscene mark that your apologists, out of a sense of modesty, will fail to mention in their biographies of you, fearing that they may reveal, thanks to your plainspokenness, the hidden foundations of the ominous notion of Power: a serpentine presence that subjugates and castrates, images of coercion concealed in the invisible depths of your soul that accompany a Caesar in his rise to glory and his fall: a destructive, monolithic tyranny, which goes back to the very beginnings of history, you tell yourself, like a story that never ends, continually circling back upon itself

super flumina Babylonis: a nomad-like search for "your self-expression in some imaginative form": abandoning the pleasant refuge of the simeonian column in order to reconnoiter the enemy territory from Antioch to Baghdad: over the prostrate body of the old empire in ruins: up the erect trunk and across the broad expanse of the shoulder blade, to the burnished column of the muscular neck, scrutinizing the enigmatic sphinx face from the protuberance of the adam's apple: the dream of Arab national unity within reach of your hand, as they say, thanks to your innate gifts as a strategist and the perfidious, avaricious aid of crass British capital: renouncing for the moment, however, the laurels of a successful campaign in order to orchestrate the full range of your emotions in a hesitant, experimental symphony, artistically and morally atonal: attacks, pillage, raids, derailments will henceforth serve you as a pretext for the subtle games of literary composition, as the futile heroism of Vercingetorix served the rhythmical Latin prose of the *Commentaries on the Gallic War:* the facts dissolved in a hazy dream, at the mercy of rhetorical devices and the insidious tyranny of the written text: discovering, with ingenuous surprise, the gap that separates the object from the sign and the worthlessness of the means employed to bridge it: your claims to authenticity are difficult to verify, and neither tears, solemn oaths, nor blood could possibly establish beyond question their relation to the slippery, elusive truth: the cleverness of the narrative takes the place of the dubious reality of the facts, your victory as an artist hallows your vain exploits as a warrior: you will therefore scornfully reject a fame based on an imposture and decide to forever abandon your empty pose of a historian: refusing to play by the rules of the inane game in order to put your own adventitious model before the reader as an exemplar in the battle against clichés: henceforth making no effort to disguise the unavoidable ambiguity of language and the omnipresent, contagious process of expression: trading rebellious deviation from the norm for inventive power: recreating your world on the blank page: the liberation of Damascus is not pressing, and ascending to the head of the Islamic body, you will tarry once again in the luxuriant foliage of the hanging gardens of Babylon: their tangled vegetation will conceal the fervor of your surrender: from the stiff, bristling hairs of the handlebar mustache you will observe the matted hair that covers the rough and rugged chin!: the devil himself could not offer you a more tempting prospect and the vertigo of passion assails you like a bolt of lightning: in the warrior's repose you will find the eighth pillar of wisdom: you will blindly hurl yourself into the burning-hot volcano of the lips

**incursions
into Nubian
territory**

Upstream or downstream: ascending or descending: borne along by the toplofty sailboat that skillfully tacks back and forth between fake natural settings: humble huts, yawning caves, groves of palm trees, slowly rippling cane fields: as though you were submerged in a terrifying, recurrent nightmare: amid scenes straight out of the old photographs of the mansion, down a succession of gloomy hallways, in the crepuscular dawn of the early days of your childhood: the images follow one upon the other in your memory as though projected by a magic lantern and you will join the polyglot throng, trying your best to conceal your emotion: ruins, ruins, a babelic archaeology, baritone sightseeing guides chattering on ad nauseam: amid the vast panorama of sunhats, movie cameras, guidebooks, and dark glasses of the groups that wander back and forth under the protection of the massive towering columns: the custodian, his head enveloped in a turban, beckons to you with furtive gestures, and abandoning the heterogeneous herd, you will decide to follow in his footsteps: a dazzling-white smile seals the complicitous tacit agreement, the necessary preamble to your dark journey!: the dancing flames of the oil lamp highlight his slim, elegant hand as the two of you make your way in silence through tunnels and subterranean galleries: the provocative, billowing contours of his galeyah alternately reveal and conceal the outline of his sturdy body underneath, his bushy eyebrows enhance the impatient gleam in his eye: tenors and choristers up above continue to recite names, dates, limp, spaghetti-like bits of serpentine erudition, and the musical counterpoint accompanies you as you descend farther and farther toward the funereal realm of Pluto: pleased to leave behind the doublets and plumed caps of the usual group of troubadours: the spirited bel canto performance that gradually grows fainter and fainter: your attention now riveted on the feline gestures of your mentor: sinking lower and lower with him, feeling yourself seized with vertigo as you fall: the textual subversion of his body drowns out the empty discourse, and the final tremolo of the diva will die away between the gaping jaws of the cavernous mastiff: your fierce joy at this moment is that of a man condemned: the whirlpool has sucked you to the bottom: you know it: you will not come up again

imagine yourself up above amid the fauna of your former life: the flourishing grandee of the illustrious local establishment, the cunning magnate of an eminent import-export company, the bemedaled pachyderm of a pompous executive committee, the smiling archangel of a remote fiscal paradise: enrolled, perhaps, along with the resurrected supernumeraries of your childhood, in a highly selective management course for industrialists: cloistered with them in the neo-Gothic lecture hall of some beautiful postgraduate institution in Massachusetts: the VIPs memorize along with you the sublime bits of advice offered by the computer and will resolve to apply them diligently, obediently, and promptly: to sign the letter dismissing the oldest employee in the company without taking into account either his devoted, selfless services or his tragic family circumstances, to go to bed and sleep soundly all night without scruples or remorse: a *jeune loup* in short, master of capital funds and human lives, the promoter of vast enterprises and undertakings, the efficient and keen-witted engineer of souls!: with the dazzling attributes appertaining to your new status: credit cards, jet travel, business equipment advertised in the color pages of *Fortune,* a red coupé with an elegant lady sitting smoking in its leather-upholstered interior: dreaming of climbing higher and higher and camping on the lonely Arctic heights: tempering the steel of your character as an invincible captain of industry in the smithy of your soul, thanks to tests more arduous than those you underwent in the carnegian course you took in New England: eliminating your own sire, worn out from overuse and become a source of profitless expenditures, throwing him unceremoniously down the toilet bowl and, mentally savoring the savings that will result from this audacious and enterprising step, resolutely pulling the chain: great men all over the world will recognize you, in open-mouthed admiration, as one of their own: never, never will you step off onto the railway platform: as the driver of the powerful locomotive of its marvelous industrial revolution, the train would promise to take you, oh dear, dearest Herr Alvaro Krupp, to the far ends of the earth

but the African subsoil is satisfaction enough for you as you follow the ritual of the suras absorbed from the lips of the dragoman and abandon yourself to its sonorous spell with crude, cruel joy

     oh infidels
     I do not worship the one whom you worship
     nor do you worship the one whom I worship
     I shall not adore the one whom you adore
     nor shall you adore the one whom I adore
     keep your religion, I've got my own!

the voices of the tenors spoil the limpid recitation of the prayers with fancy trills and tremolos and the European troop of strolling players will absorb their massive culture injection with uncommonly loud bleatings: poco a poco s'indebolì l'autorità centrale e, nel corso del secondo interregno, vi fu l'invasione degli: or: at the end of a shaft hewn into the rock: or: ce n'est qu'à l'avènement de la onzième dynastie, originaire de Thèbes, que l'empire: or else: die Könige des Neuen Reiches werden in Tal der Königsgraber zu Theben begraben: until the various choruses burst into the cave where the two of you have taken refuge, and at the sight of the abominable spectacle, a heavy silence ensues

(POSSIBLE REACTIONS

    they pretend not to see
    their faces change color
    they clear their throats or cough
    they cross themselves
    they speak of moral corruption)

according to the guides of the Cairo Museum, the pygmies elegantly depicted in the reliefs and funeral frescoes enjoyed throughout the various dynasties the supreme protection of the Pharaohs: the hunting, capturing, and transporting of them were governed by strict laws and carefully supervised by the royal intendant, and all the expenses of maintaining them were paid for out of the royal treasury: the stewards and household servants were to look after them and treat them kindly, prevent any possible attempt on their part to escape, keep them from throwing themselves into the river and being borne away by the current: received with pomp and circumstance, they were trained to perform important duties and functions, and in accordance with their preferences and tastes, they were paired with pygmies of the same or the opposite sex: they were customarily entrusted with the responsibility of guarding the royal wardrobe: their small stature prevented them from wearing in secret the garments of their masters or parading them in the marketplaces and public squares in their frequent accesses of vanity: other advantages: the smaller budget required to feed and clothe them, a proverbial talent as jesters and practical jokers: yet another, by no means the least important: their convenience: when Potiphar or his wife awaken in a lustful mood from their languorous afternoon slumbers and call for their expert collaboration in soft whispers: their pleasing, cunning little heads are located at an optimum height and hence it is not necessary for them to kneel down or squat on their heels: the hieroglyphs fail to depict this, but it is a veritable banquet: a height of four feet two inches faithfully adapts itself to the mold and spares the artist as well the painful effort of bending his neck

beginning at 00 hours on this day, you will formally declare love on Nubians: their army corps surround you, melting into the thick shadows, and the defensive-offensive operations will take place at a dizzying speed, in accordance with the conventional strategy of the blitzkrieg: an assiduous reader of Clausewitz, you will carry out your war plans with the methodical precision of a monocled officer of the Prussian General Staff: deducing the location of their command post as they ferociously brandish their swift, sharp-pointed javelins: their arching shoulders tense, ready to launch arrows aimed straight at you that threaten to turn you into a hedgehog: locked again and again in hand-to-hand combat, your parrot's claws will hold them down until you manage to disarm them: you have traded a fertile expanse of land, with gardens and meadows, for another surrounded by thorny hedges: the aridity of this desert wasteland forbids the very idea of fruit and its naked barrenness intoxicates you: your amorous imperialism recognizes no frontiers, and like a kinglet, a basilisk, or a legendary animal, you assuage your raging thirst in the implacable rigor of the struggle: granting no respite, truce, or quarter: in turn taming their perverse pride and unhurriedly savoring their bitter surrender: helmsmen of feluccas who glide over the lubricated muscles of the river or wild mountain dwellers who subjugate hostile territory: not to mention the innocent, nubile lad unafraid of the springing savage beast: prolonging the skirmishes and encounters that lead you step by step to your ultimate goal: exquisite, accepted surrender: to the servitude that calls to you with its unwholesome glamour: the voice of the almocri chanting his chaplet of suras from the Koran reaches the small room where you lie enveloped in clouds of kif smoke: insatiable, you will expand your holy war until it embraces the entire country

the omnipotent powers of writing!
with a mere pad of paper and two ball-point pens with no caps (the career of one of them has ended just a moment or so ago, its generative force exhausted), shut up in the tiny room where you customarily work (a kitchen with the necessary equipment for the concoction of your weird recipes), with no other aid save that of a multilingual guidebook of the country and a blurred portrait of your alter ego (and the voice of Um Kalsum in the background, as solemn as a poem by Cavafy), you have sailed (and will take your reader on the same journey) from the teeming Alexandria of the poet to the redeemed-by-Moses temples of Abu Simbel, drifted along on the river's waters, carried this way and that by the wind's inspired afflatus, admired the double row of sphinxes pierced like sieves by the cameras of sightseeing tours, attended an intensive course for executive directors from a distance of five thousand leagues away, recited Allahu Akbar with your hands resting on your knees and your trunk horizontal to the floor, made love in the dark, listened to a tourist guide explaining the customs at the court of the pharaoh, smoked a pipeful of kif on the propitious straw pallet of a boatman
and its cunning, suasive artifices will gradually take in all

those willing to be caught in its net, forgetting for a few moments the dismal shabbiness of their lives: a strange civilization, yours, condemned to live by proxy!: producer and consumers marked by an identical, ineffaceable stigma, like different players in one and the same game: exhibitionists, and at the same time Peeping Toms

variations
on a
Fez
theme

Lose your bearings in Fez

fast from sunup to sundown, hearkening to the sudden shriek of the siren

enter a mosque and perform the ritual ablutions

fall on your knees and recite a few verses from the Koran

smoke a couple of pipesful of kif

dissolve several grams of hashish in a fragrant glass of mint tea

take un petit taxi, get out at the Place Commerce, walk along the wall surrounding the Jewish cemetery, cross the Mellah, follow the main thoroughfare of Fès-el-Jedid, leave behind on your left the drowsy guardsmen of Dar-el-Majcén, absorb yourself in the contemplation of the old waterwheels along the river in the shade of the gardens of Buxelúd, turn off to the right along the esplanade where the tourist buses are parked, and after passing beneath the horseshoe-shaped arch of the great gate, immerse yourself in the human river running down the slope of Tala, wander off the usual itinerary and enter the tortuous labyrinth of narrow streets and alleyways

if your stubborn sense of direction doesn't desert you and unconsciously guides you à la Tom Thumb, scattering in your memory the recollection of life-saving points of reference

screw up your courage

take yet another step

rid yourself of the oppressive space-time binomial

abandon your ridiculous role of a crusader aspiring to colonize the future in order to share the common lot of

those who live as best they can in the precarious and uncertain present

feel your way along blindly, without a seeing-eye dog, a
guide, or a cane

little by little, attune the pulse of life within you to the
vibrant heartbeat of the Medina

walk on, keep walking on and on

and when a pleasant fatigue overcomes you and you suddenly have no idea where you are, and above all no idea
why you are walking on and on

pass through any door you choose, utter the ritual greeting,
feel the walls of the little dwelling with your fingertips

lie down on the furs and rugs on which those who live here
take their rest

and

without ever once removing the blindfold

make violent love with the first person you chance upon

(the sex and the age are of no importance

keep your surprise to yourself)

ah!

if you are a connoisseur

stir the mixture thoroughly

and add a few drops of liqueur to taste, plus one wild cherry

is there perchance anything as reasonable, as totally and
universally accepted, as solidly and effectively proven by logical argument, as irrefutably established, more unanimously
revered and less subject to doubt, more highly endorsed, in
a word, by the consensus of history and the vast majority of
mortals than the supremacy of erotic pleasure (physically,
dynamically, functionally) in the arms of the fierce leader of
a harka or a sentinel of the Royal Moroccan Army, preferably one who is attached to the Regular Infantry?: only a mad-
man, a malicious backbiter, or a fool would be so bold as to
maintain the contrary!: according to ecclesiastical annals and

chronicles, the last deluded soul who dared to do so was condemned ad perpetuam rei memoriam by the most celebrated
theologians of Christendom, who had met in council in
Basel a few months before a deadly epidemic of the plague
and internecine quarrels put an end to the power of the
Merovingian dynasty and its grandiose imperial dreams: his
imprudent and infantile perversity led him to the extreme of
attempting to read before that learned and imposing assembly a treatise in seventeen volumes, written in outlandish,
macaronic Latin, entitled *Brevis Demonstratio ad Rev-
erendos Ministros Verbi Dei contra impiam et perversam
Doctrinam impugnatoram Superioritas Amore in Virginis
Placentis,* in which, with the aid of a number of engravings
and colored plates, he endeavored to prove his weird theory
amid indignant shouts of protest on the part of those present,
who punished his stubborn folly by sentencing him to death:
however, in view of the evident perturbation of his mental
faculties, this death sentence was commuted at the very last
moment and the criminal was instead waggishly placed on
public exhibition in the public squares and marketplaces of
the city, wearing the ears and the tail of a donkey, whereupon the wretch, according to the chronicles and documents of the period which mention him in passing, lived
a life of misery, wandering about all the capitals of Europe:
he became the manservant and ostler of a Lithuanian prince
who enjoyed the protection of the Grand Bailli of Bruges, he
frequented for a time clandestine Scottish patriotic groups, he
founded a minor dissident sect strongly influenced by the
mysticism of the Order of Rosicrucians, he eventually joined
a half-Masonic, half-spiritualist conventicle led by a Mexican
colonel who later took part in the insurrection at Cartagena
and was obliged to emigrate to Crete, he was a contributor to
various publications and wrote a number of pamphlets, stubbornly refusing to renounce the idea of putting his wildly
eccentric doctrine before the public, though apparently he
never succeeded in attracting more than a half dozen prose-

lytes of the most humble class of society, whereupon he became a libertarian utopian, held a debate, standing atop a barrel in Hyde Park, with an obscure disciple of Fourier, had fleeting contacts with separatist movements in the Val d'Aosta and the Jura, labored in vain to establish communities of disciples in Burgundy and Nivernais, was prosecuted for rape and breach of promise in Lausanne, delivered perorations in Jacobin clubs in Paris, headed a Quaker colony in the Alpujarras Mountains, received money and other aid from a British philanthropical institution, sold copies of the New Testament that George Borrow had translated into gypsy cant, plotted vague conspiracies that came to nothing and allied himself with a mysterious Jew from Tangier with the aim of promoting an esoteric, nebulous, and unclassifiable cult without thereby attracting any new followers, until finally, overtaken by old age and misfortunes, he ended up, in rags and filthy dirty, in a lowly inn in the city of Burgos, where he was taken with a severe fever, the effects of which he eventually died of, without ever having revealed his identity to anyone, clinging to an old and battered valise in which, according to the learned scholar Don Marcelino Menéndez Pelayo, he kept safely hidden, beneath a jumble of papers and letters long since turned yellow, the seventeen unpublished volumes of his mad *Brevis Demonstratio*

if a love that rebels against all norms seeks you out, give it a warm welcome, and do not refuse it bread: reward the blind labor of the body with a few silver coins and embark once again upon the impossible search for the beloved city and its elusive shadows: in a fantastic setting of minarets mosques schools for the study of the Koran, burnooses veils jellabas will conceal the uncertain images that your memory will never be able to reconstruct: dubious itineraries, hesitant journeys through an inextricable tangle of alleyways stubbornly winding back upon themselves: an infinity of colored slippers like miters crowded together in the tiny shops along the side streets and the usual activity of craftsmen will accompany you to the arabesques of the tomb of Mulai Idrís: the devout rub the circular aperture in the copper plaque with their hands, a character out of the Thousand and One Nights nods sleepily above his goods for sale in the late-afternoon shadow of a shop: zigzagging, continually zigzagging through patios tunnels caravansaries you will cautiously hug the crenelated walls of the Karueein: through the pitch-dark alleyway of the Seven Turns, disappearing into the rough, narrow folds of its uterine sinuosities: crannies, hiding places, curves of a path endlessly changing direction, snaking along in an arbitrary fashion, leading only to a cul-de-sac: the jutting cornices on either side of the alleyway almost touch, and the sky above is the faraway edge of an evanescent knife: you will follow the example of the nameless architect and lure the future reader into the meanders and snares of your writing: you will erect blocks of sonorous stones, you will free them from the tyranny of rational use and allow them to grow and cluster together, to attract and repel one another, docilely obeying the laws of magnetic fields and the secret affinities that polarize the perilous search for the soothsayer: their joyous copulation will be the best compass: their collision with one another will set off the stream of sparks that suddenly ignites the voltaic arc: invested with the subtle powers of the magus, you will enlist your imagination in the service of new and insidious architectures whose ultimate purpose will be that of the treacherous alleyways of Fez: to attract the ingenuous intruder, seduce him, deceive him, envelop him in the meshes of an elusive verbal construction, confuse him completely, force him to turn around and retrace his footsteps, less sure now of his powers of language and his infallible sense of direction, letting him loose again in the everyday world, having taught him to doubt

the phallus
of Ghardaïa

the pharos of Ghardaïa? or the phallus of Ghardaïa?: from the terrace that overlooks the quadrangular area of the square and its bustling market, you will contemplate once again the dense conglomeration of little dwellings clustered about the feet of the splendid symbol: the men who in the phantasmagorical course of the centuries escaped to these lonely haunts in order to preserve in all their rigor the purity and immutability of their rites erected it as a solid and rugged affirmation of their faith in the striking of a terse, vibrant chord as an act of worship: its stout, tapering, oblong, exquisitely cylindrical shape is reminiscent on first sight (an illusion born of thirst, a herbivorous confusion?) of the idle chimney of a huge factory: but the industrialization that is rejuvenating the vast country has not yet reached the remote oasis and you will be obliged to admit that it is merely an ordinary turret of a mosque: the voice of the muezzin soars above the hubbub of the marketplace, and facing in the direction of Mecca, you will decide to boldly imitate the duties incumbent upon a zealous Moslem: the recitation of the midday prayers will take place in accordance with the well-known ritual: the docile texture of the jellaba adapts itself to the suppleness of one's gestures and its ample folds do not conceal the tension of your fierce disciple: freed of the ancestral yoke, you will turn it out to pasture and allow it to frisk about and rise to the furthest limit of its fervor, not perceiving what an obvious affront its uncircumcised outer rim represents: the insolent, inauspicious imposture provokes an indignant reaction, and attempting to escape this opprobrium, you will flee, like an assassin, the fallacious city: but your feet mislead you, taking you into an insidious labyrinth of alleyways, and on catching a glimpse of you through the narrow (cyclopean?) slit that reveals a single eye, the women walking in the opposite direction stop and turn their backs to you: standing, as though being punished, along the wall, they wait for you to walk past so as to be able to continue on their way, leaving you foundering in perplexity and confusion: is the stigma marking your body that of a person infected with the plague?: once again your sense of self-estrangement dizzies you, and climbing to the brow of the hill you will relive the fits of delirium and ecstasy of the Reverend Father Foucauld

all of it!: I want all of it!: from Maison Carrée to Timbuktu to Tuggurt, the moonscapes of the Hoggar Mountains, the barren plains of Tademait, the marvelous oases of El Golea! this Africa, these missions ministering to infidels call forth so irresistibly the saintliness that will be the one means of converting them: how wonderful it is amid this great calm and this beautiful natural landscape, so tortuous and so strange!: one must pass by way of the desert, and tarry there in order to receive God's grace: it is there that one empties oneself, that one banishes everything that is not God, that one throws everything out of that little dwelling of our soul in order to leave room only for God: close every last book: never take up a pen: remain a servant: and if one day you are no longer wanted, return to the Sahara, sleeping in some grotto: conversion! conversion!: everything tells me I must be converted: everything sings of the need to sanctify myself: everything constantly reminds me and cries out to me that if whatever good it is that I wish for myself does not come my way, it is my fault, my most grievous fault, and that I must hasten to convert myself: to be honey, a light and perfumed zephyr!: velvet!: something tender, refreshing, consoling, gentle for all men: slaves, the poor, the sick, soldiers, wayfarers, the curious: not to fear contact with the natives or with their garments: to fear neither their filth nor their lice: not to make a deliberate effort to be covered with lice but not to fear them either: to behave as though they did not exist: steadfastness: the desire to experience love and the giving of oneself to the limit: and to learn every lesson that they teach: I believe that that is my vocation: to descend: poor, scorned, abject: a thirst to lead at last the life that I am seeking: Saint Mary the Virgin, Saint Joseph, Saint Mary Magdalene, Saint Mary Margaret, Saint Pascal-Baylon, Saint Augustine, Saint Peter and Saint Paul, Saint Michael, my guardian angel, saints male and female, holy angels, good souls in Purgatory, pray for the Little Brothers and Sisters of the Sacred Heart of Jesus, for the Tuaregs, Morocco, the souls of the Sahara, all the infidels, and for me a poor sinner, in order that we may all crown with every possible glory the Sacred Heart of Blessed Jesus the immense, cetacean bust thrust forward anxiously and quivering like a bowlful of jelly: crying out for the tasty fruit for which the father of us all was driven out of paradise: the eternal apple, or better still the banana, the tropical pineapple, the suggestive pear: the enormous lips greedily parted: secreting saliva like Pavlov's dog: crying out for all of it: from Tamanrasset to Orleansville, from the Niger to Algiers, yes, I want all of it!

as the wretched figure holds forth, with no other witnesses (so he believes) save the dense flock of vultures hovering like birds of evil omen high overhead, you will lie in ambush awaiting his words (a bird of prey yourself), looking for-

ward to the clandestine pleasure that the flow of the pen (of
the sex organ) will create in the space of the text: constella-
tions of signs that speed up the pulsations of your (my)
most intimate self (genetic, germinative, generative, genesic) until they abolish the distance created by illusion in a
single great feast of destruction: the Reverend Father Foucauld remains prostrated before the pharos of ubiquitous,
evanescent Ghardaïa, and then resolutely raising himself to a
sitting position, he will dispense his comforting gifts and
benefactions in swift and diligent apostleship: alms, medicines, assistance, soothing words of encouragement, blessings, the balm of his caresses: freeing slaves, adopting
orphans, succoring widows, sheltering beggars and invalids
beneath his towering tutelary jurisdiction: delighted to see
such crowds, to distribute a great many remedies, to make
the acquaintance of so many people, to make the rounds
from tent to tent: the expeditions of the Nineteenth Army
Corps under the command of General Caze spread to the
farthest corners of the land the aroma of your sublime mission, and without abandoning your watchful scrutiny, you
will join the column composed of twenty-five Sudanese
sharpshooters, ten Kenaka auxiliaries, Captain Théveni-
aud, Lieutenant Jerosolini, the army interpreter Pozzo di
Borgo, Combe-Morel the telegraph operator, as it heads for
Tamanrasset: each day's journey is arduous and the welcome
that the natives will extend uncertain, but the steadfastness of
your companions will remove difficulties and obstacles and
favor the miraculous realization of your deep-rooted, stubborn dream of subservience: to descend to the rank of a
servant: submerged in darkness and abjection: surrounded
by crude, brutal, slothful, lying, thieving, depraved, perverted creatures: courageously accepting every sort of suffering, opprobrium, violence, insult, mistreatment: loving
and obeying for love's sake to the point of offering yourself
as a victim: your soul has not yet been purged of its innu-
merable faults, and lurking in the shadows of your hidden

observation post, you (from outside) will be witness to the meticulous examination of your conscience, following the rules set forth in the old schoolboy's manual: the *Primer of the Christian Child*!: the list of sins of thought, word, and deed, the proper feelings to move you to contrition!: nothing can remain hidden from the eyes of the Lord, and the holy Guardian Angel has also been witness to your despicable actions: he has seen everything you have done, and heard everything you have said: therefore you must ask for forgiveness: on your knees, at the foot of the phallus/pharos, you will recite the long list of your crimes: je n'ai pas eu une familiarité fraternelle avec les indigènes, j'ai craint la malpropreté et la vermine: and the breast-beating and acts of humility beneath the towering minaret: but this is still not the abjection that you have dreamed of: you are more and more eager each day to cast yourself headlong into the ultimate self-debasement: the scourge is within your reach, as supple as a lizard's tail, and removing your habit of rough, coarse-woven cloth, you will proceed to chastise yourself with fierce enthusiasm: habituating your body little by little to the martyrdom you have so ardently longed for: a lamb amid wolves, totally defenseless, humble and brimming over with gratitude: but the sight of the blood that gushes forth also inflames your blood, and throwing caution to the winds, you will grab the whip out of his hands, causing a ubiquitous pleasure to reign supreme in your mental kingdom: an ambiguous back-and-forth movement of the pen, that symbol of your astonishing power!: he is still on his knees, in thrall to the potency of the mosque, and will turn around toward you in surprise, with an expression on his face that is at once beatific and entreating

who are you? he asks you

never mind, you tell him: I'll lend you a hand: I like shedding your blood: whenever an occasion presents itself, I take advantage of it: as a child, I used to wear a Zealot costume in order to whip you in processions

I don't remember, he says to you

that's because I've changed a great deal, you say to him: I
used to go by another name and wrote in your language

and now? he says to you

I became an apostate, you say to him: look at this outfit I'm
wearing: the sultan himself presented it to me as a gift

the sultan? he says to you

yes, you say to him: I abandoned the priesthood and cast off
my habit: I married and have a son named Mohammed: I'm
the chief customs officer of the kingdom and majordomo of
the palace of Abu Faris Abd-al-Aziz

he stretches out face downward, beseeching you to lend him
your despotic aid, and you will test the strength of the rope
before going into action

are you ready? you say to him

wait just a moment, he will say: you haven't told me your
name yet

my name is Ibn Turmeda, you will say: and I am the author
of the *Offering of a Learned Man*, *against the Followers of
the Cross*

Father, forgive him, for he knows not what he does, he will
say

wait, be quiet, be quiet, shhh, you will say: if you're good,
I'll read it to you when I'm through

born on an island not far distant from the spacious and sor-
rowful Peninsula (may Allah restore it to Islam!), as a child
(at the age of five? six?), I chanced to witness, thanks to an
indiscreet jalousie (it was summer, it was hot, it must have
been the siesta hour), my parents' conjugal intimacy (tepid
procreative love, as dreary and tasteless as a meal warmed
over), a spectacle whose base sordidness (heightened by
their gentle, polite moans) caused me to conceive a violent,
boundless hatred (as sudden as the storm that bursts in
splendid fury and fills the crew of a frail vessel with

silent, religious terror) of the orderly sort of reproduction sanctioned by the law and its wretched and grotesque supernumeraries: from this early age, despite my tender years, I began to dream of colossal disasters, and swift, magnificent cataclysms which, with the same inexorable force as those which devastated ancient Egypt, would finish my progenitors off once and for all and rid the world of their inane and absurd presence: on gray and gloomy winter evenings, when time crept on at the same petty pace as the monotonous murmur of their devotions, I prayed with secret fervor for the appearance of some horde of enemies which, after destroying their miserable power that was slowly stifling me to death, would vent its fury on them with subtle, refined cruelty: I conjured up in my mind (in the vaguest of ways) fierce, barbarous tribes, with bodies as steely and unyielding as knives, whose copper-colored, enigmatic faces would rival the hardness of a precious stone with dazzling polyhedral, crystalline facets: pitiless, brutal creatures, such as the one described by Marcelino Amiano in a few brief, unforgettable lines, when he attacks the army of the Goths with his naked blade, beheads a youngster, and immediately places his lips on the boy's neck and voraciously sucks his blood, sowing panic and confusion in the ranks of the enemy: unmoved by the attentions and indulgences with which my procreators attempted to buy me off, I prayed for the advent of torturers who would subject my progenitors' ridiculous, anemic bodies to the rigors of their harsh pleasure, not sparing that accursed hole which the docile horde with pale, washed-out faces superstitiously preserves as a sanctuary: witnessing from inside it, in ecstasy, the charge of their swarthy, somber wild beasts: the impetuous, violent attacks that proudly disdain the propagation called for by the law: seeing them wallowing about, biting, and cruelly baring their claws as my parents would beg in vain for mercy and address their futile petitions to a powerless, deaf divinity that had selfishly withdrawn (like a retired oldster or pensioner) to the confines of his cozy and unprepossessing retreat: until the sublime moment (so often dreamed of!) when they would discover my bedazzling act of treason, and with the ardor of the neophyte devoted heart and soul to the cause of his new masters, I would actively participate with these latter in the delights of profanation: such were the visions that assailed me day and night for years and years (although outwardly I affected the air of an innocent and ingenuous youth), until finally, taking advantage of a moment of inattention on the part of my parents, I boarded a Genoese galleon, crossed the sea, and journeyed far into the African desert, anticipating that I would here find my masters, and with their help some day mete out my long-delayed punishment: and embracing the powerful knees of Ebeh, beneath the protection of his magnificent scepter, I entreat him to aid me in carrying out my plans and await the arrival of Christians such as yourself in order to brandish my bloody whip, and through the pain inflicted on their bodies, symbolically wreak my revenge on my parents

you will describe Ebeh
scimitar in hand, ready to attack the enemy with all the strength of his sturdy arm?: or in the act of subjecting another body to the imperious pleasure of his own, as the cruel echo of his laughter diffuses a solemn splendor? hieratic, rather: his sovereign self-possession frees him from the necessity of making any sort of gesture, as with a deliberate economy of movement, he stretches out on the sheepskin in his rude chieftain's den: his eyes inscrutable and hard, stealthy, cunning, those of a wild beast emerging into the light of day from the depths of a shadowy lair: his face secretive, angular, rugged, as though hacked out with violent blows of an ax: his body massive and compact, like a prismatic block of crystal, possessed of a sheer majesty sufficient unto itself: (you for your part) seeking in vain for

any sign of pity or tenderness in the stubborn severity with which he subjects men to his rule and metes out strict justice in the form of blows of a whip and kicks: his followers and acolytes appear to be resigned to his command over them and the young lads who entertain and serve him share the joyous relief of those who have found refuge in an ultimate certainty: free acceptance of an unconditional obedience: the awareness of having reached bottom, incapable of descending a single rung further on the ladder leading to sheer animality: hence savoring the sweet pleasures of this harsh treatment: fascinated by the discovery of the satisfaction they find in the slavery and degradation of their bodies: the joy of abjection, of offering to their master their flesh and blood for any and every imaginable purpose: is that all?: ah, you will add to this portrait of the Senusi chieftain a few subtle touches of inhumanity: rough, weatherbeaten skin, a face pitted with smallpox scars, teeth with gold caps, dark glasses which enhance the indecipherable enigma of his gaze: his solid, mineral density: at the precise moment (why not?) at which he unsheathes his impressive weapon, the sight of which confounds the servant: colossal, resplendent, arrogant: as he patiently waits for it to grow larger and longer and then suddenly gives up the attack and magnanimously offers it to the sword swallower as bait for his vile treachery

I / YOU

apersonal pronouns, hollow substantive molds!: your bare reality is the act of speech through which you appropriate language and subject it to the illusory dominion of your reducible subjectivity: empty wineskins, handy vessels, you promiscuously offer yourselves, to be used by one and all, for social, collective enjoyment: nuclear, hermetic indicatives, you nonetheless transmit your uniqueness, when with a mere stroke of the pen I force you to obey the dictates of my protean, ever-shifting voices: the particular range of frequencies you broadcast on facilitates this clever sleight-of-hand trick outside the limits of ordinary communication: who is it expressing himself in this I / you?: Ebeh, Foucauld, Anselm Turmeda, Cavafy, Lawrence of Arabia?: the wandering shades change in your indispensable hollow mold, and you will be able to play sly games with the signs without the ingenuous reader's noticing: submerging him in a world in flux, the object of a continuous process of destruction: distributing among your scattered egos the various roles in the chorus and continually orchestrating them in accordance with the inspired movements of your baton: the swift flight of the pen over the rectangular space of the page: your talents as a pander, your function as the joker in the deck of cards call for an oneiric metamorphosis, and with the expert skill of the dragoman, you will direct the strict rites whereby the scene will be brought to its proper consummation: incarnating in turn the latent, contradictory drives that govern human actions: the lust for absolute power and, simultaneously, for annihilation in an act of self-sacrifice: at once a caudillo and a martyr: a cadaver in the service of a cause and the forger of destinies and lives, depending on the caprices of your will: exorcising demons in bloody mock confrontations, with no other weapon save naked discourse: transmuting violence into a sign: sweeping away its odious face from the earth: turning it into an occasion for verbal prowess

the column will move off across the desert, following the itinerary of oases where the Bedouins make camp, briefly recovering their strength beneath a molten sky and starting to advance again: via Anesit, El Khenig, Usader, Tiloq, Tin Tanetfirt: the men of the harka will carefully scrutinize the wavy horizon line of the dunes, their faces hidden behind their coarse-woven neckerchiefs, the trappings of their camels swaying as they track across the yellow sand at a brisk trot: unmoved by the silent pain of the Nazarene, who, with a rope around his neck, drags himself along behind them on the road to Tamanrasset: stumbling and falling, rising to his feet again with the greatest of effort, falling face down on the sand again, rising once more: resigning himself to his miserable fate with an ineffable smile on his lips: at once tormented and filled with joy: the encounters with the enemy follow one upon the other at a fantastic rhythm, and after bitter combat the vanquished are given no quarter: the bodies of the Turks are proof of your malicious and anxious desire to do battle, and freeing the youngest and most handsome of them, the crafty Ebeh welcomes them into his rustic captain's tent: pouring forth words of encouragement with the object of gaining their confidence and lulling them into a comforting belief in his benevolent and paternal esteem: with the smiling countenance of one who pretends to appreciate the caresses bestowed upon him though in fact he is preparing to attack: innocently, imprudently, they allow themselves to be swayed by his soft words and are at a loss as to how to show him their gratitude: oaths and protests of loyalty issue forth spontaneously from their lips without their noticing that the person to whom they are addressed is already stealthily fingering the delicate, tender skin of their necks, searching for the right spot to insert his keen-bladed weapon: disguising his treacherous intent by pretending that it is a mere affectionate gesture, a soothing, kindly embrace: allowing the lad to settle down gratefully in his lap with a smile on his lips, until the moment when he unsheathes the dagger and wields it with the swift expertise of the butcher: decapitating the victim in a single stroke: savoring the look of astonishment in his glassy pupils: receiving the ritual spurt of blood full in the face: the mineral hardness of his features takes on a crystalline purity and a delicious warmth swells through you at the sight of the cruel spectacle: the brutal attack of the harkis of Ebeh, the vultures that hover in black circles above the disemboweled corpses!: still clutching his scimitar stained a bright red, firing, with twitches and convulsive gestures, at the enemy scattering in every direction: paying no heed to the urgent exhortations of Ali, who is panic-stricken at this hysterical expression of your wrath: to Damascus, El-Orens, to Damascus!: giving orders to the horde in his stead: take no prisoners alive!: avenging the affront suffered in Deráa: the resistance to the Bey's desires: the citadel of your personal integrity, now irrevocably lost with the savage pleasure of revealing, to yourself and to others, the irreducible truth of your most intimate being in a single act of real communion with the world: giving your inner violence to have free rein without fear of the consequences: setting its paroxysms over against reason, its intoxication over against the worthlessness of a false, precarious order: mercilessly finishing off the defenseless wounded, using up with feverish, dizzying pleasure every last bullet in your cartridge belts: sure at last of what you are: beneath the talismanic protection of the adamantine Ebeh and his implacable knife-blade refraction

in the footsteps of Father Foucauld

the longed-for martyrdom at Tamanrasset, the dazzling apotheosis of your career!: a visceral impulse, brooking no denial, that leads you inexorably to the assigned place, so often dreamed of since your offering to the apostolic, missionary cause: to the Roman circus on whose benches the neronian crowd sits impatiently, eager to witness the torture: the voluptuous pain inflicted on the victim before the final surrender of his soul: replaced here by the fierce harka of Senusis under the command of the angular, refractory Ebeh: in full and total possession of his unyielding, adamantine hardness: of his solid, mineral density: with his geometrically carved body, like a rock with dazzling crystalline polyhedral facets, and a lean sharp face that betrays not the slightest notion of pity: the arm that brandishes the whip gleams like naked steel and the agony of the blows slowly fills you with joy: ah, to die a martyr, stripped of everything, stretched out on the ground, naked, unrecognizable, covered with blood and wounds, killed violently and painfully!: martyrs, prophets, apostles, corpses, out of perfect obedience!: the perfection of love is the perfection of obedience!: finally surrendering, without inhibitions, to the exquisite, amorous swoon: to the ineffable ecstasies and raptures that unite in a single soaring arpeggio executioners and victims, yogis and commissars, heretics and inquisitors: everything, even your style, a consummate imitation of the burning thirst of mystics, their insatiable, savage voracity: then closing your copy of the *Oeuvres spirituelles* in order to return to the bare expanses of the Sahara: to the rigors and the harshness of a desert of sheer stone, without a trace of vegetable coloring to make it more attractive: a thousand leagues north of Tamanrasset, after following in the opposite direction the famous camel route, the path of the old slave caravans that are a thing of the past now: crossing the Tropic of Cancer to the right of the spurs and summits of the Hoggar range, beyond the dark mountains that watch over the wasteland of In Amguel, heading for the massive *adrar* of Tisnú and its triple marble dome: plateaus surrounded by high ridges whose sharp crests thrust upward like barren islands jutting up out of the sea, steep violet-colored cliffs, gorges and narrow passes, ravines of oneiric black rock: past the lunar cirques of Arak, the sierras that wall off the horizon from the wadi, the somber valleys and peaks with a forbidding, tortured beauty: reaching at last the sere plain of Tademait, and continuing along the winding paved road, the confluence of two rivers at Fort Miribel, at the edge of the mysterious Chaamba territory looming up before you: you are now in the palm grove of El Golea, and, with the permission of your obliging executioners, you will climb to the top of the old castle in order to gaze down on the oasis for the last time: the dense urban conglomeration with its jumble of buildings at your feet, the educational centers under construction, the sanctuary with the tomb of the Mohammedan hermit, the cemetery and campgrounds where the Moslems celebrate the paschal feastdays: the eucalyptuses of the Annex garden, the ocher-colored government buildings, the artesian well that gushes forth at the edge of the highway to In Salah, and eight and one-half kilometers farther north, the cupola of the Church of Saint Joseph and the ruins of the Buffalobordj: at the end of the road that leads to the deserted Christian colony, and amid abandoned summer residences that have fallen into ruin on either side, to the tomb of the Reverend Father Foucauld (the Calère district of Oran, shortly after the great disaster: the gutted buildings of the rue Philippe, hollow shells with no doors or windows, empty eye sockets: the drowsing bricks of the cathedral, the Plaza de la Perla and its deserted buildings: the traces of dynamite explosions still blacken the cafés of the Place Kléber, the façades of the rue Haute d'Orléans: everything stained, dead, useless: not a soul about save for a lonely, lost old man here and there, walking along aimlessly and blindly, like a sleepwalker

chapels shut up tight, bistros for sale, silent brothels left over from the happy, beaugestian days of the valiant Foreign Legion

the razed barracks of Targuist, the desolate and defenseless Llano Amarillo, the statueless pedestals of Xauen

the desert is reclaiming its age-old rights

the dunes' all-devouring waves are advancing

a slow, irreversible process of degeneration

vanity of vanities)

on your knees, with the rope around your neck and your hands tied behind your back, you will examine the ridiculously insignificant crosses eroded by the stubborn sirocco and the tombs half asphyxiated by treacherous arms of sand, meditating, in quiet sadness, upon the total, lamentable failure of the evangelical mission: the selfish, sterile pleasure of martyrdom: your wretched usurped glory: the view from this spot is pleasant in autumn and the cry of the sentinel announcing the arrival of reinforcements dispatched to liberate you does not dim the later vision of the palm grove and of the gentle, serpentine undulation that spreads outward from the church, vast and unreachable: when the shooting begins and the predestined executioner places the barrel of his rifle to your skull, the horizontal line of your eyes will rise, enabling you to catch a glimpse of the blurred inscription engraved on your own memorial plaque

DANS L'ATTENTE DU JUGEMENT DE
LA SAINTE ÉGLISE ICI REPOSENT
LES RESTES DU SERVITEUR DE DIEU
CHARLES DE JÉSUS

VICOMTE DE FOUCAULD (1858–1916)
MORT EN ODEUR DE SAINTETÉ LE 1 DÉCEMBRE 1916
À TAMANRASSET
"JE VEUX CRIER L'ÉVANGILE PAR TOUTE MA VIE"
PÈRE CHARLES DE FOUCAULD

(seconds, days, or years?: time is entirely effaced in the text)
mercifully, the volley of gunfire will ring out

**with Ibn
Turmeda,
back to the
open sewer**

from one cemetery to another

leaping from one gravestone to the next, you will reach the Tunisian kubbeh where the remains of Brother Anselm are on display for the silent, worshipful homage of the Moslem multitudes: the faithful come from every direction of the compass, and Ibn Turmeda in person will contemplate the scene with you and affably await the judgment of posterity: his rightful, eternal inclusion on the list of Mohammedan anchorites: popular sanction of his apostasy and proselytism in favor of Islam

clasping each other's hands in affectionate intimacy, you will plot, with the glow of pleasure of surgeons, new acts of betrayal, treacherous crimes, traps, and disloyalties: the two of you fraternally united in the accursed abjuration of the Spanish convert to Islam: dizzily enjoying the first fruits of your chosen lot: with no stupid sense of shame quant au genre de jouissance!

freed of the anathema that surrounds the abominable hole and its impure visceral emanations, indifferent to the ideal state attained by the saints and the blessed, whose residues, Saint Bernard tells us, are transformed into a sweet, refined liquid, like unto myrrh and frankincense and the essence of musk, you will henceforth disdain the steep stairway that leads from stench to perfume, from quadruped to angel, opting instead for the corporeal evacuation of plebs squatting over the effluvia of the open public sewer, the impudent, outrageous curve that proclaims its base kinship with unclean matter, the amorous promiscuity with dung, filth, and stink that conjoins the face and the ass, the Eye of God and the eye of the devil abandoning forever the illusory role of lords and masters of Creation in favor of the apparent humility of the most insidious insect species, you will combat the supposed superiority of the hominid through the use of the incisive logic of parasites

with the greatest compunction, we live and take our ease within your humble dwellings, your homes and mansions, your sanctuaries, we sleep in your beds, on your mattresses, sheets, down quilts, and pillows, feeding, when such is our pleasure, on your very flesh, reproducing ourselves and spawning in the very midst of the hair of your heads, your armpits, your beards, penetrating your nostrils and ears and thereby depriving you of sleep and rest, expelling on your bodies and your garments residues that are far more fetid than those which you abashedly evacuate in a squatting position, without troubling ourselves to conceal them as you do or emit them in a private place: quite to the contrary, we do so openly, in plain sight, sullying the fine and delicate garments that you have just laundered with soap and bleach and your skin that you have scented with cologne and sterilized with deodorant, establishing ourselves in the thickets and shady spots round about your inferior hole in order to witness, completely free of charge, the spectacle of what you so presumptuously call the act of love, the monotonous, familiar ritual intended to ensure, on propitious days, the orderly propagation of the species, when your organ, not a musical but rather a tiresome one, slowly distends in its dull, duly assigned abode and piously gives up the ghost out of melancholy and boredom, thus allowing the minuscule gene to make its way along against the current and reach its appointed destination after an eventful journey, as we swing back and forth on the bindweeds and the tangled vines, agilely coupling in pairs, quartets, dozens with a dexterity and suppleness incomparably superior to yours, depositing

our eggs wherever we please and immediately recovering our strength thanks to the gratuitous abundance of your thick, nutritious blood, simply burying in your epidermis our proboscis in the form of a tube at the precise moment at which you are pretending to moan in ineffable ecstasy or straddling the ostentatious bidet, in order to eliminate, with a morbid sense of guilt, all traces of your secretions and discharges, tacitly resigned to the fact that we enjoy ourselves, eat, drink, and take our rest at the expense of others, totally indifferent to your torments and anxieties, your toils and troubles, since there is little or nothing that you can do to us, and if you blindly and futilely scratch yourselves, you exacerbate your pain without even bothering us, thereby clearly demonstrating that you are the helpless victims of our caprices and obviously our servants, far down, very far down, on the zoological scale, lacking that nobility and dignity of your species that your priests proclaim in vain when they fill your ears with panegyrics and high-flown speeches with the aim of causing you to believe that you are essentially different from all other species and that God is setting aside an exclusive paradise for you as a recompense for your present miseries and sufferings, neglecting, on the other hand, to tell you that they too allow themselves to be exploited by us, and in the secrecy and purity of the sanctum sanctorum ignominiously bare their behinds like the desurplusvalued darkies of the common sewer, in direct contact with crude raw material, base waste products, the visceral emanations of the plebs
men the lords and masters?
please, don't make us laugh!

starting from the open sewer
from the summertime revelation of the sewer ditch being installed by the department of public works which, like the hail of murderous machine-gun fire from a plane, was dis-

embowcling the paved surface of the sidewalk and revealing the earth hidden below, scattering it along a line parallel to the wooden walkway provided for pedestrians along which you ventured as the humble artificers toiled at your feet with their picks and shovels and the chatter of the pneumatic drill in the background pierced your ears with the muted impact of machine-gun bullets

(when their heads poked out of the hole at the level of your shoes and your gaze lingered upon them, yielding to their animal magnetism)

you have gone from one end of the Moslem world to the other, from Istanbul to Fez, from Nubian country to the Sahara, changing skin like a chameleon thanks to the handy, satisfying passkey of certain apersonal pronouns, ready and waiting for the common use of your protean, ever-shifting voices

you have taken your pleasure on the enormous fat behind of the illustrious Queen Kong

rivaled the heroic feat of the Stylite atop the buñuelesque column

fought against the Turkish army on the desolate plains of Jordan

gone up the valley of the Nile from Alexandria to Luxor

crossed the desert in the company of Ebeh

suffered Christian martyrdom at Tamanrasset

whipped Father Foucauld in the tumulary minaret of Ghardaïa

beginning with that memorable Paris summer day that generously cast its heat waves down upon the enslaved laborers of the public-works crew clutching their work tools

by way of the little cafés of the Goutte d'Or and the alleyways of Belleville, through the network of urban thoroughfares that leads from the wedding cake of the Sacré-Coeur to the train platforms of the Gare du Nord

(there where the savage shriek of the girl suddenly drowned out the noise of the crowd and abruptly precipitated your hatred of certain marks of identity that had ceased to be yours, as though the liberating cry, instead of coming from her, were a mere projection of the explosive, uncontainable tension that had accumulated in your breast)

you have drifted from one continent to another like the legendary Wandering Jew, in search of the blinding clarity revealed completely by chance in the wretched public-works ditch

(bodies and more bodies enveloped in the rigor and firmness of their beliefs, clinging stubbornly to their instinctive will to live as to a clear and incontrovertible axiom)

finally arriving at the conclusion

(thanks to the warmth and aid of the Beni Snassen tribesmen and their robust and hircine constitutions)

that the conversion to their law has been absolute and henceforth all roads will inexorably lead you to Bernussi, Umm Rabia, or Uxda

IV

paulo maiora canamus

from the vast expanse of space to the no less vast expanse of
time: from the schoolroom atlas to the old history manual: barely recovered from the oneiric foray through the
phantasmagorical Mohammedan orbit and now ready, with
no other aid than paper and pen, for another invasion, an
unpredictable one too, this time of Einstein's fourth dimen-
sion: shut up, as always, in the tiny room: without ever
abandoning the confines of your own writing: focusing your
interest on the exemplary trajectory of the country that has
ceased to be yours and means nothing to you today except
this: a handy stop on the way to Morocco: a hostel, an inn,
a place to spend the night: a spot on the map: thanks to the
heap of documents piled up on the shelves of your library,
practically in reach of your hand: authentic proofs of incor-
rigible obstinacy in the pursuit of a campaign of self-mutila-
tion and punishment, prolonged for centuries with a tenacity
worthy of a better cause: from the time when, as a waggish
little character belonging to the dominant species of fauna
once observed, the now-unified Peninsula was an area popu-
lated by various multicolored, corrupt beings: a shameful
past that it was necessary to hide, like the existence of
leprous, mad, or syphilitic ancestors, from the pure-hearted,
valiant lad from the Meseta as he readied himself to generously shed his blood for the perpetuation of the kingdom of
Seneca, a dismal era of different beliefs, freedom of expression, illicit passions, in which the Most Christian King himself wore Moorish dress and endorsed, through his own
example, the crimine pessimo, finally provoking, by his in-
describable conduct, the rightful, salutary reaction of his sis-

ter the queen, clearing the way for a memorable pruning from the vigorous and flourishing national trunk of those rotten, perverse limbs, hundreds of thousands, perhaps millions, of lascivious, crude, effeminate beings, fond of bestial amusements and much given to the sins of the flesh, who, in addition to offending the sight of the pure-blooded nobility, transformed the toiling peasant class into a learned assembly of theologians and the libidinous homeland of the Arcipreste de Hita into an austere and solemn *auto sacramental,* a great theater of the world in which the masses identified their personal dignity with total mental quietude and fervidly attended the rites of execution of reprobates, Judaizers, sodomites, bigamists, and Lutherans, who, in the name of a tolerance which, as Menéndez Pelayo put it, is nothing but an infirmity or a eunuchism of the understanding, endeavored to infect the healthy portion of the country with their perverse and outlandish doctrines and their despicable and infamous vices, a life-saving intransigence and inflexibility which, beyond our frontiers, was to bring down on our heads violent hatred and enmity, repeated calumnies, persistent phobias, as our military genius extended to the farthermost corners of the earth the boundaries of our splendid Empire, a robust and vigorous attitude which, having been steadily maintained for four entire centuries, amid reverses and misfortunes, calamities, acts of aggression, disasters, has finally turned into an authentic ascetic exercise by virtue of which the gradual intercession of antibodies has freed our organism of the fatal toxins that today are poisoning societies less sagacious than ours, confronting them with the terrible dilemma of slow death by asphyxiation or a brutal, extremely painful amputation

the voice of the little character has gradually drowned out your own, and you will listen to his monotonous, imperturbable oration as, from the books piled up alongside your worktable, on your crude set of file shelves, in your cramped library, other anxious, frantic, discordant voices cry out to you reproachfully, demanding in their turn the inalienable right to be heard, denied them for years, decades, centuries in the pitch-black solitude of the dungeon or the torture chamber, the heavy silence of an abode that is continually besieged by slanderers or the hoarse shouts of the mob gathered round the stake, stifled, snuffed-out voices, a clandestine history of thousands and thousands of ex-countrymen who, unlike you, were not able to escape, a history never divulged, buried in the sanctuary of their eternally defiled consciousness, lived in anguish, against their will, by a cast of sober, dull little figures, or overexcited, hysterical, grotesque ones, conquistadores and hidalgos, nobles and inquisitors, virgins and prostitutes, picaresque rascals and squires, an entire people, a sleeping-beauty society turned to stone by a sorcerer's spell, which from the time of poor Juana the Mad to that of Carlos II the Bewitched, prognathous and sterile, gave its consent, openly or tacitly, to the expeditious, unquestionably effective methods of a most reliable instrument of repression intended to create an impenetrable, hermetic cordon sanitaire around the stern, forbiddingly grim country, denunciations, confessions, trials, confiscation of property, recantations, death sentences, burnings of books and documents, of apostates, Jews, heretics, practitioners of that abominable sin which, though now exposed to public shame, still merited the pious attention of the inspired muse of Quevedo, a lifeless, stone-dead history, a demented epic, a lugubrious chanson de geste, recited against a changeable backdrop of processions, one-act farces, comedies, bullfights, sporting events, joyous operettas, sound and fury, an interminable bolero by Ravel, vain and empty gesticulation, prolonged for century after century, with no real logical continuity, out of sheer historical inertia, until the birth of the stranger, which is what you were, within the bosom of an atrophied, extemporaneous bourgeoisie, a little more than forty years ago, and hence an involuntary supernumerary of an embittered and bloody saga, three years of frenzy, destruction, and pillage, a cruel civil struggle, a celebrated million dead, the crowning achievement of a nation that is now only a stopping-off place for you, where dissident, vindictive voices persistently claim your attention, invite you to stretch out your arm, take up the book or the volume in which they are shut up, leaf sadly through its pages, and hear their testimony to times in which, as the liberated Poet once wrote, their congenital unreason, today become madness, struck them as an admirable paradox

still listening nonetheless

continuing to listen

until that glorious epiphany that we all remember, when stubborn domestic subversion, with aid from abroad, tried to abolish marriage and the family, subordinate the spirutual to the material, impose committees on us to replace brotherhoods, substitute a dirty astrakhan cap for our beloved statue of Faith atop the Giralda, a deliberate attempt to destroy us which, although it met with total defeat on the battlefield, nevertheless persists in its work of sapping and undermining through new and more subtle devices, seeking to obtain by peaceful means what was unobtainable by taking up arms, through intellectual corruption, eroticism, pornography, decadent theatrical spectacles, literature that was vulgar and unwholesome and very often prejudicial to our political and patriotic ideals, endeavoring to contaminate the country by way of drugs, the confusion of the sexes, the proliferation of morally unsavory public dance halls, a mortal threat to our bright future, to our most noble and most sacred patrimony, against which we must defend ourselves, tooth and nail if necessary, in order to prevent our sworn enemies from achieving their goal, namely, the creation of soft and effeminate youths who may one day be destroyed by a sudden invasion of cruel super-male peoples from the East

animus neminisse horret

it all began with baths

whenne the Infante Don Sancho perished during the greate rout of Zacala, the king summoned his wyse men and byshops in order to ascertaine why the martiall spirit of his warriors had suffered a decline, whereupon the former gave answer that the latter had fallen into the habit of frequenting publick bathes and were much given to vyces and unbrydled appetytes of the flesh

> and doth this not serve as a selfe-evident notorious and palpable example to any man who would reflect upon this lewde vyle filthie and horrible sinne of fornication and accursed copulation beyond the holye bonds of matrimonie according to God's law, the ynfynite harm it doth occasion today, both to the bodye and to the soul, inasmuch as any man who doth immoderately give himselfe over to such carnal delectation loseth his appetyte at table and out of heate and a thirste that naught can slake taketh the habit of drinking more than is his wont, for love and lust bring on many ynfirmities and abbreviate men's lives, cause them to grow olde before their tyme, their members to tremble, their five senses to undergoe change so that in consequence they lose some of them, either wholly or in parte, and hence human bodyes grow debylitated, whereupon men called upon to take up armes and perform other arduous labours are found grievouslie wanting in power, cowardlie as Jewwes, abject vanquished creatures possessed of little strengthe, and as in our present tymes our sinnes are moltiplied with each passing day and evil ways persist without correction and as the most common of sinnes is lycentious love in the publick bathes, which thus entrain violent contentions, homicides, deathes, scandales, and perdition of goods as well as perdition of persons, and what is

farre worse, perdition of miserable souls, inasmuch as the abominable carnal appetyte respects nothing and inasmuch as many lovers instead of seeking out the female prefer the companye of males for their vyle act, like men in their many evil deeds and like women in their comportment and like little harlots in their lewde appetytes, and hence it would appear that the ende of the world shall soon be upon us, there being no feare of God nor of His justice, and shame a thing that has compleatly dissapeared from peoples heartes, that the heavens and the earth ought rightlie to tremble and adjudge such as these like unto vycious brutes in soul and bodye, lacking in sense reason and understanding in view of their ynfamous workes and sodemmitical deeds, all these things being sinnes which by way of publick bathes bring great harm and confusion to our realm, and thus the publick goode doth urgently require that they be destroyed and closed, and may it please our allpowerful Lord, Jesus Christ, incarnate, God's on-lie begotten Son, engendered by the Word of God the Father in that virgynal womb of Our Reverend and Blessed Mother, to open our eyes that we may see and protecte ourselves against Satan our enemy and correct our vyces and repent wholeheartedlie of our sinnes, in order that we may be deemed worthie of entering with Him in that precious celebration of that blessed nuptial feaste amid the gloryie of paradise forever and ever amen

de vita et moribus

this expression, popular throughout the globe today thanks to the careful and efficient labor of our consulates and travel agencies, is not simply a highly successful advertisement: rather, it is a reflection, alas, of an indisputable reality that only the mad or the blind would dare question: what other country besides ours would in fact offer tourists so rich a folk tradition, full of picturesque rites and customs that have no parallel or equal in any of the five corners of the earth?: what other nation besides ours would be capable of affording the curious visitor, eager for new sensations and heady emotions, such colorful, lively, and original spectacles as those which he may witness, free of charge, on Sundays and holidays, after complying with the precepts of Our Holy Mother Church, in the public squares and arenas of the principal cities of the Peninsula?: an extraordinary dépaysement, a fantastic breakaway that suddenly transports him thousands of leagues away as he contemplates, absolutely fascinated, the preparations for our typical, most unusual fiesta!: a gloomy ceremony and yet at the same time a joyous, incomparable ritual of life and death that sends the most serene souls into raptures and justifies the liturgical atmosphere, the religious attentiveness of the countless familiars, advisers, and aficionados who fill the balconies and stands all year long: as our authorities and pillars of society, in full regalia, squeeze together on the platform and in the boxes with their cassocks and broad-brimmed hats, their hussar's dolmans, their medals, their curved tortoise-shell combs, their mantillas: moments of restrained emotion and silent, anxious expectation that allow our sensual but chaste females an opportunity to slowly and effectively display their solemn, entrancing coquetry!: their extremely resourceful, inspired language of come-hither looks, glances, blushes, smiles, gestures, flutterings of their fans: but tender, human compassion as well, that wells up in their huge dark eyes, like those of pharaohs' wives or sultanesses, when the actors and extras in the drama majestically enter the arena, accompanied by the huzzas and cheers of the audience: constables, judges, inquisitors, the condemned, the priest who delivers the homily, those handed over by the church authorities to the secular arm of justice: these latter dressed in and adorned with the garments and symbolic objects that identify them, as is the tradition in our country: sambenitos, dunce caps, gags, yellow or white habits: locked up in a wooden cage and chained to a sort of coffin, or else sitting astride a donkey, with a grotesque paper cone atop their heads: and even though it is a ceremony performed in accordance with a very strict ritual, those who regularly attend it and connoisseurs from abroad will always find, we guarantee it, that note of subtle improvisation that ensures that the rite will inevitably have an element of novelty about it: one condemned man, for instance, may walk to the auto-da-fé with aplomb, dignity, and sangfroid, and when they remove the gag a few moments before setting fire to the faggots, he may recite one of the Psalms in a ringing voice: another may abjure his crimes at the very last instant and, as a consequence of his sincere though belated recantation, be granted the merciful favor of being garroted: a third, deeply moved by the explanations and arguments put forward by the priest in his homily delivered at the foot of the stake, may fall silent and, with a noble gesture of expiation, humbly place the faggots atop his own head: another, finally, may stubbornly remain deaf to the exhortations of his confessor and his judges and willfully persist in his faulty syllogisms and errors, indifferent to the executioner's preparations and the hoots and insults of the crowd: the motive for the crime and the subsequent punishment also vary, thus avoiding the monotony of the déjà vu and introducing into the auto-da-fé an element of surprise which, as you have doubtless learned from personal experience, keeps the real aficionado in suspense and obliges him to hold his breath until the dénouement: yesterday the tourists who had come to contemplate the beauties of our incomparable Andalusian capital had the singular privilege, on returning from an instructive and enjoyable visit to the famous cellars of Jerez, of attending an auto-da-fé in the old Plazuela de San Francisco, which was honored by the presence of the bishops of the Canary Islands and Lugo, the cathedral chapter, the judges of the royal tribunal, the Duchess of Béjar, numerous ladies of high station, and countless numbers of hidalgos and caballeros, and in which twenty-one Lutherans were turned over to the secular arm and another eighty condemned men were put to death on the rack and the wheel: day before yesterday members of the Club Méditerranée were present at the solemn burning, in Madrid, of five convicts found guilty of the abominable sin: a court jester, a valet of the Count of Villamediana, a little mulatto slave boy, another of Villamediana's manservants, and a page of the Duke of Alba: our damsels and matrons lamented their extreme youth and their unfortunate lack of discretion, and there were moments of intense emotion when the executioner bound the very young and most contrite page to the stake and lighted the pyre with a stern frown: naturally we are cognizant of the fact that this imposing, virile spectacle, precisely because of its sudden ferocity, may perhaps temporarily disturb members of the audience who come from other countries, particularly those of the gentle sex: hence in our guidebooks and tourist folders we recommend that persons who have delicate sensibilities or are overly impressionable refrain from attending: the initial shock might be too great: but we do not want a missed experience to mar the memory of your vacation in our sunny and hospitable country, which we hope will be a most pleasant one, and therefore for such persons we offer a vast variety of other diversions and entertainments that we are certain will delight them: on the other hand, however, we will make no compromises simply because of the obsessive, stubborn campaign on the part of a certain sector of the foreign press that regularly calls us brutes and makes a great hue and cry about our "barbarism": this hypocritical humanitarianism, worthy of a menopausal old maid or the president of a society for the prevention of cruelty to animals, fails to take into account the complex and eminently cathartic nature of our expiatory, educational fiesta: in point of fact, in order to properly appreciate the auto-da-fé it is indispensable to embrace it in its tragic and redeeming totality: admittedly, at first glance the spectacle of a man roasting on a stake seems unbearable and horrifying: yet if we take into consideration the gravity of the offense of which he has been found guilty, his terrible agony contains a positive, compensatory element which, even in the cases of the greatest abjection and baseness, confers upon the condemned man a prestigious aura of dignity: the writhing, the screams, the odor of burning flesh are mere accessory details of the staging of the tragedy and only the true aficionado can judge them at their proper worth: examining them not in isolation, but, rather, assigning them their rightful place in the overall, global picture: as the celebrated author of *Death in the Afternoon* (who had as intimate a knowledge of our fiesta as did Lope de Vega) put it so well, the audience that attends burning ceremonies possesses an innate sense of tragedy, thanks to which the secondary aspects of the spectacle are seen and appreciated as integral parts of the whole: and this sense is something as personal and fortuitous as the possession or nonpossession of a perfect sense of pitch: in the case of the listener who lacks this latter, the principal impression he will retain of a symphonic concert will be that produced by the gestures and movements of the bass violinist, thus precisely resembling the spectator at an auto-da-fé who remembers only the agonizing death throes of the condemned man: but this latter's writhings and the screams he emits, judged separately, lack aesthetic purity: if the listener attends a concert with the same humanitarian spirit that he brings to bear on autos-da-fé, he will find there too a vast field on which to focus his anxieties and charitable impulses: he may dream of bettering the salaries and the standard of living of bass violinists, just as he might have wanted to do something for the convicts sentenced to the redeeming flames of the stake: but if he is a real man of parts, a scholar and a gentleman, and knows that symphonic orchestras must be considered as a whole and accepted in their totality, he will probably manifest no other reaction save one of pleasure, approval, and delight: he will not evaluate the bass violinist apart from the orchestral whole, nor will he think of the condemned man, even for a fraction of a second, as a human being who is thinking, suffering, writhing, and screaming

finis coronat opus

and the condemned men?, you will ask me: are they not perhaps human beings like the rest of us?: do heretics, sinners, and members of impure and degenerate castes not suffer?: and even though physicians and scientists universally agree that depraved men and individuals of mixed blood and tainted origins do not possess the same sensitivity to pain as upright, pure-blooded persons, we shall now set aside such an argument in favor of that of the prodigious benefits that torture bestows upon those brought to justice: listen, my sons, why do you believe that we have bound you to the stake if not to redeem you through suffering and show you the arduous and difficult path to Christian salvation?: therefore do not curse the pains that you are called upon to endure: your bodies will be burned and reduced to ashes: but your souls, by virtue of sincere repentance, will be free to fly to the eternal and blessed abode of the elect: it is for this reason that we subject you to tortures by water and cord, the pulley, hot bricks, the thumb screw, and deprivation of sleep and lead you to the auto-da-fé with chains, shackles, a gag: so that the devil will not tempt you to relapse into your perverted doctrines or yield to the execrable promiscuity of the most brutish animals: protecting you against yourselves: in order that one day you may sit at the right hand of the Father, absorbed in the joy and ecstasy of a thousand sublime visions: with souls as white as the silken mantilla, trimmed with lace, worn by those damsels and matrons who witness our fiesta from the boxes or the stands: the Most Exalted Defender of the destiny of the country will then look upon you with a smiling countenance and no one will reproach you for your past opinions, your stupid contumacy, your bestial pleasures: that is where your errors, your wretchedness, your vile deeds will lead you in the end: the Immaculate Virgin will invite you to her table and offer you her own delectable viands: instead of continuing to live your degenerate, depraved, abject lives and eternally suffering because of your tainted blood, you will temper your spiritual lineage in the flames of the pyre and free your souls of disease and affliction: the Lord who is our master has taken pity on your dejection and will rescue you from the gloomy darkness in which you live, thanks to this opportune, providential crucible of pain and penitence: what an intoxicating and comforting prospect!: the auto-da-fé is the merciful divine stratagem whereby you will enter heaven in a state of exquisite, immaculate purity: like unto those who have unfailingly lived a peaceful and virtuous life: you will mingle as equals, without discrimination, with the illustrious members of our caste: the refined, purified, immaculate, perfect soul of the contrite criminal, of the docile condemned man, is like the native gold found in the sands of rivers, in the form of bright nuggets or flakes, which, when alloyed with copper, is used for making jewelry, for decoration, or in dentistry: but no soul of a Moor, a Jew, a heretic, a bigamist, or a sodomite ever attains this exquisite, perfect, exemplary state without first undergoing a long and rigorous process of purgation: you know, do you not, of the existence of goldbearing ore that it is necessary to extract, wash, and beat in order that it may at last yield up its noble yellow substance?: in like manner the soul of the criminal is purified and refined for days, weeks, months, or years through the careful, precise torture of our dungeons and jails: nonetheless, my sons, the mineral thus cleansed of its impurities is not yet perfect: in order to reach the superior, ductile, incorruptible state, it must be made to undergo a series of complicated operations that require the delicate skills of smelters and goldsmiths: and likewise we inquisitors must separate good from evil, the gold from the dross: the patience and resignation of the condemned as they are brought face to face with the executioner in fact causes the residual, impure matter to trickle away: with the notable difference that, whereas the melting and refining of the gold takes hours and hours, that of the soul of the criminal sentenced to the stake lasts scarcely ten minutes: and what does this ridiculous lapse matter compared to the immortal glory offered you by the Eternal!: the hypocritical, overly sentimental reaction of foreign critics neglects this fact and therefore fails to take into account the most important factor of all, since the real meaning of the sufferings that you undergo is revealed only when we examine them in the light of the fate of your souls: Father Vosk, you will say to me: why must we suffer and not you others?: must we deduce from your words that our arrogant, criminal, or impure actions were predestined ab eterno?: O unfathomable Mystery!: although God knows the future, he respects our freedom, and if he tolerates evil he does so in order that the elect may voluntarily choose to follow the path that leads to redemption: have you perchance heard of the diamond fields of the Transvaal, in which carbon naturally crystallizes in the form of admirable octrahedrons?: there too the Lord, in His infinite wisdom, has decreed that while some crystals will be transparent, gleaming, iridescent, refractive, others will merely be translucent, and the immense majority opaque and black, resembling coal: and on Judgment Day the Mine Superintendent will classify the three varieties according to their purity and value: the dark souls of the hardened sinner will be like the carbide that is used to drill rocks, but that all buyers disdain: repentent sinners, so-called bort, coarse crystals used for grinding precious stones: and those who accept with Christian joy the drastic and redemptive sentence of our most holy tribunal, the beautiful gems, with dazzling facets, which all of us admire in the display windows of jewelers or diamond dealers: saved souls, arctic snow fields, eternal glaciers of a nordic whiteness!: and is there any one of us who still dares to complain?: if so, you may rest assured that he deserves his fate and even the extreme rigors of infernal damnation

salus populi suprema lex esto

the results of our thoroughgoing, effective therapy are
abundantly clear: governments throughout the globe envy us
this sovereign purifying agent which, adapting itself to the
problems and needs of every era, preserves our moral health
for century after century, thanks to the radical elimination
of suspected carriers of germs and the establishment at our
borders of a hermetic, impenetrable cordon sanitaire: today,
within the civilized Christian world, our country is the one
that has the smallest number of eternal damnations, both in
relative and in absolute terms: only some twenty per cent of
our citizens were condemned this past year to the eternal
sufferings of hell, a really ridiculously small proportion if we
compare it to that of the eternally damned in the liberal-
democratic countries, whether pagan or atheist: and likewise we are situated at the bottom of the list with respect to
the total number of years of expiation being spent by our
blessed souls in purgatory: recent studies carried out by our
computers reveal a noticeable decrease in the number of forbidden books, attendance at unwholesome theatrical spectacles, dances cheek to cheek in promiscuous public halls,
impermissible strokings-rubbings-caresses: as for manuscripts submitted for approval by our Department of Orien-
tation and Consultation, we rely on the following criterion: if
the legitimate Reproductive Couple could read them aloud
to each other without either of them blushing and, above all,
without becoming sexually aroused, we authorize their publication, and all others are sent back stamped Not Ap-
proved: a procedure as fair as it is sensible, the merit of
which has been demonstrated not only by an appreciable
decrease in adultery, as might seem at first glance to be its
sole aim, but also a considerable decrease in carnal enjoyment not connected with the act of procreation: our adoles-
cents today do not indulge in heinous solitary vice, as is the
case in other nations, and as for those guilty of the abominable sin, one must search for them with a magnifying

glass: their odious caste is growing smaller and smaller with each passing day, to such a point that the historical continuity of our glorious national fiesta is endangered: the authorities of several provinces have recently voiced their alarm and are recommending a more lenient policy in order to ensure the solemn celebration of autos-da-fé in years to come: numerous official delegations and tourist groups experienced a most cruel disappointment last summer when at the last moment the fiestas to which they had been invited were canceled by the masters of ceremony of several cities, for understandable reasons of pride and prestige: the number and the pedigree of the criminals were not up to the minimum standards and therefore the convicts had to be returned to their dungeons amid the indignant hoots of the audience: inquisitors and judges with solid, well-earned reputations in the professional world of burnings had regretfully found themselves obliged to bring to justice foreigners caught in flagrante delicto or to pay an exorbitant price for condemned men from other provinces who were of an obviously inferior quality: the gap between supply and demand is widening daily, and being convinced of the superior results of rational planning on a national scale, our technocrats are arguing for a bold policy of priorities and economies that will henceforth guarantee normal reserves in tourist areas: the debate has spread from government circles and pressure groups to the general public, and our daily papers are printing hundreds of letters from readers in which the latter protest against this grave state of affairs and propose all sorts of expedients and solutions to the problem, with that proverbial ingenuity, so characteristic of our people, of which other nations are so envious: some of them are in favor, for example, of the gradual incineration of the condemned man, that is to say, the abrupt extinction of the flames before his burns are fatal in order to permit his prompt recovery in one of our comfortable and ultramodern hospitals, so that, after having been treated with all the careful attention and pampering that his condition requires, he may again play the principal role in the fiesta in other arenas: others suggest that the dramatic decrease in the number of the guilty handed over to the secular arm be compensated for by a prolongation of their punishment, through the use of some substance that slows down the action of the flames and lengthens the life of the condemned man for the space of several minutes: the most foresighted propose the creation of reservations of the sort established in the U.S.A. for Indians, on which future convicts will be permitted to indulge in the bestial sin and barbarous copulation, and be allowed heretical manuscripts and forbidden books: and some, finally, despairing of the viability of these remedies and persuaded that active moral prophylaxis will forever uproot this sin from our hallowed soil, favor the institution of a lottery system that will select condemned men from among the lowest social classes and grant their families an annual pension larger than the wages that the dead man has customarily earned, as well as a series of physical and moral privileges equal to those of soldiers who have died a glorious death on the battlefield: the advantages of this daring proposal: it would galvanize national emotion, satisfy our traditional predilections, maintain the country's prestige abroad, ensure the continued influx of foreign tourists: our government agencies and travel bureaus would have no difficulty guaranteeing that the fiesta would take place as advertised, just as they guarantee sunshine and clear skies, the hospitality so characteristic of our way of life, the sensual attraction of our women, the incredibly low prices in our country, and that vague, mysterious je ne sais quoi, whose fascination is more easily experienced than described, which is the very foundation of our unique difference as a people: the disadvantages?: an apparent cruelty and injustice which, though quite superficial, nonetheless present an easy target for the acerbic pens of our eternal enemies, permitting them to wax indignant at our presumed savagery, as meanwhile they carefully conceal from their readers the reverse of the coin: the much more cruel and tragic consequences of their famous policy of tolerance toward the inhabitants of their own countries: the really frightening number of souls irremissibly condemned to eternal punishment through their lack of imagination: for if the torment of the stake, regardless of whether it lasts ten, twenty, or forty minutes, provokes their whines of commiseration, how ought they to react to the idea of a fire that does not last a day, a week, or a year, but an entire, absolutely an entire, lifetime?: well, hell is more agonizing still, and lasts a whole eternity!: so who are the real barbarians then?: we or they?: who will have shown more compassion, mercy, and tenderness, the fans and aficionados of our burnings, or that motley crew of defenders of human rights in which there is not a single minister of the gospel, not a single devout old-maid Anglican, not a single overly sentimental titled lady who does not shed copious tears over the expiatory, and essentially benign, fate of those sentenced to the fleeting punishment of being burned at the stake?: but let us repeat again: a hypocritically humanitarian mentality will never be capable of understanding the noble, purifying, and virile sentiment that motivates our fiesta: if during the course of the auto-da-fé a person possessed of such a mentality prefers, out of masochism, to identify with the condemned man, let him do so: we for our part, however, will limit ourselves to asking him what intelligible criterion causes him to find such an attitude compatible with his stony insensitivity to eternal suffering: can it be that tortures endured outside the borders of our country do not move him or disturb him?: medice, cura te ipsum!: are you or are you not familiar with the saying about the mote in another's eye and the beam in our own?: I suggest that you reflect on it, mister critic, and stop spouting that nonsense of yours once and for all!

monstrum horrendum, informe, ingens

our parched and somber Peninsula has always been a land fertile in heretics, illuminati, apostates, and all manner of queer characters, as well as saints and wise men, the illustrious scholar Menéndez Pelayo writes, and there is no gainsaying the fact that there is something turbid and troubled and corrupt about the genius of an energetic race whose history, though studded with the glorious names of kings, conquistadores, and prelates, is also darkened, as though by shadows or stains, by small groups of individuals who, straying far from the beaten path, have endeavored since the very earliest times to perpetuate a secret worship of reptiles and other lascivious creatures, denying God, His law, and His saints and taking instead the devil as their lord and master, in the form of a hairy simian at times, and at others in the guise of a dashing Moor, celebrating with him unspeakable witches' sabbaths at which they adore him with osculations and genuflections, as a prelude to strange and unheard of collective diversions in the course of which they engage in bestial couplings and filthy acts of all sorts, on which we shall not dwell, out of aesthetic decorum and a respect for the boundaries of good taste, crimes described in minute detail by the guilty parties themselves, and their testimony corroborated by numerous witnesses, before our just and infallible tribunals, that, for instance, of a pertinacious convict recently burned at the stake who, after a shameless defense of his execrable devotion to the serpent, confessed that male ob strepitus audiebat nocturnos, prima nocte incubum sensisse, sed cum olivas nigras coena comedisset, naturale existimasse, and continued to proclaim, in his mad delirium, the advent of an enormous and monstrous gorilla whose power would extend to the farthest corners of the earth, an ominous prophecy, a gloomy prediction which, although uttered in a monotone, filled the learned and august members of the assembly with terror, leading them to cast horoscopes and call upon the services of warlocks and excommunicators, who, after organizing an imposing, spectacular procession grouping the entire population around the miraculous image of the Virgin, proceeded solemnly to excommunicate ophidians, obliging them, with powerful spells and incantations, to take wing, hiding the sun like a dense cloud and flying off in great flocks in the direction of the African shores whence, in an evil hour, they had come, in search perhaps of that fantastic avenging simian whose succor the condemned man, in his agonizing death throes, vainly implored, blasphemously addressing him by the barbarous, absurd name of King Kong

hoc volo, sic jubeo sit pro ratione voluntas

in order that there may vanish from our soil even the remotest idea that sovereignty resides outside of my royal person, in order that my peoples may know that I shall never accept the slightest alteration of the fundamental laws instituting monarchy, and in view of the various customs sanctioned by long observance or by ordinances many centuries old, I have decreed the creation of a Council, consisting of sages, royal officials, delegates to the Cortes nominated by the male heads of a household, and other authorities, whose function it shall be to explain to my beloved subjects the supremely suasive arguments and reasons attesting to the divine and providential nature of the executive power incarnated in my august and majestic will, and have formally instructed them to impress upon the people a small number of notions which are primordial and basic, and thus fully accessible to even the most dull-witted and simpleminded souls, so as to counteract the clandestine diffusion of foreign doctrines according to which citizens are responsible before the law alone and must decide on the future of the nation in conformity with the insidious arithmetical rule of the majority, setting aside for the moment the prodigious mass of historical proofs to the contrary, accumulated over the many centuries of our venerated dynasty's rule, in order to focus attention on the philosophical meat of the subject: the scientific basis of our indisputable though benevolent superiority, manifested not only in the most unusual circumstances of our eminently poetic propagation, thanks to a subtle, highly refined procedure which, lying at a thousand leagues' remove from the viviparous, placental reproduction of the plebs, involves a stupendous series of processes of florescence, pollination, and fecundation, at times similar in nature to plants possessed of neither a calyx nor a corolla which are pollinated by the gentle, discreet action of the wind, and at times similar to that of bright-colored flowers endowed with ambrosial perfumes that attract the winged creatures of various multicolored species of insects, but also, and most important, in an exquisite, quintessential digestive system that precludes, ab initio, any fetid visceral emission or base evacuation of filth: do those presumptuous, mendacious little gadflies who boldly propound their wild and abstruse theories think, perchance, that my royal person and that of the members of its revered family defecate in stinking common sewer ditches and then rinse their assholes with a bucket of water?: such an idea would be amusing were it not also sacrilegious, and those who would argue in favor of such an enormity would be incapable of proving their hypothesis, since simple natural reason suffices to show that visceral eliminations, be they solid or liquid, not to mention all the other corporeal eliminations such as hairs, sweat, fingernail parings, secretions of mucus, would necessarily partake, should they have actually existed, of the sovereign nature of my august person and would have been lovingly preserved by my most trusted servants and my most faithful subjects as emblems or signs of my invincible power: but inasmuch as we find no mention whatsoever of such precious tokens in the annals of History, we are obliged to conclude, consensu omnium, nemine discrepante, that they never existed and that my exalted person and that of the members of its family were not subject to the animal needs that afflict ordinary men and force them to squat down in shame in the act of restoring to the earth, in such a base and filthy form, that which they have received from it in the form of savory viands and refined, tonic, mellow drinks: for it is here that the malicious absurdity of the egalitarian hypothesis becomes manifest: it is common knowledge that there is one respect in which animals and humans are patently inferior to plants and trees: the fact that the superfluities of these latter are pleasurable and delightful whereas those of bipeds and quadrupeds are nauseating and abominable, and if those of plants and trees attract us and satisfy us with the aroma and savor of their fruits, who, pray tell, besides the devil would find the sordid and horrible product of animal and human entrails pleasing?: this is the quid of the problem!: and who will dare argue that my illustrious and enlightened person is qualitatively inferior to mere vegetable species?: a three-year-old child would indignantly reject such errant nonsense!: naturally, however, some presumptuous smart-ass democrat among you will be so bold as to ask: don't Your Gracious Majesties eat?: daily papers, magazines, and news broadcasts teach us the contrary: so tell us then: what becomes of the food that your royal person consumes if it does not evacuate it?: ah, you fops and pedants, that is precisely what I was leading up to!: if the metabolism of the vegetable kingdom is different from that of animals and humans, what's so strange about the fact that the metabolism of your just and exalted sovereign is also different?: while the republican and plebeian eye secretes corruption and impurity, that of your venerable dynasty exhales fragrance and harmony: the Lord, in His infinite wisdom, has ordained that terrestrial creatures shall rise above the animal condition and its impure secretions, in accordance with and in proportion to their merits, until they attain the ideal state of the saints and the blessed in Paradise, whose residues, Saint Bernard tells us, are transformed into a sweet, refined liquid, like unto myrrh and frankincense and the essence of musk: God, through His Divine Mediatrix, elevates His creatures step by step to the fragrant superior state, and in recompense for the services done Him by our holy and devout family, He has permitted it to rise one step higher on the steep stairway that leads from stench to perfume, from quadruped to angel, and has proved it in the eyes of the world by means of a simple and edifying miracle: the act of expelling, with neither sound nor fury, in a noble and exquisitely refined manner, a highly varied assortment of aromas, essences, and balsams which, artistically presented in little vials and bottles designed by our most talented artists, may be acquired at a price that none of our competitors can come close to meeting, in the principle pharmacies and toilet-goods shops throughout the country: their inimitable and exemplary quality has immediately earned them the public's favor and has put an end to the traditional predominance of certain chic but synthetic French products, their place having been taken in our flourishing market by a half-dozen authentic brands whose prestige is well earned: "Royal Breath," "Dynastic Bewitchment," "Prince's Smile," "Nights in the Palace Gardens," "The Sovereign's Kiss," "Fleur Monarchique": no lady of high estate or gentleman à la page would dream of not purchasing and using them, proud to give off in the presence of others a fragrant aura that is at once a mark of personal distinction and the majestic synthesis of the splendor and grandeur of our monarchy

natura non fecit saltum

such a lofty and eminent example has little by little spread
to the most modest classes, giving rise among their members to a noble emulation with respect to the place that they
occupy in the echelon of odors: such a classification in steps
or layers presents the characteristics of a singular theogony
whose base is the shamefully squatting, vulgar plebs and
whose apex is the winged, sublime royal majesty: between
these two extremes, a most rigorous scale of dignity fortunately takes the place, in our country, of the social strat-
ification, of economic origin and hence regrettably precarious, which prevails in other lands: in place of the
principle of "you are what you possess," which is the rule in
basely materialist nations, we have established the principle of "tell me what you smell like and I'll tell you who
you are," which is the official criterion of our immutable
caste system: each individual in his proper place, according
to the aroma or the stench that he gives off, in obedience
to the wise and provident decree of The One who directs,
from the wings, the staging of that solemn *auto sacramental* in which the Great Theatrical Spectacle of the World
culminates: thus sparing us the tumult, the agitation, the
passions of the tempestuous sea of history, with its continuous uprisings and armed struggles, its upheavals and
revolutions, while granting us the awareness of the fact that
life is a dream and that everything is uncertain, mutable, and
ephemeral in the face of the naked reality of death: some
taking their ease on the seat of a neat, secluded toilet, others
hunching down in a humble cabinet à la turque, and the most
wretched obliged to visit that evil-smelling and corrupt
common sewer ditch into which they dump their dung, their
ordure, their stinking turds, delighting in the filth of defecation and shamelessly and unblushingly giving themselves
over to the execrable vice of sodomy: a criminal and barbarous act, which, although typical of infamous, degenerate,
or dark races, has always also had its proselytes among our

people, possibly in conformity with a divine plan to ensure the continuity of autos-da-fé, whereby its utility, which at first glance is an unfathomable mystery, becomes understandable: as a matter of fact, those individuals who occupy the upper rungs of the ladder have succeeded, through an arduous and rigorous process of purgation, in reducing the volume and form of their behinds, converting them into an organ that is superfluous and merely ornamental, thereby differentiating them from those posteriors whose insolent, brazen curves proclaim their vile relationship with obscene matter: thus invested with their brand-new dignity, these individuals may devote themselves to those tranquil, fruitful labors of study and meditation for which all foreign university professors and scientists admire and envy us: in place of the usual disciplines of mathematics, physics, anatomy, natural history, et cetera, whose eternal repetition eventually becomes monotonous even to the dullest and most parochial minds, our great intellects prefer to plunge into the bottomless wells of casuistry or explore the fascinating world of ethereal syllogisms: there are classroom discussions, for instance, on the constitution of the heavens: are they made of the same metal as church bells, or are they as liquid as the lightest wines?: in our daily papers two eminent theologians are carrying on a running debate as to whether angels can or cannot transport human beings through the air from Lisbon to Madrid: and recently a pioneer of the extraspatial aviation of the future, after having subjected himself to a strict diet suitable for birds and having pondered the problem of the number of ounces of feathers necessary to support two pounds of flesh and arrived at the precise figure of four, pasted onto different parts of his body the quantity of the former corresponding to his weight, fabricated two wings that he could tie to his arms and flap, and thus plumed, leaped into the breeze from the tower of the cathedral of Plasencia, flying directly cloudward according to his disciples, or falling and ipso facto getting his balls busted according to his rivals, but in any event breaking a path for the progress of modern structural and generative angelology, a discipline in which, as in the study of the Paraclete and its faculties, we have taken a lead over the wise and learned men of other nations that we believe to be definitive, thus consolidating for our country the unique place that it today occupies in the world history of science

video meliora proboque, deteriora sequor

and thus the Creator, situating man, who is His handiwork, in the middle of the universe, that is to say between heaven and earth as regards his physical location, between eternity and time as regards his duration, between Himself and the devil as regards his liberty, and between the angels and the beasts as regards his nature, He has made of him the nucleus of Creation, so to speak, the necessary point of convergence of an extremely dense network of internal relations through which he is united to all things and all things are conjoined with him in a complex and subtle architecture in which each stone, each brick, each apparently insignificant or minuscule element nonetheless fulfills a capital role, to such a degree that its disappearance would mean the total collapse of the magnificent edifice, the perfect product, as we have said, of the unknowable will of the Lord: and one of these factors, at first glance so petty as to be beneath our notice, is doubtless our powerful inclination to return to the earth, in a sad and distressing posture, the sustenance and nourishment that we have received from it in the form of savory morsels of food, in obedience to a careful divine plan intended to emphasize our dual or intermediate condition, halfway between sublime celestial creatures and vicious brutes, an extremely strong, and to judge from superficial appearances, irresistible inclination, yet one which we must master and overcome if, taking as our example numerous noble and wise men, exalted monarchs, and distinguished caudillos, persons to whom Our Merciful Lord has granted great prerogatives, decreeing that they are to be honored by our veneration and making of them the finest flour among men, whereas the rest of us are merely what remains in the sifter, we are to continue to fight with immovable and heroic stubbornness, refusing to yield to the mortal depression that frequently follows a fall, rising once again with stout hearts and an unshakable trust in God: Father Vosk, some of you will say: the resistance that you preach is utterly, completely, and totally impossible: we have tried not one, but hundreds, thousands of times and have always relapsed into evil: it has availed us nothing to lead a healthy and abstemious life, avoiding occasions that bode ill and the many roads that lead to the latrine: in vain have we driven scatological thoughts from our minds and closed our eyes and ears to the dalliance of those who take pleasure in gross, crude animality: temptation assails us day and night, our very vitals seem to dilate, our senses urge us on, our intelligence begins to cloud over and a shameful weakness overtakes our bodies, unleashing a series of reflexive movements that lead us almost blindly to the public sewer ditch and force us to cower like savages and capitulate in the end with a relief and satisfaction that floods over us, inundates us, completely depriving us of reason and judgment for the space of several minutes, following which we come to our senses again, sad and disconsolate with contrite souls and broken hearts, beating our breasts and begging for pardon: this is the unhappy reality, Father Vosk: we want to fly, as free as angels: we strain mightily, but the devil pulls us down by our abominable eye, forces us to squat over, and after widening with his perverted arts the black culvert that we infamously, ignominiously offer him, he triumphantly witnesses our miserable spasm, taking delight in this frailty of our human will which subjects us to his fateful tyranny and leads us away from the love of God: I know all this, and to him who comes unto me in tears after yet another sudden relapse, I shall simply say: my son, never lose hope: quantumvis multa atque enormia fuerint peccata tua, nunquam de venia desperabis: corruisti?: surge, converte te ad Medicum animae tuae: et viscera pietatis ejus tibi patebunt: iterum corruisti?: iterum surge, geme, clama, et miseratio Redemptoris tui te suscipiet: corruisti tertio, et quarto, et saepius?: surge rursum, plange, suspira, humiliate: Deus tuus non te deseret: and one day, unexpectedly, the miracle will take place: you will cease to shit!: suddenly your anxieties, your writhings

and wrigglings, your anguished contortions will disappear: a
physiological and psychological quietude, a corporeal and
spiritual serenity will slowly saturate your soul, raising you
up from the sad and wretched masses to that wondrous
abode where only the elect dwell: your residues will then be
eliminated cutaneously and they will be possessed of an
exquisite perfume: and surrounded by monarchs, warriors,
and saints, you will live eternally, in a realm of fragrance,
harmony, and peace

etiamsi omnes, ego non

there is no denying that a really moving example of heroic perseverance in the path of righteousness, both on account of the peculiar circumstances of the case and on account of the extremely tender age of the noble protagonist, is that of the blessed child Alvarito, whose process of beatification in the Roman Curia has now won the advocacy of eminent theologians and the ardent support of thousands and thousands of devout, religious, and pious souls: born in the bosom of an illustrious patrician family, which through the most honest of means amassed a modest fortune in the Pearl of the Antilles and is there celebrated for its apostolic zeal and its philanthropic spirit, the future saint received the careful Christian education that was the usual privilege of heirs apparent of his social station, manifesting from his earliest years a profound and charming devotion to the Mysteries of our revealed religion, in particular that of the Immaculate Conception of the Virgin: instead of giving himself over to happy, innocent childhood games like his schoolmates, he preferred to retreat to the family's private chapel, far from the noise of the city's feverish commerce and the world's frantic hustle and bustle, spending hour after hour on his knees at the foot of the altar, absorbed in grave and recondite meditations: his acute awareness of the corrupt nature of the human body, with its strong inclination toward animal-like alleviation and its impure secretions, caused him many a sleepless night: he mentally compared the sad reality of visceral expulsion with the beautiful ideal of those saints and blessed of Paradise, whose residues, Saint Bernard tells us, are transformed into a sweet, refined liquid, like unto myrrh and frankincense and the essence of musk: the daily act of defecation in his splendid enameled porcelain chamber pot, the handiwork of a noted craftsman, filled him with anguish and sore affliction: the merry eye painted at the bottom, with the inscription I AM WATCHING YOU, made him feel that the slow dilatation from his very vitals down into that odious and black culvert that the devil covets would be an irremediable disaster: irresistibly, his imagination evoked that other Eye which in his governess's manuals of piety symbolizes the omnipresence of God, and the idea of its sacrilegious profanation was so overwhelming that his abdomen instinctively contracted, thus causing him to be unable to pass fecal matter: this state of affairs grows worse with each passing day, to the point that finally his parents, fearing for his health, endeavor to remedy it by any and every possible means: called in for consultation, the most famous physicians prescribe vigorous purges: the number and violence of his temptations increase, but our future saint joyously accepts the trials and obstacles that make his undertaking a difficult one and temper his force of will: sitting on the chamber pot, with his nether linen undergarment slightly raised and his velvet breeches pulled down to his knees, he remains motionless, resisting for hours on end the base and insidious promptings of his body, silently beseeching the aid of God and His Celestial Mother: nursemaids and chambermaids hover about him with enemas and topical remedies, hoping to glimpse on his angelic and impassive face the triumphant signs, to hear from his lips the boastful cackling usually induced by the proverbial glycerine suppository: they will vainly oblige him to stand up, in order that they may scrutinize the expected happy results: but again and again they will spy in the bottom of the receptacle only the pure and undefiled watchful eye: nothing, still nothing!: Alvarito sits down yet again, with the utmost dignity and decorum, with that sober, mature expression that surprises even those who know him merely by sight, refusing to allow his inner anguish and the fierce battle of his contradictory impulses to surface even for the space of a second: he will proudly disdain the advice of the cunning serpent, in a splendid tableau which his biographers paint with a wealth of detail, and which we shall permit ourselves in turn to reproduce in extenso, in view of its intense drama and its paradigmatical nature: on the right, God, the Most Blessed Virgin, and their retinue of servants and archangels: on the left, a throng of evil serpents, grouped around the fearful, monstrous gorilla from Africa: in the middle, sitting on his enameled porcelain chamber pot, a child with an exquisite face and fair hair witnesses the verbal joust of the irreconcilable opponents, beneath the weightless, subtle protection of a magnificent halo, as broad as the ring of Saturn, miraculously suspended over his comely head

THE SERPENT: why do you stubbornly resist your instincts?: don't you see that you are torturing yourself in vain?: if you listen to me, you will experience immediate relief and be enormously happy

THE GUARDIAN ANGEL: the pleasure that he promises you lasts only a few seconds!: think of your eternal soul!: of the pain that you will cause the Virgin!

THE SERPENT: let your muscles go slack! relax your intestines!: let yourself go!: you will see how easy it is!

THE GUARDIAN ANGEL: no, no Alvarito, don't listen to him!

THE SERPENT: don't suffer any more!: stop constricting your rectum!

THE GUARDIAN ANGEL: no, no, he's trying to fool you!

THE SERPENT: do as I tell you!: yield to your impulses!: satisfy your body!: you'll die of pleasure, you'll see!

CHOIR OF ANGELS: no, Alvarito, no!

and our future saint, with that powerful self-control granted him by his serene and unclouded faith, contracts his colon and keeps his hole tightly closed, fervently invoking the aid promised him by the Lord: the Massah on High meanwhile swings back and forth in the hammock, dressed in a suit and a panama hat exactly like those of the great-grandfather, and the Virgin, nervous, petrified, feverishly watches for the result through her opera glasses

Marita, my girl, do you hear me?

yes, Papa

what is that precious child, that lovable offspring of the masters of the plantation at Cruces, doing now?

he's still sitting on the chamber pot

is he resisting?

he'd rather die than excrete!

very good!: may he persevere! and what about the doctors?

they've just given him another suppository

poor little fellow! do you think he'll be able to hold out?

he has an iron will

will alone does not suffice: tell him to pray to Me!

he's already praying

do you know if he's recited the petitions to the Most Holy Trinity?

yes, I believe he has

well, tell him to recite them again: that is what my most competent theologians advise

very well, Papa

the hymn to the Trinity will help him to resist: and if the temptation is very great, find a scapular and put it around his neck!

I've got a very nice one here

well, go and see him and tell him that my thoughts are constantly with him and that I bless him

the Virgin readies herself to descend with two pieces of fine-woven cloth jointed together with ribbons when a simple, moving miracle crowns Alvarito's superhuman efforts: the act of eliminating, with neither sound nor fury, in a fragrant and noble manner!: there is intense emotion and tears of joy well up in the eyes of numerous spectators: whereupon King Kong and the serpents recoil and flee and the celestial choirs and hierarchies raise their voices in prayers and antiphonies amid soft arpeggios and the rustle of wings

what's happening?, the great-grandfather inquires what is the meaning of this agitation among my angels?

they're singing hymns in celebration of the victory!

what victory?

he's won, Papa, he's won!

who? the child?

yes, Papa, I swear!

oh, daughter, how happy you make me!

he has just emitted, cutaneously, an aromatic substance!

does it smell good?

better than French perfume!

collect it in a vial: it will be a true relic!

I'm going to put it in my own atomizer

does it please you that much?

it gives off a fragrance that makes me giddy!

would you mind bringing the chamber pot a little closer?

yes, smell it for yourself

you're absolutely right

ah, quelle volupté divine!

what's that you say, daughter?

it's sublime, Papa: exactly like a poem by Lamartine: it's enough to make one believe in God!

ad augusta per angusta

the insistent, nasal voice annoys you and you will cease to transcribe it, suddenly but nonetheless deliberately, like someone who, protecting himself against a radiophonic act of aggression, violently silences the blast by furiously pressing the button: again returning to the mountain of testimony that has accumulated in your minuscule library and on the shelves of your improvised filing cabinet: in the room with the dormer window in which you stubbornly devote yourself to the expert onanism of writing: the inveterate, unproductive act of clutching the pen and letting its filiform generative secretion flow in accordance with the impulses of your will: from the masterwork of that astute archpriest of Talavera who, apparently subjected to the servitude of moral discourse, found a way to plow down at an angle and bring to the surface the latent genius of a language that thereafter lay fallow after having exhausted itself in an extraordinarily fruitful century, down through the writings of pachydermous provosts and daring iconoclasts, to the paperbound volume published in Havana which x-rays and reveals the exploitation of your sucrocratic family: stopping for long stretches at those authors whose acute awareness of your country's wretched state led them to sadly ponder its decrepitude and the possible remedies for it: scrupulous diagnoses, with corresponding medicines, prescriptions, proposed cures: recommendations that it open outward or turn in upon itself: modernism or self-absorption: panaceas suggested not once but dozens of times, in different keys and registers, without (like you) taking into account the fact that neither our prolific and illustrious Benedictine, nor our worthy prisoner of Bellver, nor our melancholy self-banished Spaniard, nor our lucid visionary who committed suicide, nor the much-celebrated generation of the owl of Salamanca, nor those generations which followed (and still continue to follow) in its footsteps, ever managed to discover the real roots of our ills: the image of the blond, angelic heir apparent majestically sitting on his chamber pot has perhaps set you on the right path and given you a hint of the correct answer: that of a country (his) that has been constipated for centuries, it too established on a self-sufficient throne whose satin cushion conceals from the eyes of the audience the secret of a double circular cavity beneath which, shielded by the sides of the canopied throne, there awaits in respectful but impatient expectation the sublime and sublimatory artifact, the today-discarded chamber pot which historically precedes the beloved son of puritan concealment, the dernier cri of the once-mighty English industrial revolution, as a horde of presumed healers and licensed disciples of Galen vainly attack the patient with suppositories, enemas, physics: a national reality that should rightly be represented not, as is usually the case, in the hieratic figure of the victor portrayed in *The Surrender of Breda* or in the solemn *Gentleman with His Hand on His Breast,* but in the form of an austere, grave, silent hidalgo, who has also stepped straight out of some canvas by Velázquez or El Greco, shown, however, in a squatting position and leaning slightly forward, so that the folds of his underpants of fine cloth hide the round edge of the receptacle theoretically destined to receive the offering, indifferent to pleas and entreaties, sirens' songs, and the pressure of the world's opinion, praised by his panegyrists for his exemplary patience and his Christian steadfastness, and to sum the matter up briefly, tight, niggardly, and stingy, deaf to the urgent exhortations of those physicians who with purges, cathartics, laxatives attempt unsuccessfully to loosen up the canal and facilitate the long delayed discharge, as meanwhile he responds, as august and imperturbable as the second Philip, to their feverish activity and anxious concern with a mere cavernous "calm yourselves": his long-standing rectal contraction, his hard, painful, miserly offerings are thus probably not the result of an innate metaphysical predisposition (as the orthodox mastodon had believed), or of a most effective, draconian regime (as his victims maintain), but, rather (you now conclude), of a persistent digestive anomaly, which through faulty diagnosis and a lack of proper treatment, has turned into an incurable chronic illness: this would at last explain the poor quality and quantity of his output (in particular if we compare it to that of his historical rivals): those indigestible, compact, heavy, dull works that have always been characteristic of his literary-scientific production and (why not?) the miraculous secretion of dense, fragrant pearls, whose aroma no nose (divine or human) could breathe in without an impression of intense delight, of helpless, wholehearted admiration: a country (his) in which a sense of malaise, pains, disorders, which have slowly become endemic, insidiously morbid, have now entered an extremely contagious phase, whose paroxysms, acuteness, and virulence are merely symptomatic, the premonitory signs of new and aggravating complications that preclude all hope of relief or lenitive surgery in infirmaries, clinics, or hospitals: an apparently fatal process, with no known cure or treatment, which leads renowned physicians to use the term irreversible, even though the solution is at hand (and with no need for learned specialists), in popular medical manuals and encyclopedias: all that is needed is to consult (as you are doing) the chapter devoted to the infrequency or paucity of evacuation and the causes (internal or external) thereof: improper nourishment, lack of liquid, insufficient intestinal musculature, a lack of peristaltic reflexes: and immediately proceed to the application of the various measures that are so patently necessary: gymnastics, abdominal massage, outdoor exercise before and after meals, alternate hot and cold showers in the lumbar region: not to mention the usual diet of vegetables (raw or cooked), fruits (cherries and grapes in particular), one hundred and fifty grams of honey, a glass of cold water or milk taken on an empty stomach: ah, and above all, abandoning forthwith the use of a chamber pot or a flush toilet in favor of the much-disdained ancestral method of evacuation!: an improper position during the process constitutes a serious obstacle to the proper freeing of the intestine: instead of settling down comfortably on a horizontal seat some eighteen inches off the floor (or somewhat less than that in the case of the chamber pot), the constipated subject (or country) must squat down with his feet preferably resting on a raised step twelve inches high: such a posture (we guarantee it!) aids the functioning of the abdominal muscles that are responsible for serpentine circulation and constitutes a weighty argument when forthcoming from the lips of those who recommend the optimum relaxation of the canal and the return to the old, intimate pleasures of emission in common sewer ditches

V

I

You will leap into the verbal future: a prescription, an obligation, a certainty?: a subjective mood in any case: without the assurance of the aorist tense, characteristic of historical statement, and its gleaming varnish of truth: adding yourself with a mere stroke of the pen to that small though smiling pleiad of airy utopian dreamers who since the Century of Enlightenment have attempted to rescue the grim land of your forefathers from its proud natural unreason?: to the eminent encyclopedists, promoters of agricultural and industrial development, members of prestigious corporations, virtuous citizens useful to the country who, following the number-one mastodon of your orthodoxy, candidly believed, with dovelike innocence, that merely by handing over deeds to farm land and setting up economic enterprises there would spring up artificial meadows, cotton manufactories, and trading companies, thus turning the deserts and uncultivated fields into edens where prosperity and abundance would reign?: idyllic dreams, bucolic illusions which, extended to all areas of social existence, gave rise to fantastic plans for education and communal life, modeled on Greco-Roman antiquity and completely alien to the hostile, teeming masses of a nation that was not only far more ignorant and brutish than most but also a past master at scornfully spurning the offerings of the native species of philanthropists: rustic aristocrats, pastoral monarchs, clever experimenters in the field of abstruse pneumatic machinery who were immortalized in etchings and canvases, posed against the background of a pleasing, prosperous, industrious Swiss landscape!: a utopia promptly ruined and as promptly reconstructed in the course of the bourgeois industrial revolution, as meanwhile in the stony and gloomy land there were repeated scenes of violence, captured or dreamed in a delirium by the great deaf painter, amid a sinister splendor of smoke and gunpowder, the prelude to other, now inextinguishable fires: a series of dark events which, by betraying all the bright hopes for the future, perhaps occasioned the outbreak of boils that so afflicted the most lucid spirit of the age: the author, as is well known, of rigorous scientific analyses which, although idle fantasy played no part whatsoever in them, were nonetheless to engender, by sheer paradox, those grandiose social constructs which history offers us as a model, in which the captains of two opposing camps, with juvenile, stubborn passion, hoist as the battle flags that flutter over their baggage trains the discoveries of Thomas More: humani nihil a me alienum puto: a rational creature, a perfectible being, a most lovable new man, a brain free of base necessities and instincts, simple, sociable, good, who continually advances along the rectilinear paths of order, progress, felicity!: as society and the individual cease to be antagonistic terms and pernicious individualism resolves into one unanimous, majestic social arpeggio: with chaste, wholesome Valkyries working side by side with tractors: the ear of grain that transforms itself into a song, a song that becomes an ear of grain: vast seas of blond wheat rippling in the wind, as though waving in time to a joyful military march!: happy couples of brilliant hydroelectric engineers, or a wife who is the manager of an ultramodern oil refinery and a husband who soars through the vastness of interstellar space, portrayed in the company of countless, eternally smiling progeny, staggered like the steps of a ladder: child after child with eyes opened wide, seemingly dazzled by a shining future, par l'avenir lumineux of a life plan sans bavures, the guarantee in its turn of an existence unmarred by cares and anxieties, where the vices and defects of the previous decadent society will never take root: no one will exploit anyone: love will be equivalent to a freely accepted contract: man will be a peaceful, harmonious, honest creature: the previous separation of the face and the ass abolished, a completed sublimatory process!: individuals without destructive drives, not subject to the tyranny of physiological laws, without spasms of violent erection!: a paradise that forbids duality and rejects dichotomy, snatches the bestial slave out of the dark pit of his activities that require a squatting position, and projects him to sublime heights of saccharine, pure, perfect whiteness: bodies that neither enjoy or are enjoyed, being deprived of the pitch-black hole and its infamous use: in the sweetly sentimental colored postcard of the present-day utopias without asses: a boundless sea of faces that laugh, sing, listen, recite the works of the leader, but neither fuck nor shit, neither couple nor excrete: blind in their inferior and most useful eye: shorn of the radically generic common denominator which makes men equal and denies their false hierarchy: a deceptive, fake eden, whose functioning necessarily presupposes those hidden and shameful holes, like those in Swiss cheese, through which, as in the kitchens and cellars of the middle class, the repressed breaks through and the banished ass takes its vengeance: asylums, cells, tortures, the vehicle of crude impulses which openly, generously find expression in the mephitic expansion of the common sewer ditch and its feverish, labored panting: defecation, sodomy, filth, attributes of the tortuous drain that permits and encourages the sage reconciliation!: not a homo sapiens separated from his dung, ordure, and stinking turds: the face and the ass equals, free and bare, the utopia of a complex world, without asepsis or concealment: a world in which the impudent, brazen curve that proclaims its vile relationship with obscene matter leaps from the old plantation yard to the supreme direction of the sugar factory: a paradise, yours, with an ass and a phallus, where a metaphor language subjects the object to the verb, and at last words, freed from their dungeons and chains, treacherous, elusive words, vibrate, dance, copulate, strip naked, and assume carnal form

||

without a guide or a tovaritch interpreter, you will enter the Plaza de la Revolución (a physical, physiological, anatomical, functional, circulatory, respiratory, et cetera, revolution, according to the visionary genius interned in the asylum of Rodez), and making your way through the thick, variegated human carpet that covers the vast square (an image captured dozens of times by the harmless camera of the paparazzo), you will approach (as though you were his double) the dais symbolizing the happy lot of those who have now gained their freedom

take a good look at them: you will find that you recognize their faces: announcements over the radio, in newspapers, on television have brought them together in front of the improvised podium, and the urgent blare of loudspeakers summons those stragglers who have been dallying in the recreation and copulation centers of the suburbs to a privileged, direct witnessing of the portentous event: the tropical sun beats down on their heads and they shield themselves from it as best they can, with colored handkerchiefs and crude woven palm hats: mingling with them, the females fan themselves with feminine gestures, eternal coquettes despite the dust, the filth, and their now threadbare play clothes: comrades whose function it is to preserve order direct people to the last remaining empty spaces, and volunteer comrades of both sexes carefully inspect the podium decorated with tapestries and rugs where in all probability, when the hour has struck, the executive committee will appear

you will interrupt your train of thought for a few seconds in
order to sketch in the décor: sofas, rocking chairs, hammocks, a grand piano for the girl with musical talents, pots
of ferns, baskets of fruit, bouquets of flowers?: the portrait
in an oval frame of some imperious great-grandfather, a
little mulatto obsequiously chasing the flies away with a
palm-leaf fan?: period-piece descriptions of novelists of the
era of Cecilia Valdés, which you will be spared the obligation of dwelling upon at length by the cheerful strains of a
catchy, comical march: as the careful mounting of the scene
by the stage director focuses the attention of the worthy
spectators on the row of empty thrones, which, mounted on
damascened pedestals and protected from the sun by graceful canopies, also obviously await the sovereign presence,
which, like the monstrance amid the gold of the tabernacle,
will immediately confer upon them their very reason for
being and crown them with the august power of its radiant,
magic splendor: liturgical symbols which by their mere
existence overpower and fulminate, enslave and awe: fitted
out perhaps with satin pillows whose exquisite embroidery
hides from the suffering masses the secret of multiple circular cavities beneath which, shielded by the sides of the
canopied thrones, there await in respectful but impatient
expectation the sublime artifacts, the beloved sons of puritan
concealment, the swan song of the dying English industrial
revolution?: certainly not!: purposely placed in such a way
that their virtual occupants may gaze, through the little
round peepholes in the backs, lined up as symmetrically as
a row of deck chairs on an ocean liner, upon the exultant
mass of citizens in the apogee and glory of their inalienable,
triumphant liberty: a fraternal order without degrees or
hierarchies, forever united thanks to the conscious possession by its members of that inferior and common face whose
single, watchful eye disdainfully contemplates the laughable, grotesque efforts of anyone who foolishly insists on
distinguishing himself, rising higher, taking command: an-

thems, ballads, songs pour forth con brio from the loud-speakers in order to calm the impatient crowd or perhaps pave the way for the plump, bi-convex apparition: the simultaneous appearance of a dozen or more faces of the modest executive committee, protected by the anonymity of their perfect and exemplary dignity: neither pilots, captains, nor guides: at intervals of precisely three feet, thus conforming to the norms of careful staging: in all likelihood in a squatting position, in order to offer the happy assembly a glimpse, through the handy peephole in the backs of the seats, of those round, jovial bodily parts which certain naturalist photographers of the beginning of the century were wont to capture on film for the enjoyment and the delectation of connoisseurs, in the act of rivaling, in a festive group, the rubicund, chubby cheeks of Aeolus: skill-fully playing their varied panoply of wind instruments: flutes and fifes, flageolets, oboes, clarinets, saxophones: obediently following the conductor's baton of the anonymous taker of the snapshot who, like you, ecstatically observes the asses, buttocks, behinds, posteriors prodigiously invested with supreme, executive power: attempting in vain to also associate these derrières and hind ends with the letters of the Latin alphabet which in sibylline fashion identify the unnamed members of the directorate: the secretarygeneralesque face of A in the climax of poetic effort, the mirthful countenance of B, softly whistling a tune, the chubby moonface of C, contracted in a graceful pout: absolutely interchangeable faces, which, as in those backdrops in stands in an amusement park, wherein the painter leaves an empty space corresponding to the face of the figures represented on the canvas so that customers may have themselves photographed in the costume of a clown, sailor, or boxer, seem to proclaim the incontrovertible truth of their merely temporary function, precarious and impersonal in its very essence, open without exception to all individuals of society: an office that is neither titular nor permanent, neither rotating nor perpetual, but ephemeral and transitory, purely because of the its holder's common and simplest eye: a picture on a postcard which, despite all its lyrical effusion, only half reflects the political import of the scene that you are meticulously attempting to depict: the delightful, delectable succession of rotund, plump-cheeked faces that contemplate you and the excited masses, as though seeking to photograph all of you while at the same time making fun of you in the same way in which you are all making fun of them, with the sudden spasm of someone who bursts into a roar of laughter and thus dissipates his prolonged tension in a brief and violent discharge: the friendly mockery is mutual, and once the pedagogic demonstration is over and the offering deposited, the joyful donors will proceed to reach to one side and eliminate the traces of their impulsive euphoria with the simple gesture of someone passing his hand across his face in order to wipe away the traces of a smile: then submerging the hand in the corresponding washbowl beneath the approving gaze of the audience, which during the requisite pause for the washing of hands will have occupied the dais with ingenuous spontaneity: great-grandfather Agustín and his spouse, the young master, the girls, a group of poor but respectable relatives, the house slaves, a fluttering swarm of nursemaids?: no, the sovereign people now, the masters and creators of their own destiny, whose playful African instinct has replaced the chains of centuries of slavery with the delights of idle leisure: face after face, uniform, identical, analogous to those which at the end of the confrontation withdraw in a disciplined manner from the circular openings in the thrones and again assume, without fanfare, the duties and charges of their office: obscure, unknown, anonymous: voluntarily submitting to humble public exhibition in a squatting position, to the bain de foule which unites them to the multitude streaming off like trickles of ink: happy blacks abandoning the vast expanses of the square, heading for the recreation

centers as the captive rational lunatic preaches in your ear
the program of genuine subversive Revolution

one of the most notable features of our system (if such is the
proper word for the series of rank exceptions deliberately
and purposely deviating from all principles or norms) is
our unique method of combatting bossism and the sordid,
scandalous consequences of the foolish cult of personality:
instead of skirting the problem, by banning for example the
posters, statues, photographs that in other countries reproduce the inspiringlyresolute, rodinesquepensive figure of the
chief and his crew of bold helmsmen, we have elected to
multiply the active signs of their presence while at the same
time limiting these latter to those strictly sequestered parts
of the body which, despite their noble physiological function, a deeprooted, ancestral prejudice has taught us to
scorn: the elitism, the authority, the hierarchy inherent in
the superior biocular face has been replaced by the ordinary,
plebeian, humble genius of its symmetrical inferior counter-
part: that other bisected, lunar face whose polyphemic,
penetrating eye is favorably disposed toward digestive and
reproductive pleasures, simply winking at them indulgently
and frequently combining them in an act of profligate,
gratuitous pleasure: with no petty concerns as to spending,
waste, or profit: deliberately enthroning its image in government offices, bars, dormitories, sports centers, on public
monuments and thoroughfares: giant photographs in full
color, intended to remind today's fortunate citizens of the
popular, democratic nature of our spontaneous collective
leadership: the minimum common multiple that cancels
out the superior difference in features and rallies the masses
of the liberated around its firm, unitarian emblem: prefer-

ably caught by the camera's eye in the grandiose act of offering its first vernal poetic fruits, cheeks tense with effort, a grave, illustrious countenance possessed of a modest and noble dignity: or else whistling with contagious hilarity a soft, piping melody, the prolepsis of the jovial, irrepressible explosion: a felicitous likeness also duplicated on the stamps issued by our otiose republic and fondly treasured by philatelists who are lovers of rarity and singularity: not to mention lithographs and playing cards, medals, banknotes, gadgets, record jackets: a ubiquitous profusion of anonymous, bare, acephalous physiognomies, whose uncertain identity is the basis of a unique lottery system and of the placing of wagers whereby our idle citizens thrive and prosper without working: merely by establishing a relationship between the beatific exposed face and the letter of the alphabet that stands for a given member of the executive committee: the winner receives a pile of money, and if he has the requisite physical qualifications, he will be promoted in turn to the ephemeral dignity of leader and to the glories and servitudes of public gluteal exhibition

IV

another feature: neither a flag nor a national anthem: a radical, incisive opposition to everything which institutionalizes, mummifies, disguises: acting in accordance with the idea that man is a mutable being, who will fit into a formal schema only if we have first extirpated his natural inclinations to change and to distinguish himself: hence we offer this counsel to our diplomats and delegations invited to international congresses or sporting events: refuse any sort of misleading identification with emblems, flags, and musical themes: abandon your risible role as spokesmen: define yourselves negatively: but if the participants in congresses or the audiences in sports stadiums insist and demand that you display a standard on the flagpole assigned our nameless republic, do not hesitate: satisfy them: choose any old piece of cloth (a pair of men's undershorts that are dirty in the back and stained with semen, the nylon panties of a girl who has not yet reached puberty, a matron's scabrous sanitary napkin, even though it may be as bright red as a soldier's bandages), and solemnly hoist it on the staff to the stentorian strains of a catchy, ironic tune: a brief list of suggestions: "La Madelon," the march from *The Bridge over the River Kwai,* the Beatles' "Come Together," Lupe's rendition of "Fever," reminiscent of a hurricane: oh, we almost forgot: "El Congo" or "Mi Coquito" as sung by the luscious rumba dancer whose voracious, pagan mouth smiles from the shiny jacket of the hi-fi record, wouldn't be bad either

V

accept your own material condition: overcome your complex-ridden, hysterical relation with your inferior facial double and its tender, beloved creature: put an end to the process of wretched puritan capital and its absurd, nefarious consequences: retention, accumulation, constipation, and at the same time asepsis, abstraction, lack of contact: the innocuous mediation of paper in the gleaming toilet bowl that stems from the remote ideal of those saints and blessed whose residues, as Saint Bernard once told us, are transformed into a sweet, refined liquid, like unto myrrh and frankincense and the essence of musk: on the steep stairway that leads from stench to perfume, from quadruped to mediating angel via the act of elimination with neither sound nor fury: without dung, ordure, stinking turds: a collective schizophrenia that in our day has reached its paroxysm thanks to the well-orchestrated promotion of detergents, bleaches, deodorants destined to efface every guilty trace of its most obvious and most basic function: implacable, merciless self-denial, whose morbid imprint reveals the aggressive, compensatory nature of omnivorous modern societies and their efficient repressive apparatus: compulsions, contractions, censorships that cause the human organism to atrophy and brutally divide it in two: above: what is visible, rational, tolerated: below: what is abominable, unspeakable, hidden: therefore, in order to escape the same fate, proceed immediately, courageously, to a healthy reconciliation with the hidden face of the body and its intimate, extremely personal fruit: put an end, once and for all, to the unwholesome interposition of toilet paper, re-establish manual contact: the ancestral use of a can of water, the return to the humble but worthy pleasures of emission in the common sewer ditch: the democratization that you yearn for will thus be absolute, and should you be one of those persons nostalgic for the good old days of wanton consumption, we have foreseen your needs and produced, especially for you, different models of portable wash basins, in white or in color, which we regularly advertise in the pages of *Elle* and *Le Jardin des Modes*

VI

our inexorable enemy: the Couple, settled in its warm, homey nest, happy and satisfied with itself, and what is worse, ready to increase in geometrical progression and multiply on the face of the earth, in accordance with the foolish decree of the Creator: the source and origin of new little hermetic honeycomb cells: of an infinity of soft, fluffy silken cocoons: of a sea of symbols indicative of the good life and voracious possessive appetites: lipsticks, Kleenex, deodorants: Coca-Cola, ice-cold beer, whisky on the rocks: electric refrigerators, tape recorders, cars: travel, psychiatric treatment, credit cards: diets, health clubs, rest cures!

our remedy?: very simple: an ars combinatoria of disparate elements (individuals of all sexes, races, ages) in accordance with the very special principles that govern artistic construction (including the imponderables of improvisation and chance): trios, quartets, septets, decades, whose structure is capricious and variable: thereby avoiding the mechanical quality displayed by the rapt figures shown in the illustrations of collectors' editions of the Kamasutra, with their dizzying rhythms, worthy of that of those immense factories in the United States based on time and motion studies, in which copulation is a sad parody of production: adopting, rather, the flexibility of Calder's airy mobiles, the conjoining of whose parts is ruled by a secret, multilateral flow, consisting of attractions and repulsions, centripetal and centrifugal forces: architectures in fleeting, precarious equilibrium, like that of the acrobat, the professional dancer, the tightrope walker, calling forth the playful virtuosity of the consummate artificer: a magnetic field in which the divinatory search of the poet-soothsayer takes place, with its subtle rhythmical alternations and its unexpected associations: the one series that is excluded: the logicoprocreative: the kingdom of semantic anomaly, of sterile and unproductive enjoyment: sheer pleasure, prohibited, accursed, condemned, contrary to law

VII

our inexorable enemy also: the proles: the ubiquitous, devouring hydra with countless heads that boldly crops up, sending forth vernal new shoots even after fierce, ruthless pruning: the repository of the faults and vices of the old system, its prolific, contagious nature makes it a virtually mortal adversary and forces upon us the cruel necessity of resorting to a crude, radical therapy: the preventive slaughter of unbaptized innocents: of the future battle-hardened army of little incurable Vosks: a general elimination, methodically planned, with no silly deadbabytalk: buttando l'acqua sporca con il bambino dentro and resolutely flushing it down the drain: sparing only bastard progeny conceived in passion or those who are the chance by-product of censured, abominable love: thanks to the inspired resolution of the disciple of Changó when he lets loose the wild beast hidden in the delightful cavern of the devil and allows it to graze in the shady thicket which the entire Christian flock lawfully visits in order to ensure, on propitious days, the orderly propagation of the species: forcing it to slowly distend in its dull abode and there give up the ghost out of melancholy and boredom before returning to the wide-open hole in the pearly, poetic cheeks of the hidden face of the body: the plebeian, ancillary, democratic face: only these tangential, peripheral children merit our confidence and into their hands we commend the destiny of our heroic and invincible Revolution

VIII

work plans?: none: means of subsistence?: those of the ritual economy of the potlatch: sacking, robbing, pillaging industrious neighboring peoples, great orgiastic fiestas that last for months on end, and once the cycle has been completed, the spoils consumed, war once more, and the whole thing begins all over again
another unusual feature: the inclusion in our body of laws of a most enlightened provision destined to protect idlers, as dreamed of by the unjustly forgotten son-in-law of that

profound but human prophet whose somber, dire predictions with regard to Victorian capitalism were to cause those parasites who were living most comfortably on the product of their insectile workers to spend many a sleepless night, forcing them from that moment forward to retreat to defensive positions that to all appearances were generous and altruistic, but in reality were designed, as the facts have demonstrated, to subtly mask their spoliation and to prolong their privileges sine die: indirectly giving rise, in countries that were immense but unfortunately autocratic and backward, to egalitarian societies which, inspired by their imperfect model and thanks to the prodigious talents at organization of the efficient, modern Saul, put an end to the old form of exploitation, though not to work: collectivities obliged to produce and create wealth in order to resist the economic depredations of their adversaries, and compelled, because of the deep-rooted, natural tendency to proceed from the making of necessity a virtue to taking heart in the face of adversity to an almost Job-like acceptance of evil as a sort of smiling fatality, to propose as a paradigm of proper conduct the exemplary behavior of the castrated and submissive squirrel that proudly puts in hours and hours of gratuitous, extraordinary toil: an alienated brain, a perfect hymenopteron, which the stern patriarch with the bushy mustache nonetheless called the new hero, and on the podium of the supreme, finest-floured directorate, solemnly bedecked with medals: an edifying episode which we always call to mind when the parrots and parakeets of productive bifrontal society reproach us for our playful nature and our ringing praise of relaxation: we have purged ourselves of the accumulative process once and for all, refusing to yield to the arguments that perpetuate it in honor of a far-off paradise: we are active in the present, and the present is all that interests us: asserting our rights to idleness as the santiago-cuban, dusky-faced son-in-law of the prophet urged: encour-

aging games, recreation, and dissipation: roundly condemning work, indeed condemning it without appeal

IX

it is important to determine, statistics at hand, who it is who
stealthily, cynically benefits from the modest surplusvalue
of the ant: is it the traditional grasshopper absorbed in his
vague, sonorous, repetitive task?: or is it the venal, individ-
ualist locust that tirelessly lays up treasure for the simple
pleasure of so doing?: the majority accuse the bumblebee
of proxenetism, since he is the suspect protector of a remote,
nebulous queen: the responsibility of the cricket is an open
question, though there are those who speak of possessing
conclusive proofs in this regard: official resolutions and reports demand of the dragonfly a precise and clear program
of action: his flightiness is suspect and is not his showy
manner of dress an anachronism in these times of struggle
and sacrifice?: the glowworm also has his detractors: his
nocturnal, elitist, cliquish activities apparently alienate the
sympathies of many: and finally, there are those who blame
the ant himself and his love of work: if he simply folded
his arms and didn't fuck around working, they say, nobody
would live off his surplusvalue

X

repression?: none: we hold the collectivity directly responsible for the delinquent acts of the individual, and instead of
punishing the latter according to the old scheme of things,
we consider it more logical to reform society: how?: by hit-
ting it in precisely the places where it already hurts the most,
so as to oblige it to take corrective steps and avoid in the
future those injustices that traditionally give rise to criminal

activities: destroying, for instance, its most celebrated monuments or the symbols of its glorious past: razing the cathedrals of Cologne or Canterbury, Chartres, the Duomo in Milan: ripping up the most famous canvases of the British Museum or the Louvre, the Prado or the Galleria Borghese: blowing up Michelangelo's *Pietà* or the *Dama de Elche,* the Arc de Triomphe, the Statue of Liberty: not to mention exhuming the remains of some literary or scientific genius, some illustrious prince or father of his country, following a carefully planned mise-en-scène: calling the entire population together in front of the Pantheon, removing from it, to the sound of drums, the urn containing the sacrosanct ashes, taking it in silent procession to the nearest river, stopping on the Bridge of Sighs, calling for a moment of sobs and tears, and majestically casting it into the waters like the bodies of sailors who have died at sea: in the past year the bones of Manzoni, Kipling, and Victor Hugo (among many others) have departed from among us: this year we have mourned the disappearance of those of George Washington, Garibaldi, Bismarck: and who knows whether fate does not have even more painful losses in store for us!: Napoleon, Metternich, Catherine the Great?: Pasteur, Edison, Santos-Dumont?: but one meager consolation, for which we are most grateful, remains to reconcile us to such sadness: criminality is not on the rise as in the biform productive society, and according to the calculations of the Department of Statistics, after decreasing in geometrical regression year after year, in the coming decade it will have died out altogether

#

other announcements from the Department of Statistics: a spectacular increase (not only in quantitative but also in qualitative terms) in the type of copulation that is abominable and fruitless (at the expense of the productive love that was the rule in the old class societies): the right to idleness extended to all citizens: the free exhibition (thanks to little slits in the backs of skirts or the seats of trousers) of those glorious convexities whose solitary and ineffable eye enhances and glorifies the discreet inferior face: a few dark spots as well: an alarming reduction in the number of heads of cattle, the regrettable abandonment of traditional varieties of cereal grains and pasture grasses: but the violent appropriation of the surplusvalue of our neighbors (that is to say, of the fruits of their toil and strain and heroic efforts) more than compensates for such deficiencies and restores the balance in our favor: on the other hand (and we should like to make this abundantly clear), we apply no elitist criterion to the various flora and fauna: we give equal opportunities to all vegetable and animal species, including those which, with errant egocentrism, the men of the past deemed noxious and useless: bedbugs, lice, and other parasites now live peaceably off us as we live off the fungible goods of the soil: following the precepts of the venerable Ibn Turmeda, we have democratized the animal hierarchy and no longer take ourselves to be, as we once did, the lords and masters of anyone: those species once considered vile and abject flourish without impediment in our society, and with fraternal solicitude we ensure the reproduction of all varieties of reptiles, particularly of hatedandfeared serpents: the number of these latter is steadily increasing, and according to the most reliable predictions, voracious, enormous specimens will little by little infiltrate the family nests of bipeds and silently creep across the conjugal bed itself

#

Michelet reports in his celebrated History:

>   it was beneath this banner of moderation and compassionate justice that on the following day the new

religion was inaugurated: Gossec had composed the melodies of the hymns, Chénier the words: a Temple of Philosophy had been hastily knocked together in two days in the extremely narrow choir of Notre-Dame, and decorated with the effigies of sages, of fathers of the Revolution: a mountain supported the temple: on a crag there burned the torch of Truth: the magistrates sat beneath the columns: there was no honor guard, no soldiers: two rows of girls of tender years were the only ornament of the celebration: they were dressed in white, and crowned with wreaths of oak leaves, and not, as some have said, with wreaths of roses

Reason, in a white robe with a blue mantle, emerges from the Temple of Philosophy and takes her place on a simple seat of verdure: the little girls chant her hymn: she crosses to the foot of the mountain, casting a gentle glance, a sweet smile, in the direction of the audience: she withdraws into the temple once again, and the singing continues: the audience waited expectantly, but that was all there was to it

a chaste, dull, lackluster, boring ceremony!

we shall not fall into such a gross error: on the ruins of churches and ideologies we shall give ourselves over to the intoxicating pleasures of clandestine, nocturnal worship of the mighty gorilla of the film and his paradigmatico-explicit, categorical-imperial COCK

VI

In the dense silence of the kitchen-study the night moth flutters about the lamp: it soars, hovers, flits round and round, describes obsessive circles, retreats when you shoo it away, but then returns again and again to the brilliance that fascinates and attracts it, totally absorbed in its hallucination, paying no attention to the movements of your hand: in like manner, from the moment that you return from the bathroom, the oft-rehearsed, chimerical idea appears and assails you repeatedly, vanishes when you chase it away, stubborn, persistent, silent, certain that patience will bring it victory, knowing that you will soon tire: you resign yourself then and bid it welcome: solitude is propitious to its flight and the parallel is blindingly clear: why should you continue to resist tracing it?

initiating, tantalus-fashion, your own personal trial of the novelistic canon and the x-raying of its vain camp followers: as you feel your way along, searching for the secret, guadianesque equation, the mighty subterranean stream that feeds both sexuality and writing: your obdurate gesture of grabbing the pen and allowing its filiform liquor to flow, prolonging the climax indefinitely: leafing, for inspiration, through the pages of your copy of *The Seven Pillars* slumbering on the plank laid across the sink, on top of a pile of books and newspaper clippings: as independent and free as a Bedouin chief yourself: master of the air, the winds, the light, the vast emptiness: above, the subtle, colorless sky, and below, the trackless sand, like a glistening glacier: the shadows of the camels move along the ground as you advance across the plains of Jordan following the railway line: from the platform of the dilapidated station the harkis fiercely brandish their weapons, and with theatrical jerks and exaggerated fits and starts (as if all the screws of its structure had suddenly loosened), the locomotive will start up: accompanied (you, that is) by the whistling complicity of the engineer, the deafening din of the cars of the train: into the darkness of the tunnels and defiles that the echo proclaims to the point of paroxysm, thus enhancing the atavistic rhythm of the divertissement for one hand that you are playing: the windows throw little squares of light on walls and cliffs, allowing you to witness the animated spectacle from an oblique angle: magic lanterns make Chinese shadows, suddenly hurtling you back to your childhood and the stuttering glories of hollywoodian technicolor: a slave-girl market in Damascus?: the polychrome back streets of Baghdad?: any hypothesis is plausible and the jolting of the Dogü Eksprés multiplies the clues and hints: the witness of the adventures of Aladdin?: of the prodigies and marvels of Ali Baba?: past the embarcadero of Eyüp, beyond the little ancient square, along the edge of the great cemetery: a path leads into it and branches off among the symmetrical tombs: grass grows everywhere, wild and untended, velvety moss blurs and softens the Arabic inscriptions of long ago: ridiculous Nazarene pretension has no place here: death is peace and oblivion: bodies return to the earth and nourish with their substance the modest flowers that an exemplary little gypsy girl, a fierce, untamed little animal, is gracefully tucking into her hair: you will follow her, hugging the wall of the mosque, intrigued by the enigmatic invitation of an arrow that laconically announces the unsuspected presence of Pierre Loti in the vicinity: the little urchins of the neighborhood have remarked your humble presence and shout out the name of the homme de lettres as you laboriously make your way up the hill and take in at a single glance the Golden Horn and Istanbul, the Bosporus, the Sea of Marmara: minarets and cupolas glisten in the sun and the delirious chaos below rises, fluttering like a flag: a mirage?: a hallucination?: the little wild animal has also stopped now and is waiting for you to catch your breath before continuing on up the funereal hill, walking alongside the old blurred inscriptions: you are panting like the stupid lordling puffed up with his own importance who managed to make the illustrious rector of Salamanca laugh: the biped scaler of the heights of Guadarrama and Fuenfría, Gredos and the Peña de Francia: until you finally arrive at the vernal terrace of the café, where a girl dressed in a peasant costume is dispensing, with a liturgical gesture, a fragrant, dark infusion to a group of admirers of the Great Man, who have come to the very nucleus of his radiant inspiration to gather the dew of his word

yes, I work here: by fits and starts, so to speak: I listen to the tales people tell me: I study their mores, their habits: their loves, their desires, their hatreds: I note down what they say: I build my characters little by little

are your stories true?

credibility is never one of my aims: I depict what I see, and then I invent: I set up situations

what are the reasons for your success?

not boring the public: that is the sole law of the novel: a carefully constructed story line is imperative: in a novel something should be happening all the time, all the time, all the time: the European novel of our day is dying of anemia: it is incumbent upon us to return to the source, as the Americans are doing

how long does it take you to write a book?

much more time than you think!: I begin by letting it simmer for a considerable period: I think about it, and it bubbles and steams within me: I recount it to myself: so long as there is even one little detail that troubles me, I do not set a single line down on paper: but once I have everything well in hand, I don't change a word: I am thoroughly familiar with my plot, my characters, all the situations: from time to

time I put in phrases in Turkish: that makes it seem true
to life, and lends a touch of local color
Monsieur Pierre Loti, what does writing mean to you?
it is our last remaining virginity: the virginity of paper: writing is entering upon a mariage d'amour with the white page!
what clarity of expression! what depth of feeling! what a
command of words!: the French accent is perfect: those
present greet these declarations with murmurs of admiration,
and as no one seems to notice your presence, you will dis-
creetly steal away from the pushing and shoving mob of reporters, and going around behind the medals and the in-
signia of the Immortals, you will pass through the pretentious
drawing rooms with their carved ceilings, their walls with
gilt moldings and mythological frescoes and descend the
stately staircase carpeted in red that leads others upward to
the lofty heights of fame and takes you down, step by step,
to the vestibule, where the liveried servants are obsequiously
lined up in a row, just inside the portico in front of which
the official cars have stopped and are depositing their precious cargo of minks and sables, opera hats, top hats, two-
cornered hats, and cocked hats in the hands of an armada
of lackeys and ushers, who, under the precise, musical direction of an awesome chief of protocol, are performing their
function of announcing them and leading them into the
superior and perfect circle that you have just deserted, so
that they may exchange polite remarks, smiles, and witti-
cisms with the finest flour of academic Parnassus while you
(disgraziato!) irremediably drift away from them, cross the
lovely versaillesque garden by way of paths that wander
among beds of flowers, sculptures, and pools, continue onward across lawns shaded by linden and horsechestnut trees
and finally end up on a vast, inhospitable, bare expanse
strewn with rocks and boulders which little by little will be
transformed into a harsh, desolate wasteland with towering
dunes like ocean waves: your Immortal's costume will gradually become covered with dust, and as you walk on and

on, sweat will soak your snow-white shirt front and your starched wing collar will cling painfully to your skin as the mirror polish of your formal dress shoes dims beneath a layer of sand and the gleam of your two-cornered patent-leather hat darkens with the suddenness of a solar eclipse: the ribbons of your decorations hang down like miserable tatters and your laurels fade and dry up, victims of the dirt and heat: you will mournfully seek a resting-place in this stony and rocky desert, and when, with the aid of a convenient cittern which you have happened upon by the sheerest of chances in these purlieus, you make ready to express your woes and cares with no other witness than these rough and rugged solitary haunts, you will be surprised to hear the plangent, harmonious lament of an exquisite voice

VERSES OF ENCOURAGEMENT
ON HARM DONE AND ITS REMEDY

What arm is it that makes you writhe?
  The scythe.
What leaves the blood drained from your veins?
  Grievous pains.
And what is it that keeps you tense?
  Patience.
If this be so, your grave malady
Requires an immediate remedy
For hope will have no recompense
If you dwell on the scythe, pains, and patience.

What causes you such sleepless nights?
  Spite.
What eats your liver like a vulture?
  Fake culture.
What keeps you then from taking wing?
  The sympathy you bring.
If this be so, I fear, my friend
That this strange complaint will be your end
For, conspiring to do you ill
Spite, fake culture, others' sympathy can kill.

To what victory can you lay claim?
  Fame.
To be more truthful: what's within your range?
  Change.
In your defense, who are the leaders?
  Readers.
If this be so, you may be sure
That for your passion there's a cure
For its remedies, eternally the same
Are simply readers, change, and fame.

orienting yourself by the sweet sound of the guitar, you will make your way among rocks and boulders, eager to meet its divine master, amazed that such delicate harmonies should pour forth amid this wasteland, lulled by the soft plaints and laments, which, although addressed to heaven's mercy, would be capable of melting the stoniest of hearts as well, turning sternness to tenderness and harshness to clemency, such is the mournful sentiment that inspires them and the admirable decorum with which they are expressed, as though their author were not a rustic villager but a discreet courtier, a learned connoisseur of the arcana of rhyme and skilled in the playing of instruments, thereby causing your astonishment and amazement to grow even greater, since such environs, however much the novels of yore may argue to the contrary, are not normally propitious to such fortuitous events, and nothing about these surroundings possesses a sufficient degree of verisimilitude to prepare the imagination for the reality of such encounters: and on rounding a cliff you will see before you a maiden clad in the simple costume of a peasant girl, whose beauty and chaste demeanor leave you speechless: she is sitting in the shade of a little grove of trees, through which there runs a quiet brook gently flowing from a crystal-clear spring: her hair falls like thin gold filaments about her alabaster cheeks and her slender, graceful hands seem to be sculpted from the purest snow: the whiteness of the instep of her feet rivals that of the finest Italian marbles, and on dolefully raising her face in a fit of amorous delirium, she will display two miraculous jewels that would make Phoebus himself pale with envy: having ended her sad lament, the damsel will proffer a profound and prolonged sigh, and although you wait attentively for a few moments, wishing to regale your ears once again with such celestial sounds, since the music now has given way to cries and moans that grow more and more lugubrious, you will decide to ascertain the identity of this angel who is uttering them and determine what extraordinary misadventures have brought her to these remote and wild precincts: walking on a few steps farther, you will enter the verdant meadow and fall on your knees at her feet, on the smiling green grass wet with drops of dew like unto shining pearls

hearken unto me, milady, whoever you may be, for he whom you see here before you, humbling himself before your greatness, desires only to serve you to the end of his days and to offer his unworthy person to rescue you from your unhappy fate

and as the startled damsel timorously rises to her feet and covers the bareness of her shoulders with a simple home-spun shawl, you will admire the regal simplicity of her ges-tures, which, belying her humble garb, betray with a clarity as bright as the noonday sun the nobility and purity of her ancestry: she will modestly tuck the gold of her hair be-neath a little rustic cap, and decorously lowering her gaze and thus preventing you from glimpsing her incomparable eyes, she will sit there, silent and perplexed, in an attitude of modest, shy reserve, which, being far removed from any sort of lustful thoughts, proclaims the integrity of her person and her credit in the eyes of others

the causes of your misfortune, my most gentle lady, cannot have been slight ones, for only the most severe and extreme trials can have obliged you to clothe yourself in the humble garments with which you are vainly attempting to disguise your extraordinary beauty and to seek refuge in the solitary fastnesses of such haunts as these, better suited for the lairs of fierce wild beasts than for protection for damsels of your estate, lineage, and virtue, accustomed as they are to the splendor of palaces and the softness and smoothness of silks and satins

the girl will listen to you as if spellbound, still not willing to break the silence that she has observed since your sudden and indiscreet appearance on the scene, but then after utter-ing a number of even more painful sighs and allowing price-less pearls to glide down her marmoreal cheeks, she will again settle herself comfortably at the edge of the spring and delicately dry her eyes with the tip of her handkerchief

since you so desire, gentle stranger, I shall offer you a brief account of the reasons for my misfortunes and misadventures, though I implore you not to call me wayward and wanton if in the exposition of the facts to which the thread of this sad and true story will of necessity lead me, I may chance to refer to events and acts that apparently cast discredit on the tender modesty customarily expected of any chaste damsel

and as you promise and solemnly swear that you will not do so, charmed as you are by the grace and eloquence of her words, the girl will lovingly pluck the strings of her guitar, and with her gaze lost in the liquid crystal of the brook, she will express herself in these words

my name is Vosk: my home one of the most famous and illustrious cities of Sunnyspain: my origins, noble: my progenitors, rich: my profession, critic and professor: my misfortune so great that neither the arms furnished me by my solid fund of knowledge nor the power of a vast inherited fortune have prevailed against it: from my most tender years, I devoted myself to reading works of literature which, with exemplary patience and care, my industrious and upright parents had collected in their personal library of more than ten thousand volumes, installed in a spacious and commodious country villa that they possess, set amid fertile fields where Pales, Ceres, and Bacchus harmoniously offer their gifts in turn, and there, beneath the beneficent tutelage of so great a number of celebrated writers, I began to purify my predilections and my tastes in the crucible of reading and experience, and so it was that there was born within my breast an ineradicable love for those novels which, combining instruction with delight, are a truthful and sincere reflection of the societies in which they are created, thanks to

the introduction of vivid and authentic characters, subject
to the passions and the vices of men of flesh and blood,
and like them, capable of ascending to the heights of sublime heroism or descending into the abysses of degradation
and wretchedness, our inseparable companions through all
the peripeteias and adventures in which the plots of these
masterpieces involve them, the authors of which, having
deliberately forsaken allegories and obscurantist myths of
that primitive novelistic art typical of remote and archaic
communities, endeavor, through systematic doubt and the
use of reason in the service of the most pressing human interests, to reveal the defects and the shortcomings of the
society of the period with the laudable aim of correcting and
eliminating them, instilling in the minds and hearts of readers a multitude of sentiments and ideas that forever unite
them with fictional brothers as profound and as complex as
they themselves are, be they proletarians or aristocrats, members of the impoverished seminobility or the well-off petty
bourgeoisie, accomplishing this by means of episodes that
are representative and valid on a national scale, and embrace
as well the entire immeasurable breadth and depth of the
human comedy in their dense, substantial, moving, pathetic
pages, full of animation and overflowing with life and a
faithful mirror of harsh and raw truths, a love, I repeat, that
led me to the diligent study of the sacred texts of realism,
in particular the incomparable apothegms and maxims of
the evangelist Saint Lucaks, thanks to which my powers of
ratiocination grew stronger, my doubts evaporated, my arguments became better reasoned, and my conclusions more
firmly supported, eventually taking on a theoretical solidity
and consistency that made them practically unassailable,
thus turning me into the ever-victorious paladin of numerous
novels and characters that were soon to become, without my
knowledge, the object of a treacherous and carefully planned
attack on the fundamental principles of their being, as meanwhile I, hapless creature that I am, continued my reading

and my studies, and in the palaestra of the press or public forums repeatedly involved myself in brilliant jousts with the followers of a retrograde and obscurantist ideology, whose escapist myths are merely the sad reflection of the sterile subjectivism of the writer: oh, heavens, how many articles I wrote!: how many sweet and hard-earned victories were mine!: how many letters and discourses I composed and how many weighty treatises in which reason set forth its proofs, revealed its solid and firmly established first principles, and refuted the unfounded opinions of certain elitist, diseased, and desiccated brains!: the public cheered me, the ignorant criticized me, authors congratulated me, the sharp-witted defended me, with the result that I triumphed over my enraged and spiteful enemies and my fame spread to the farthest corners of the globe and redounded to the credit of my ancestral name, until the unfortunate day when, by virtue of a fashion imported from abroad or thanks to a cruel caprice of fate, the favorable wind that had always blown in my direction suddenly shifted and swelled the sails and breathed courage into the souls of the armada of my adversaries, causing the pens of those who wrote in conformity with my dictates to fall silent and unleashing those of a host of authors devoted to the cultivation of a formal and abstract style of writing, merely the deranged, frequently schizophrenic, expression of personal obsessions and complexes which, rather than being an objective reflection of the world, represent nothing more than a desperate and incomplete attempt at liberation on the part of a sick mentality: I did battle, I argued, I insisted, I persevered, to no avail: my vigilance proved futile: and although out of a sense of duty and friendship toward youth, I endeavored to set them on the right path once again and dissuade them from carrying out their lamentable intentions, employing to that end the best reasons I was able to summon up and the most vivid examples I could marshal, they nonetheless gradually deserted my camp and swelled the ranks of that of my rivals, the victims of a pessimistic, negative vision of things which not only abandons the struggle to change them but also inadvertently aids in perpetuating them by giving rise to the fabrication of evasive and hermetic products which, since they endeavor to combat alienation through the use of typically alienated forms, both aggravate and exacerbate the inner contradictions of the artist and fail to offer the reader any acceptable solution, in view of which, after bidding my aged and afflicted parents a tender farewell, I purchased a sorrel horse on whose back I rode to these wild and lonely haunts in the company of a faithful and persevering disciple, after having first allowed my silky blond hair to grow long and changed my male attire for that of a mountain shepherdess in order to protect my natural chasteness against the dangers and snares of nomad Bedouin tribes, who, inflamed by the rigors of the climate and devoid of the moral restraints imposed by our Christian civilization, shamelessly give themselves over to the abominable vice and to other very black sins that it would be otiose to mention here, and thus, having joined company with other shepherdesses and servant girls, though I know not whether they be real or imaginary, I traverse with them these solitary environs proclaiming our luminous doctrine and lamenting our harsh fate, with the sweet, secret hope of coming upon writers lost in the labyrinths and blind alleys of subjectivism, who, scorning the wholesome tastes of the public and neglecting their own social responsibilities, fruitlessly preach in the saharan desert: and were you to dwell here among us for a time, gentle stranger, one day you would hear these trackless expanses and these steep gorges resound with the disillusioned plaints of editors, readers, and critics: not very far from where your grace has journeyed from, I know an oasis with a few dozen palm trees, half of whose fronds have fallen off, and on the scaly trunk of each of them there are carved and inscribed the motifs of our school, and moreover, at the very top of the mutilated trunk of one of them is a braided crown, as if its maker had wished to make it abundantly clear that realism is the crowning glory of all literary creation: here a professor sighs: there another whimpers: yonder, fierce panegyrics are heard: over there, anguished dirges: we know of one poor creature who spends the entire night sitting at the foot of a cliff, and it is there that the sun finds him in the morning, bemused and lost in thought, never once having closed his tear-filled eyes the whole night long: and there is one, such as myself, O noble and obliging sire, who, unable to repress his continual sighs, lying stretched out on the burning sand amid the heat of a fretful summer siesta, addresses his laments, as you are witness, to the merciful heavens

corroborating the truth of these words, you will hear the soft, harmonious lament of an inspired voice which, rising from the inaccessible desert crags, seems a mirage of the senses or a chimerical fantasy because of the absolute mastery with which the litany of woes is recited and the gracefulness, elegance, and charm with which they are accompanied on a stringed instrument, leaving all the little birds in the sky and the forest animals spellbound: witnesses like you of the portentous miracle, they too lend their ears and sip with gentle delight the gifts of its poetic numen

O Literature, soaring on strong and sturdy wing
Leaving our little local-color stories far below
Thou hast reached the heights, amid an objective glow
And feast at splendid banquets where the Immortals sing

From there on high, with impartial finger signaling
The true path, hidden by illusion's veil, to show
The weary, struggling writer the way he needs must go

To skirt creation's quicksands, whence his ghastly novels
   spring

Return among us, Literature: I pray do not permit
The formalist to preen himself, decked in thy livery
Nor cut off my vocation ere its flower sees the light

If perchance thou dost not find it meet and fit
To strip these lackeys of their mediocrity
I'll take this role upon myself, and plunge the world in
   night

the sonnet will end with a deep sigh, and you will spy, standing out in sharp contrast to the monotonous, arid, rocky expanse, the figure of a nubile damsel, clad in no more than the
garments that modesty requires in order to decently cover
certain corporeal parts that shall remain unmentioned,
though this attire of a rustic shepherdess fails at the same
time to fulfill its intended purpose of disguising the superhuman perfection of her features: her hair, gold: her forehead,
marble: her eyes, precious stones: her cheeks, coral: her lips,
rubies: her throat, alabaster; her hands, snow: as though in a
trance, she will contemplate the lonely crags to which her
singular misfortune has brought her, and lost in thought, she
will caress the strings of her rebec as though she were consid-
ering continuing the recital of her woes, but she will change
her mind, and gracefully turning her countenance in your
direction, she will cast her incomparable eyes upon the person accompanying you, whereupon she will manifest
signs of profound perturbation, and after emitting an ear-
splitting, lusty shout, she will exclaim
O merciful heaven!: what is this I see?: what creature is this
that presents itself to my gaze?
these words are uttered in a voice that has changed so radically that the spurious damsel who is escorting you will in
turn manifest intense surprise, and running into each other's

arms, the two will greet each other with an extraordinary show of joy, delighted at this chance meeting in such an unbelievable and unlikely place as a wasteland ordinarily peopled with predatory animals and other fearful wild beasts: immediately thereafter, the two maidens will come over to you, and once the requisite exordiums are terminated, Vosk will question the surpassingly beautiful and modest damsel as to the causes of her flight to the desert and the unusual humbleness of her garb, urging her, with clear and well-founded logical arguments, to tell you the true story of her life, which will necessarily be new and pleasing, as can be deduced from the occasion and the conjuncture of circumstances that have brought all of you together, to which she will give answer by saying that she will do so most willingly, in order to satisfy her questioner's curiosity and that of the gentle stranger, there being no need for pleas and entreaties, so great is the inner force that compels her to recount her story and so eager is her desire to offer for the world's consideration certain facts which ordinarily, placing no trust in mere human confidants, she shares only with a kind and merciful heaven: whereupon the three of you will settle yourselves comfortably on a convenient little shaded meadow whose delightful coolness beckons invitingly, when suddenly the alternate strains of a shepherd's pipe and a rustic flute will attract your attention, and turning your eyes in the direction from which their plaintive melody is coming, spellbound by the compelling reality of the scene, you will spy a most attractive retinue of what look to be nymphs or naiads who, making their way across this rocky wilderness where no other humans have ever trod, clad in silken tunics and crowned with laurels and tendrils of grapevines, are carrying on a bier decked with garlands and greenery what would appear from a distance to be a youth immersed in deepest slumber, but to judge by the mournful countenances of the retinue and the doleful sighs of the damsels, it is, rather, the unburied body of a lad who has died in the flower of his youth, a self-immolated victim, perhaps, of the cruelty of unrequited, blighted loves, and unable to resist the natural temptation to ascertain the reasons that lie behind such an unusual circumstance, you will all approach the grief-stricken chorus of keening damsels and inquire who the departed lad might be and what unfortunate concatenation of events has brought an end to his life, just as the exquisite bucolic creatures deposit the bier alongside a grave recently dug at the foot of a massive, imposing crag whose surface is entirely covered with inscriptions engraved with a burin or a pocketknife in praise or defense of the literary school to which your two illustrious companions belong

CHARACTERS WILL NEVER DIE

THE NOVEL IS THE OBJECTIVE REFLECTION OF SOCIOHISTORICAL REALITY

DOWN WITH MYTHS THAT HIDE THE TRUTH

THE WRITER'S SUBJECTIVE OBSESSIONS ARE A MYSTIFICATION

NO TO FORMALIST AND ONEIRIC EXPERIMENTS!

REALISM IS THE ACME AND THE CROWNING GLORY OF ART

arrived at the edge of the grave, you will together contemplate the corpse of a noble youth dressed in shepherd's clothing, who despite the cruel rigidity of death gives every sign of having been in life a person of genteel mien and gallant spirit: around him, on the same bier, a number of books and many hastily penned farewell missives are evidence of the thwarted passion of a writer, and in answer to your inquiry, the damsels in disguise will reply that indeed such was the case and that one need seek no further than this deep devotion to his art to discover the origin of the sad chain of events that led him to the fateful decision to put an end to his life: the injustice of the attacks by the self-styled avant-garde of which realism is today the victim and the undeserved discredit into which its practitioners have fallen thanks to know-it-all mandarins, they will add, impelled him to interrupt a promising and brilliant career as a novelist and take refuge in these vast, wild badlands, adding, day and night, the moisture from his eyes to the waters of a fresh, crystal-clear brook where animals are accustomed to come to quench their thirst, but as neither this private retreat nor this fluid relief brought peace or calm to his tormented soul, a few weeks before, after having confided his woes to a manu-script that he lovingly kept close at hand, an inseparable com-panion that he never let out of his sight, he had scaled the rugged face of a bald mountain and had there allowed him-self to be slowly consumed, the victim of the fatal bite of serpents or of the rigors of the climate, leaving grief-stricken and inconsolable all the shepherdesses and mountain lasses who, wishing to help him forget his cares, had chastely courted him or read him novels and tales which, in obedience to the laws of the singular perspective embraced by his school, deal with society and its contradictions from an ob-jective point of view

and would your graces perchance know where this manu-script of which you speak may be found?, Vosk will ask

silently, the maidens will lead the three of you to a hole dug in a small bare clearing nestling between two rocky cliffs and show you an old and battered valise which, once opened, will be found to contain a few linen garments and a handsome doublet of crimson velvet beneath which, amid a heap of letters, you will discover a sheaf of papers tied together with a simple ribbon, each and every one of which, from begin-ning to end, is covered with writing in a fine and delicate hand

this is the last text that the hapless youth penned, and in order that you may see, sir, the state to which his misfortunes had reduced him, pass a few pages to your comrades so that they may read them and take pleasure in them, for we shall have time for it while they are digging the grave

I am most desirous of doing so, Vosk will say

and as the damsel and you share the same desire, each of you will choose a page, and with the three of you seated in a circle, you will begin to read

CHAPTER XVII

IN WHICH THE PORT OF TOLEDO IS DESCRIBED ALONG WITH
OTHER DETAILS NECESSARY
FOR THE UNDERSTANDING OF THIS TRUE STORY

"Before following the thread of events that make up this chronicle faithfully copied from real life and describing the reactions of our characters—who thanks to a happy coincidence have been drawn from life, as we have said, and have had no traits whatsoever added to their portrait on our part —it is only fitting that we should tarry for a few moments and dwell at some length on the environmental features that underlie the plot, for otherwise its development might risk appearing somewhat improbable and slightly arbitrary to the reader, inasmuch as it obeys no social or psychological law that would account for its seeming anomaly, thought in point of fact quite the contrary is true, for it is clearly motivated by a complex concatenation of circumstances that in turn depend in large part on the human context within which the action takes place. Therefore—leaving Feliciano and Prudencia absorbed in their violent quarrel with regard to the future of their son Frasquito—we shall briefly describe the seaside district of Toledo, where our heroes have sought refuge

"As the lovers of this ancient and noble Castilian city are well aware, when the ocean waves dash violently against the seawall that protects the fishing vessels in the harbor, the idlers who are accustomed to saunter along it, among whom we may often glimpse a fair number of smugglers and petty ruffians . . ."

what a hand of a true writer!: what raw but heartfelt emotion!

growing more and more enraptured, Vosk keeps commenting on the contents of his page, and accompanying the more and more perceptible movement of his lips as he reads, his voice will reproduce, in a soft murmur at first and then in clear and distinct tones, the rapid and spirited dialogue of the characters

extraordinary, he will say, simply extraordinary!

he will rummage mechanically through the pockets of a plaid vest with an ostentatious watch chain draped across the front of it and take out a wrinkled handkerchief, with which he will wipe away the beads of sweat on his forehead, having first freed his head of the oppressive bondage of a derby hat, of the sort worn by usurious moneylenders or stockbrokers

what vitality, what richness, what profundity!: what admirable fidelity to the reality that surrounds him! what masterful skill in the creation of types, the detailed description of various milieux, the scrupulously accurate transcription of spoken speech!

breaking with emotion, his voice will suddenly fail him and you will take advantage of the necessary pause as he hawks and coughs and tries to clear his throat in order, all eyes and ears, to depict him in accordance with the canons of his own school: and using as a convenient source of inspiration a well-known novel that by the sheerest of chances happens to be among the books piled up next to the table on which you are writing, you will go on in this vein: our man is one of those individuals of indefinite age who may appear either young or old, depending on the strength of the light or the expression on their countenances, which is a mirror of their innermost mood: his face is clean-cut, irregular, and somewhat depressed in its upper portion, due no doubt to his serene, slightly receding forehead, furrowed by a thin network of tiny wrinkles which extends from his scalp to the edge of his well-defined eyebrows, above a pair of small, dark eyes that are half closed but are nonetheless piercing and searching, and a pinched, hooked nose which, when he turns his face to one side, gives him the noble profile of an illustrious grandee: the slightly sunken mouth, with fine, supple lips ordinarily twisted in an affable smile that never leaves them even in the gravest circumstances and highlights and enhances the whole of his grim countenance: he is of medium stature and his hands, encased in kid gloves, are frequently clasped together over his abdomen in a protective, self-satisfied gesture: before scating himself, he has carefully parted the two rear flaps of his velvet evening jacket, and his cane with a silver handle and his elegant boots that are meticulously fitted to follow the subtle line of his instep give him the air of a wealthy tradesman or a hidalgo who has reached the higher echelons of the government bureaucracy: but the whole of his physiognomy bears a marked expression of aristocratic hauteur, and in his gaze is the fire and determination of geniuses of the old stripe

his world is dense, vast, and complex, he will conclude: the author has a profound love for his contemporaries and reveals this love in the fidelity, affection, and infinite care with which he transposes them to the novel: our first impression on reading him is that of finding ourselves confronted with a teeming multitude of characters whose outlines are just a bit blurred, but as we immerse ourselves in the work, we see how their profiles become sharper, how their traits of personality stand out more and more clearly, how the components of this great mass take on concrete individuality by way of a gesture, a retort, a smile, a silence: and do you know why all of this is so?

Vosk looks you straight in the eye with ill-disguised anxiety, and since you merely sit there waiting, saying nothing, he will answer for you

because he has faith in them!: because he believes in the existence of their actions, their phrases, their thoughts, and allows them to grow and take on a life of their own, converting them from mere paper creatures to flesh-and-blood beings, resembling in every respect those whom we meet on the street every day: with the selfsame passions, virtues, and vices: with the selfsame apparel, gestures, words: not like those pseudo-writers who have lost their faith and celebrate their empty rites without transforming bread and wine into real body and blood, thus sapping, through their irresponsibility and their cynicism, the very foundations of the novelistic order and opening the door to every sort of license, excess, and extravagance!: but you are not like them!: I have seen the light that shines in your eyes and I am certain that I am not mistaken: you believe in the novelistic character, isn't that right, my boy?

Vosk anxiously awaits your reply, and fearful of disappointing him, you will choose to immure yourself in a cautious silence

yes, I am absolutely certain that you believe!: you have just a touch of self-pride and hence are averse to confessing the fact to your bosom pals, but you believe: your soul is not dry and shriveled like those of hardened unbelievers: at bottom it is good and has preserved the smiling innocence of childhood: don't tell me that's not so, my boy, because that won't wash with me: I've talked with literally hundreds like you, and I know your secrets very well

for a few instants there will be a suspenseful silence, and without abandoning his visual attack, Vosk will thrust his torso forward with kindly solicitude and paternally place his right hand on your shoulder

yes, you have faith: because even though you have yielded to theories, methods, and styles that are foreign, exotic, and imported, you have not forgotten in the slightest the ideas we have instilled in you: your conscience pricks you and you are eager to believe as you once did: you are making your way along blindly, but nonetheless you are seeking: and he who seeks has in truth already found: it's no use playing the rogue or the blusterer: the expression on your face gives you away: you believe, my boy: and if you listen to me and pay more attention to what you do and explore situations more thoroughly and develop your characters little by little, you too will be able to see into their very heart of hearts and plunge into the most arcane secrets of their consciences: just imagine, my boy: giving life to hundreds and hundreds of novelistic beings!: creating types, personalities, milieux, episodes, settings!: composing violent, passionate, dramatic scenes!: rivaling the état civil!: forging positive heroes!: being an engineer of souls!: ah, what an intoxicating and comforting prospect!

his enthusiasm is contagious, and climbing to the heights with him, you will soar on swift, light wings above the wondrous tropical islands, the handhold and refuge of your timid youth: your youth?: no, that of the other: of the precious child (later executed) possessed of an ecumenical eagerness to proselytize and fervent desires for regeneration: dressed in snow-white garments like the Petits Frères of the likewise martyred Reverend Father Foucauld: with a cassock (white) and a pith helmet (also white) that form a harmonious contrast to the dark skins and earthy bodies of the unfortunate natives deprived by celestial decree of the glorious benefits of Redemption: distributing blessings, advice, alms, comforting smiles, soothing words of consolation on every hand: aiding widows, succoring orphans, freeing slaves: surrounded by a cloud of African children, tout noirs, oui, mais doux et intelligents: fleet-footed coolies bear the lightweight palanquin with an immaculate canopy in which he travels, and a slender, graceful catechumen fans him and refreshes him by deftly waving a pay-pay: in one or another of the countries to be evangelized minutely described in the publications to which the holy and pious family subscribed: as meanwhile he (the other) rests beneath the lily-white veil of a mosquito net, and the governess and maid-

servants, believing him to be asleep, inspect his toy priest's
set and exchange flattering murmurs of approval
the little angel has just celebrated mass
he said yesterday he wanted to be a missionary
he's continually poring over the map of Africa!
doesn't he look like a little saint though?
shhh, don't wake him up!
yes, he has a vocation
savoring (the other, that is) within his bosom the delicious
joys of his triumph: conferring divine grace on countless
creatures otherwise condemned to the sad monotony of limbo
or horrendous eternal torments: accompanied wherever he
goes by a mobile, weightless nimbus such as those shown in
books of prints, as he traverses savannas, jungles, and
steppes, acclaimed by the cheers and applause of the natives,
who kneel and kiss his redemptive pastoral ring: the spiritual
father of a vast census of flesh-and-blood beings, capable of
competing with and besting those of the real and natural
order!: delineating with one swift stroke of the pen their
physical features and their characters: and then plunging
them into violent, tense, dramatic situations!: seated (as you
are) at his worktable, with the genesic organ at lance rest:
but without falling into the abominable solitary vice of imagination that leads to the illusion of personal liberation: to
gratuitous and empty writing that is mere self-reflection and
self-consummation and lacks any sort of social justification
whatsoever: maintaining instead a fecund relation with the
world: similar, remarkably similar, to that of the noble and
licit procreative bond: engendering living, profound, complex, authentic characters who impose their existence and
truth upon the immutable novelistic orb and oblige the reader
to commune with the reality of their words and deeds: a
sinful and feverish adolescent?: no: an eminent engineer of
souls!: finally abandoning vain, onanistic pleasure in favor of
the fruitful coupling of the nuptial bed and a paternity

blessed with a multitude of scions possessed of the attributes of the état civil

look, Vosk will say: I have turned into a character of flesh and blood!: I have forebears, a past, a house, furniture, a family: a name, surnames, wearing apparel, a face, a character, a body: I am an individualized, three-dimensional being, with sociological solidity and actions that are entirely self-consistent, the index and the expression of a personality that is my own inalienable property: novelists and readers believe in my presence and have little by little endowed me with numerous attributes and prerogatives: I eat, I drink, I smoke, I love, I suffer, I think: the innermost secrets of my soul and conscience are the subject of public-opinion polls and methodical, exhaustive analyses: despite the natural contradictions inherent in every man, the sincerity of my feelings of compassion and my solidarity with those who live lives of toil and misery add up, when all is said and done, to a positive, substantial balance in my favor: I am subject to vacillations and doubts, to be sure: but I take myself firmly in hand and act: and what is more: these same conflicting traits have helped to transform me into a tremendously popular type, for whom the public has conceived the greatest affection: look, my boy, at all the correspondence I receive!: letters, postcards, and telegrams from the five corners of the earth!: my fans are eager to know what has become of me since the latest episode of the serial or after my entering into the holy bonds of matrimony in the penultimate chapter of the work: are you happy?, they inquire: have you had children?: or they ask me to send them a photograph of my spouse, and if they suspect that I am short of funds because of the intrigues of my adversaries, they generously come to my aid with money orders, checks, and letters of credit: just take a look: I have here the postal receipts for a number of

them: do you think for one moment that they would be sent to me if I did not exist?: since you first met me at the edge of the spring where I was giving voice to my cares I have changed a great deal: I have taken on weight: and all the episodes and events in which I now find myself involved stem from entirely probable reasons and facts, determined by the laws and circumstances of a complex and contradictory social order: touch my forehead, my boy: do I not sweat?: and my eyes: tell me, are they not bloodshot?: because last night I tossed and turned in bed for hours, not sleeping a wink, all on account of your marvelous manuscript!: in a word: I am natural and human, and for this precise reason I am liked: because novelists and readers can divine my thoughts through my skull and penetrate to the sentiments nesting in my innermost heart: after a while they know me better than their own relatives and friends and eventually have an intimate knowledge of my whole family background and my entire personal history: they know that I am a professor and a critic, that I am a proponent of the doctrine of realism, that I am related to eminent families in the hinterlands, that I frequent the most distinguished salons in such provinces as Galicia and Asturias, express myself in the pure language of the man in the street, adore doughnuts dunked in chocolate, write verses, am the pen pal of a Swiss lass, smoke mild Virginia tobacco, admire sunsets and Italian landscapes, suffer from chronic renal dysfunction and cryptorchidism, am subject to attacks of dizziness and vertigo, have a hearty appetite, read books on aesthetics and treatises on economics, have a mole on my left arm and a wart on my groin, possess a watch purchased at the flea market in Madrid and leather puttees that my cousin Bette sent me from France: I am normal, absolutely normal, like those persons with whom you are on friendly terms in everyday life, isn't that so, my boy?
yes, you will admit

ah, and whether Toledo is or is not directly situated on the ocean is a minor detail of no importance whatsoever!

with cordial firmness: with that discreet smile of the friend who knows one's weaknesses but does not excuse them and fervently desires that they be overcome: with that clear-sightedness tinged with melancholy of a person who has lived life to the hilt and knows how things are and realizes precisely how difficult it is to hew to the straight and narrow path: with the simple generosity of a father toward the son who has gone astray and traded his inheritance for a miserable mess of pottage: with the silent pain of a mother confronted with the dilemma of inclinations of her offspring which are totally at odds with her inflexible conception of duty, Doktor Vosk will guide you down the aisle past the rows of spectators seated in the comfortable, ultramodern studio of the National Radio and Television Network and up to the circular platform, bathed in the harsh glare of floodlights, where the press conference that has been announced is about to begin

MODERATOR OF THE PANEL DISCUSSION

      (after calling the meeting to order with a little bell and repeatedly clearing his throat)

      ladies and gentlemen: we are gathered together here this evening with an eminent group of critics and readers in order to examine the work in progress of a writer who is also present here with us, a novelist possessed of a certain talent and merits which, although exaggerated, were nonetheless genuine in earlier stages of his career, but who is today confused or, if I may venture to say so, disoriented because of the unfortunate influence of sick, foreign theories and arguments which in no way obey the principles and norms of our community: the members of this panel are, as you know, extremely hard-working, self-abnegating colleagues who labor ceaselessly to organize occasions such as this, meetings such as this in which the narrator lost in the labyrinths of a mystifying subjectivism is offered a marvelous opportunity to change course and publicly engage in an objective, sincere, and faithful self-criticism

(turning around toward the participants seated on the platform) you have the floor, ladies and gentlemen

A SOCIOLOGIST WEARING GLASSES

if I am not mistaken, the action of a large part of your novel would appear to take place in the Sahara: would you be so kind as to tell us, please, what the desert means to you?

A STUDENT FROM THE SCHOOL OF JOURNALISM

I find in your work no depiction of the human or social background, none of the drama of the struggle for existence: is this due, in your opinion, to the fact that the life of the Bedouins in a cruel and hostile environment presents no problems?

(murmurs of approval)

A YOUNG GIRL WITH BIG BREASTS

your characters are hollow, empty, lifeless nonentities: neither I nor anyone else can possibly believe in them: would you be so good as to explain to us where you got them from?

A LAD WHO IS STILL BEARDLESS BUT EXTREMELY CHEEKY

lots of people are convinced you write that junk of yours when you're stoned out of your mind, and judging by what I've read of it, I think they're right on!

(laughter)

THE DEACONESS OF A PARISH SODALITY

do your characters have a soul?: they certainly don't as far as I can see!

A SARCASTIC, OUTSPOKEN MEMBER OF THE AUDIENCE

what seems equally bad to me is that they don't have a body either: there is absolutely nothing to them whatsoever: they are not even shadows: in a word, they slip right through a person's fingers because you are totally incompetent!

(applause)

A MIDDLE-AGED GENTLEMAN

what qualifications do you have for the role of public prosecutor in the field of the novel that you have taken upon yourself?: frankly, no matter how diligently I search, I can find none at all: and this being the case, don't you believe that your behavior is indicative of a lack of modesty?

(voices: hear, hear!)

A LADY WITH A HEARING AID

why do you manifest so much bitterness, pessimism, and resentment in your work?: are you really convinced that life hasn't a single positive or pleasing aspect?

A DOCTOR OF PHILOSOPHY

your writings reveal extremely serious psychological problems: they betray a self-satisfaction, an overestimation of your own role that would doubtless be of interest to a psychiatrist: but in your considered opinion, are these elements that are mere scientific curiosities, so to speak, sufficient for the construction of a real novel?

(voices: very well put!)

A PROMINENT ART CRITIC

the pages that I have read amount to nothing but a dull accumulation of aberrations and defects that do not and cannot move our readers: would you mind telling us, mister novelist, if you don't write for the public, who the devil do you write for?

(thunderous applause)

(silencing the uproar with the aid of the little bell)
we trust that this acrimonious but affectionate discussion by his colleagues and friends will have made an impression on the mind of the person criticized, and it is our hope that after sleeping on it, he will abandon his egocentric and negative attitude and generously admit to his errors: let us therefore allow him a few hours of reflection and tomorrow we will hear what he has to say: ladies and gentlemen, the meeting is adjourned

well, my boy: what do you expect me to say?: you've seen for yourself: the outcry is unanimous!: and in your heart of hearts you know that your readers are not unfair: that they have every reason in the world to criticize you: isn't that right?: how much do you want to bet that a little inner voice is telling you the same thing?: I know that it is, and the one thing I have to say to you is this: don't be proud, listen to it: what else would you have me say?: bravo, my boy, you're on the right road, persevere, press on?: but I couldn't possibly bring myself to do that: I am forced to put duty before the bonds of friendship: I am a critic, and hence I am obliged to censure you
Vosk will sorrowfully bow his head, and on so doing will reveal, beneath the splendid, neatly combed toupee he is wearing, a little round bald spot, the size of a priest's tonsure
yes, I realize it's hard to admit the truth, that a sense of false pride causes you to rebel against common sense and says to you: no, no, pay no attention to all these carping critics, you have created a marvelous, unique work and must defend it against wind and tide!: isn't that right, my boy?: ah, what intoxicating words that pride of yours whispers in your ear!: and how beautiful and admirable they would be if only they were true!: but they are not and your own heart tells you so:

what is there for me to do then?, you will say to me: my soul is rent, all the artful castles in the air that my vanity has constructed have come tumbling down with a deafening roar!: must I break my pen in two?: must I end my own life? his voice has gradually become higher in pitch and echoes amid the columns towering above this spot that lies in deepest shadow

ah, no!: never!: listen to what the little worm gnawing at your conscience tells you: abandon once and for all your accursed pride: admit your faults frankly and resolve to correct them: and if you feel like crying, do so: you needn't feel ashamed with me, my boy: that's what I'm here for!: there is no need for pretenses or maybe you think it's not manly to cry?: well, you're wrong, my boy: I've had lots of experience along these lines and I can tell you straight out: all real he-men bawl like babies!

Vosk wipes away a furtive tear, and grabbing you familiarly by the arm, he will lead you off to a dark and quiet corner, far from the men and women who are silently reading or going about their usual business

do you see, my boy?: why reproduce only the ugly, negative side of things?: life is made up of both lights and shadows: thus far you've painted everything black: why not use light tones from now on?

his heavy breath reeks of the tavern or the refectory: fascinated, you will contemplate the tufts of hair growing out of his nostrils and just below the bump at the rims of his ears

your stories are decadent, unwholesome: they lack pleasing details: you run the risk sooner or later of alienating the few readers who are still on your side, don't you think?: the moral and human universe that you put before the public is terribly flat and dull: there is not so much as a trace of charm, of tenderness, of poetry, of profundity in the situations or in the characters: your work isn't a hymn to life, but a satire!: a desolate wasteland!

the tenor voice now reaches the upper tones of its register,

and with a protective gesture he will stretch out his fat hairy
hand and place it paternally on your shoulder
all sincere critics say the same thing: your present universe
is monotonous: the characters are eccentric, scarcely representative at all: the situations that you describe are wildly
improbable: believe me, my boy: you must change
there is a silence
you still have time, my boy: all you need do is firmly resolve
to do so: the path is steep and arduous: but you must take
the upward way: eminent personalities of all persuasions
have already pointed out to you your limitations and faults,
your lamentable stylistic shortcomings
your friend has pulled down the interminable zipper of his
garment and rummages around in the inside pockets until
he finds a yellowed sheaf of clippings that he will sadly wave
in your face
an overwhelming burden of proof, my boy: shall I read these
to you?
his gaze eagerly seeks yours, and once contact has been
made, he will forbearingly cast his eyes downward toward
the pieces of paper
macte animo, post nubila, Phoebus!
his gaze travels from one review to another with a serious,
pained expression as his lips utter the magisterial reproaches as though he were telling the beads of a prickly
rosary
(a) excessive use of foreign phrases
(b) lack of linguistic rigor
(c) suspect representation of reality
(d) inability to communicate the facts coldly and objectively
(e) meaningless accumulation of sick, morbid personal obsessions
(f) deliberate employment of substitutive myths
(g) abandonment of all claim to truth
(h) style that becomes more and more incorrect with each
passing day

(i) continual erosion of his native tongue

Vosk mercifully cuts his reading short and will return these implacable public prosecutors to the inferior hiding place of his garment

you can judge for yourself, my boy: what desolation!: what a distressing vacuum!: you are in a blind alley, do you realize that?

yes, you will stammer

writers younger than you have already received all manner of praise and prizes: admiration pursues them wherever they go: their countrymen are proud of them and the cities in which they have lived vie among themselves for the honor of erecting a monument to them

a brief pause

e tu, dizgraziato, che?

nothing!

precisely, he says: absolutely nothing!: criticisms, reproaches, accusations!: instead of creating solid, real worlds and thus attracting the interest of readers, you keep going all around Robin Hood's barn, getting lost in oneiric labyrinths, getting all involved in your own absurd messes!: and the result is plain to see: neither honors nor rewards nor laurels!: a total disaster!

your professor sighs in the secret darkness of the little booth and will gently hoist you up into his lap

the eagerness to apprehend reality by way of an irrational language leads to egregious errors in judgment, to absolutely delirious hypotheses: promise me that you will change, my boy: you are still young, you have a future ahead of you: do it for my sake, my boy

the prayers and antiphonies of the faithful end the gradual transformation of the place and the odor of incense of your childhood (of the other child, the dead one) will insidiously envelop the line of penitents standing at a distance of nearly twenty-five years away

is there anything else, my boy?

well, you say: I also broke the sixth one
the sixth one! he exclaims
yes, the sixth one
one time or several times?
countless times!
in thought or deed?
in thought and deed!
alone or with others?
alone and with others!
with men or with women?
with men and with women!
with children? he murmurs
with children! with boys! with girls! with old ladies! with old
men!
it's not possible! he moans
yes, yes, you cry: with every sort of creature imaginable!
good heavens!
with dogs! with she-goats! with swans! with dromedaries!
cunnilingus?
cunnilingus!
immissio in anum?
immissio in anum!
coitus inter femora?
coitus inter femora!
fellatio?
fellatio!
eiaculatio praematura?
eiaculatio praematura!
receptaculum seminis?
receptaculum seminis!
in vast distress, he will cross himself repeatedly: the horrendous visions occasioned by your recital appear to have addled his brain, and making a violent effort to control himself,
he will address the Mistress of the Sugar Plantation on
High in a quavering voice that every so often abruptly breaks

altogether: but this time young Mistress Fermina will not take a vial of smelling salts out of her corset nor will she cover her ears in horror: her smiling eyes, delicately delineated by the artist, will narrow in visible disgust, and pointing downward with the thumb of her right hand, like an emperor at a Roman circus, she will clearly indicate that in her opinion the case is hopeless, and that for the good of all concerned, and in particular that of the apoplectic pater, it is best to put an end to little niceties and sentimentality and finish off the guilty party as expeditiously as possible

stripped of the splendid majesty of Changó, you will dedicate to the immaculate Common Mother the first fruits of your poetic offering

> labyrinth of errors
> ora pro nobis!
> fearsome desert
> ora pro nobis!
> haunt of wild beasts
> ora pro nobis!
> lagoon full of slime
> ora pro nobis!
> stony field
> ora pro nobis!
> meadow crawling with serpents
> ora pro nobis!
> flowering orchard that bears no fruit
> ora pro nobis!
> fountain overflowing with afflictions
> ora pro nobis!
> river of tears
> ora pro nobis!
> sea of miseries
> ora pro nobis!

work without recompense
ora pro nobis!
sweet poison
ora pro nobis!
vain hope
ora pro nobis!
false happiness
ora pro nobis!
true Queen Kong

if they were to condemn you to remain shut up in a dark room without a single opening, unable to see even the feeblest ray of light, with no place to lay your head

if the ground you trod were strewn with broken glass, with brambles bristling with thorns, among which poisonous serpents slithered, ceaselessly biting you, and flames enveloped you on all sides, and all this not just for a day or for a week, but for all your life long, is it not true that the very thought would horrify you?

well then, Hell is much more terrible still, and will last for all eternity

an opportune voice will distract you from your terror-stricken perusal of the old manual of piety buried among your papers, and gratefully raising your eyes, you will discover on the other side of the table, in the aseptic and comfortable office painted in soothing pastel colors, an affable and handsome speaker dressed in a surgeon's white smock: sitting next to him, in a more roomy armchair, a colleague of his, also in a surgeon's uniform, gives you a friendly smile and holds out a package of Marlboros to you
would you care for a cigarette?
no, thank you, I don't smoke

you are quite right not to: tobacco is a real poison: but I
don't seem to be able to give up the habit: I've tried a number of times and failed miserably: unfortunately we physicians are not supermen as some people are inclined to believe: we also have our contradictions, our weaknesses: but
we are able to distinguish wheat from tares: so I won't insist
and urge my vice on you as being one that is shared by many
others and hence harmless, for that is a simple-minded argument: it's enough that I'm ruining my own health: but now
that I've said all that, would it bother you if I had one?
not at all, you will say
that's very kind of you
without taking his eyes off you, he will take a Ronson out of
his left pocket, slowly light a cigarette, voluptuously inhale
a mouthful of smoke and then exhale it after a few seconds,
making a perfect spiral in the air
allow me to introduce the two of us: I am Doktor Vosk, the
director of the Normalization Institute in which you find
yourself: my colleague here earned a diploma in psychiatry
after a residency at Bellevue Hospital and has shown great
interest in your case: he is a most faithful disciple of mine,
with whom you may unburden yourself with the utmost
confidence
you will note, as he speaks to you, that the window of the
room has dull gray shatterproof panes and iron bars over it,
and unobtrusively turning your head, you will discover, with
a certain uneasiness, that the doors have no latches and close
automatically from the outside
yes, your medical history interests me, the disciple will say:
the obsessions that plague your writings appear to me to be
extremely dangerous: but I am persuaded that with a little
patience and cooperation on your part they may still be
cured
do you really think so?, you will murmur
yes, through an intensive treatment that gets to the very

bottom of the problem and combats the root of the evil: but we need your willing and sincere collaboration: that is absolutely essential, believe me: you must trust us, and convince yourself that our one concern is your good: we wish to help you to emerge from the mire, and in order to do so you must undergo various tests and answer my questionnaires honestly look, Doktor Vosk will say: here is the first one: unfortunately it's written in English: would you like me to translate it for you?

that isn't necessary, you will say

all right then, read it: make a cross alongside each illness or defect that you now have or have had in the past: ah, and above all don't lie!: don't try to hide anything from us!: in such a case, even with all our experience, neither my disciple nor myself would be able to do anything for you and would find ourselves obliged to declare you officially incurable

Doktor Vosk will shake the ash off his cigarette: and then he will politely hand you a rectangular, carefully typewritten form

MEDICAL EXAMINATION OF APPLICANTS

I certify that I have the following conditions:

Dangerous contagious diseases:

Actinomycosis
Amebiabis
Blastomycosis
Chancroid
Favus
Filariosis
Gonorrhea
Granuloma inguinale
Keratoconjunctivitis
Leishmaniasis
Leprosy

Symphogranuloma Venereum
Mycetoma
Paragonimiasis
Ringworm of scalp
Schistomiasis
Syphilis, infectious stage
Trachoma
Trypanosomiasis
Tuberculosis
Yaws

Mental conditions

Insanity

Mental defect

Psychopathic personality

Narcotic drug addiction

Sexual deviation

Chronic alcoholism

Previous occurrence of one or more attacks of insanity

Patient's signature

Docktor Vosk and his faithful and self-abnegating disciple observe you with a penetrating gaze, and in order to prove your humility and good faith as well as your fervent desires for redemption, you will mark every item on the list with a cross and sign your name at the bottom of the page: the two of them will look it over in silence for a few moments and add a few comments in the margins, then once their examination is concluded, Doktor Vosk will smile with cordial approval

good!: excellent!: I can see that we're on the right track!: your case is serious, extremely serious: but you must not despair: science today works veritable miracles!

our percentage of recoveries is really fantastic, the disciple says

the treatment that we employ has cured cases even worse than yours, Doktor Vosk says

our patients lead perfectly normal lives today, the disciple says

thanks to the frankness, generosity, and warmth of our staff of male nurses, they have clearly seen their errors and we have given them the opportunity of correcting them, Doktor Vosk says

after a few weeks of persuasion, all of them tear up their pretentious manuscripts and begin feverishly to write about their new experiences, in a sort of desperate catharsis, the disciple says

they express very beautiful thoughts amid their anguish and melancholy, Doktor Vosk says they are now writing in a rational and objective manner, the disciple says

they have rid themselves of their obsessions and myths and are faithfully reflecting the outside world, Doktor Vosk says you wouldn't recognize them! the disciple says: they are people as normal as Doktor Vosk or myself!

they have wives and children! Doktor Vosk says: they participate fully in the productive process!: instead of the fleeting erection of a textual pleasure that is purely masturbatory and barren, they plow a fecund, genesic furrow in an alert and attentive public!

and believe me, they owe all of this entirely to us, the disciple says

to our fabulous treatment, Doktor Vosk says

the same one that you are now about to follow!, the disciple says

the very same one!, Doktor Vosk says

a few weeks of intensive care for the normalization process and then a few more weeks in order to avoid a relapse, the disciple says

we isolate the patient from all dangers and risks until the treatment has taken hold and he has adapted to new environmental conditions, Doktor Vosk says

you are a fortunate man, the disciple says

not just fortunate, incredibly fortunate, Doktor Vosk says

a brilliant future awaits you!, the disciple says

we are giving you back your innocence, Doktor Vosk says: here with us, you'll feel like a child!

to the park, running to the park, holding a nursemaid's hand or that of the dead governess, along remote paths covered with fine gravel, winding among flower beds and boxwood hedges, leaving behind little rustic bridges, pavilions, kiosks, little pools and lagoons, statues, heading for the meeting place, where the other children are shouting, tussling, hopping and skipping and leaping, making sand castles, playing on teeter-totters and slides, as nearby nuns laugh excitedly, flutter about in their starched white coifs, organize games of hideandseek runsheeprun hopscotch dance contests, surround him like butterflies of some gigantic extinct species, and Mutter Vosk invites him to join the joyous circle of those who are singing songs together, he's a liddle fraidykatz who doesn't like to play games with his gumpanions at regreation time, am I recht?, she says in her unmistakable teutonic accent, trying to shame him for his shyness, komm on, repead afder me now, mein kind; beep, beep, tell me, liddle bird, vat's this sound that ve haf heard? I'm off to heaven, you vill see, that's vy I beep, vun, two, tree!, leaning down over him so that he will join in the song, beep, beep!, and giving his arm a hard pinch, listen, you sdroke your liddle bird, nicht wahr?, every vunce in a vile, I'll bet a thaler, and don't you play papass and mammass too, you naughdy boy?, whizper in my ear, because these are oggly, oggly thinks, and if the poor Plessed Firgin sees you, she'll chop you hant right off!

the solitary pleasure of writing!
to gently wield the pen, to caress it with adolescent fervor as in the half sleep propitious to manual diversion, to allow its filiform liquor to trickle over the whiteness of the blank page, to attain the delicate perfection of the soloist, to prolong with subtle artifice the tumulary rigor, to postpone the climax indefinitely, to consume your own energy without moderation, to do away with the stubborn avarice of the real order of things: abandoning yourself to the chance inspiration that guides your footsteps in their festive Sunday afternoon wanderings: through Ghardaïa, Istanbul, or Fez: Belleville, Barbès, or the Gare du Nord: like unto a rapine bird hunting for prey, you enter the labyrinths of the urban jungle with the vigilant promptitude of the falcon: awaiting

the sudden magnetism of the body that will irresistibly attract your own and couple the two of them like words joined to each other by the poet in versatile, fleeting conjunction: transforming semantic deviation into a voltaic arc, turning your back on pedestrian logic and its petty contempt: until the moment when the parallel paths of your mutual search come together, the word becomes incarnate, and the amorous copula glows like a resplendent metaphor: disdaining the threatening proximity of the religious, socialist-realist, or psychiatric critic who, firmly entrenched in his erudition, points an accusing finger at the little shrine and loudly proclaims that he has been witness to the mutual and deliberate pleasure of Onan: of the abominable act of wielding the pen without benefit to the public and its multiple and pressing necessities: accompanied by a chorus of upright citizens who appear at the windows and contemplate the spectacle presented by these dregs of humanity with exclamations of virtuous indignation and outcries of fascinated horror

oh, comme c'est dégoûtant!

take a look

it turns my stomach

disgraziato!

monsieur, vous n'avez pas honte?

shoot them, that's what, shoot them!

oh, snap it

please, don't move

regarde, il jouit!

filthy pig!

un momentino, per carità

look at the camera

andiamo, è troppo orrido

when the babelic crowd disperses, the Faithful Disciple will cast his gaze in the direction of the Mistress of the Sugar Plantation on High and young Fermina will frown and point downward once again with the thumb of her right hand, like Caesar after a gladiatorial combat, to clearly indicate that in her opinion the case is hopeless and that for the good of all concerned, and in particular that of the novelistic order and its stipendiary guardians, it is best to put an end to little niceties and sentimentality and finish you, the contumacious, indecent guilty party, off as expeditiously as possible

the Faithful Disciple remains seated in a rigid posture on the other side of the office desk, and after contemplating you with a grave expression, tinged with disapproval, he will nonetheless silently hand you TEST NUMBER TWO

> *Read the following text written by the director of our establishment and comment or expand upon three points of it which have particularly attracted your attention*
> "Today, when the self-styled critical vanguard proposes to 'free literature of the intolerable tyranny of genres,' thus throwing overboard centuries of progress made by the human spirit, it is merely going round and round Robin Hood's barn insofar as it repeats the same tired, timeworn, and now discredited arguments that the surrealists, among others, propounded at least fifty years ago. With a thousand subtleties and otiose hair splitting worthy of the ancient Hellenic sophists, we are told that 'language cannot be a faithful copy of the world,' that 'literature and life are entirely different things,' etc. Resisting the temptation to tell them to go peel a grape, we shall merely leave these elitist mandarins free to divert themselves with their illusions and mirages that obey no rules whatsoever, and shut up in their ivory towers, give voice to a swansong that fortunately no one finds moving. Today's readers still possess an

> unswerving faith in characters: if the novelist loses
> this faith, tomorrow it will be they who will ardently
> write, in real life, the plot of their own novels."

the Faithful Disciple scrutinizes you through his dark glasses,
and eager to ingratiate yourself with him and win at all costs
the coveted normalization that will earn you the applause of
the public and assure you a place of honor among the Giants
of Literature, you will seek the aid of a travel guide, and following the instructions of the test, you will proceed, firstly,
to describe with the maximum possible accuracy the path
that leads directly to Robin Hood's barn

> the road to Robin Hood's barn leads through Sher-
> wood Forest, the typical features of which are tower-
> ing oaks and beeches, with occasional copses of ash
> and yew, and a ground cover in spring of such
> exquisite shy flowers as violets and trilliums . . .

you will interrupt your laborious task of copying, allow the
Disciple to leaf through your commentaries, and without
waiting for his nihil obstat, you will consult various cook-
books, searching in vain for instructions on how to peel
grapes, in view of which, after timidly and respectfully pointing out what must be a slight error on the part of the chief
psychiatrist, you will pass on the comment of a well-known
gastronome with regard to the culinary uses of PEELED
GRAPES

> Grapes may be used in fruit salads, prepared with
> whipped cream or a marinade of fruit juice. Kirsch,
> cointreau, or other liqueurs may be added to the
> latter.
>
> Grapes are also used in the preparation of sauce
> Véronique, to be served with fish, and as a stuffing
> for quail.
>
> They may also be used as a garnish for fresh fruit
> plates.
>
> Small seedless green grapes which do not require
> peeling are to be preferred for all of the above dishes.

this time the Disciple will manifest unmistakable signs of anxiety, but being determined to see your normalization safely home to port and faithfully adapt your writing to the exigencies of the état civil, you will proceed to the third part of the test and ready yourself to paint, with the minuteness of detail of the great masters and their natural and simple style, the living conditions characteristic of habitation in an ivory tower, when suddenly your examiner will snatch the paper out of your hand, and in a fit of anger start to rip it to pieces

listen, young man!: he will say: the way you're going about this is enough to make me tear my hair!

may I point out, sir, that you are absolutely bald?, you will reply

wait a minute, he will say, regaining his composure: let's not confuse things: I'm addressing you in plain, simple Spanish, which you understand just as well as I do: it's no use trying to sell me a cat for a hare

I'm not offering you either one of those two animals, you will say

come off it, he will say: quit playing games, you're not a child any more!: you know very well where the shoe pinches!

on the bunion on my right foot, you will say

stop this nonsense, he will say: I am referring to your answers to the test: you're leading me a merry dance

would you prefer an Aztec two-step?, you will ask

no, no, a thousand times no!, he will shout: isn't there any way to make you understand?: I've been trying my best to explain to you that we speak two different languages!: there's a fly in the ointment, wouldn't you say?

certainly, you reply: though I am unable to determine whether it's a housefly, a tsetse fly, or a horsefly

I'm at the end of my rope trying to get you to see what I mean, he will stammer helplessly

well, perhaps they didn't want to give you enough to hang yourself, you answer all this is absurd, he will say: it's as though you and I were broadcasting on different wavelengths: someone has doubtless prejudiced you against me: otherwise I can't explain all this: there must be a nigger in the woodpile!

poor thing, you will say: shouldn't we try to get him out?

I'm losing my bearings, I tell you, he will say

well, if you lose them, you need only buy some more

I don't know where you went to school, he will say: but your manner of expressing yourself is vulgar: watch your step though!: I warn you I know of more than one way to skin a cat!

does that go for hares too?, you will ask

there are limits to my patience, he will say: mend your ways or I'll wash my hands of you!

the lavatory is straight ahead, you will say

all right!, he will shout: you'll pay for this!

cash or credit?, you will ask

you are impudent and impertinent, he will shout, and I'm sick and tired of your shooting your mouth off!

I don't even have a hunting license, you will point out

leave me alone!, he will say: you can go jump in the lake!

I'd be happy to, but I don't happen to have my swim trunks with me

I can't stand this!, he will howl: I'm about to explode!

and that is literally what happens, without your being able to do anything to prevent it: a bland, gelatinous substance spurts out of his head, as though it were a bursting shell, and splatters all over the walls and ceiling of the ultramodern office painted in restful pastel colors: you wipe the spatters off your face with the third test sheet and calmly walk out, thanks to your skeleton key, through the silent, well-oiled doors of the Normalization Institute (the literal and the figurative meaning blend and become indistinguishable: the possibilities of discourse cancel out with one stroke of the pen the supposed impossibilities of the referent) my disciple!: where is my disciple?, the director will shout my treatment has had a bad effect on him, you will say: while setting me on the right path his brain got overheated and he's been the victim of a terrible explosion

something dreadful is happening to me, V says: intercede in my behalf, I beg you: hurry up!: do something!: those thieving penny-a-line scribblers have gradually stripped me of my assets, my substance, my inalienable possessions: I have lost weight, stature, expression, attributes, character: they have expropriated my typically middle-class family mansion, described in minute detail in countless novels: with its line of balconies with wrought iron railings, its magnificent staircase fallen into ruins, its pretentious drawing room, its table with a brazier underneath it and the wing chair where I went over the accounts of the shop and read the editorials in the newspaper on the crisis of the parliamentary system: and not only the house and furniture, but also my clothing and personal effects: my bowler hat that made me look like a usurious moneylender or a stockbroker, my plaid vest, my velvet evening jacket, the cane with the silver handle, the kid boots and gloves, the leather puttees, the pocket watch and chain bought in the flea market in Madrid: I now lack a past, a profession, typical traits, lineage, ambition, friends: I neither eat nor drink nor smoke nor love nor suffer nor think: I have ceased frequenting literary salons, writing verses, exchanging letters with Swiss lasses, being subject to attacks of dizziness and vertigo, studying books on aesthetics and treatises on economics: they have removed a mole that I had on my left arm (a detail that on many occasions had served to identify me on meeting a close relative whom I had lost sight of) and (this is something I'm most reluctant even to mention, something downright unspeakable) even the scar of an old operation I had on my groin!: but hang on, because I still haven't finished!: those soulless creatures (I am unable to find a politer term to describe them), not content to have robbed me of my real property and my chattel, have also gone so far as to deprive me of a face and a figure! I look into the mirror and see nothing at all!: neither my serene, slightly receding forehead, nor my small dark eyes that are half closed but are nonetheless piercing and searching, nor my pinched, hooked nose which according to the most reliable descriptions give me the noble profile of an illustrious grandee: I have lost the smile that does not abandon my lips even in the gravest circumstances, my expression of aristocratic hauteur, and that gaze of mine full of the fire and determination of geniuses of the old stripe: today no one recognizes me on the street or takes any interest in me or bothers to see what has happened to me: I no longer receive letters, telegrams, postcards, checks, letters of credit, or money orders: I neither sign autographs nor dedicate portraits of myself: my ruin is absolute, my solitude total: and as the final crowning touch (for my misfortunes are comparable to those which overcame patient Job, as we are told in the Bible), they have taken away the last three letters of my name and refer to me only by the initial: they call me just plain V, can you imagine?: not even the blackest totalitarian doctrines which attempt to undermine, with marvelous, glowing promises, the stability and the values of our chaotic contemporary world have gone that far in their plots to erase all distinctions, to do away with individuality, to eliminate, purely and simply, the soul itself!: I have ceased to be a complete, three-dimensional entity, and have instead become V: an initial, a letter, a number!: tell me, mister novelist: is this the paradise to which your revolutionary siren songs lead?: the abolition, the death of the ego?: this is worse than Mao's China!: I am nothing but a voice now: you have reduced me to the murmur of a vague and unidentifiable discourse: not even my voice, but yours, the voice of my master: have you the heart to abandon me like this?: have you no pity for the tears welling up from my broken heart?

as the little voice becomes hysterical and grates unpleasantly in your ears, you will repeat the simple gesture of the Mistress of the Sugar Plantation on High and point downward with your right hand, like an emperor at a Roman circus: whereupon the pitch of the little voice will rise until it resembles the shrill scream of cattle being led to the slaughter: but fortunately it will soon die away, and when you let go of your pen and get up to urinate and wash your hands, this time it will be Our Lady of the Bosque, alias Mistress Fermina, who will have gone straight to the devil

the king is dead, long live the king
once the brief responsory for the eternal repose of the character is concluded, you will descend the first flight of steps of the Sacré-Coeur and stroll in the direction of the Place du Tertre, along the little streets of the Free Commune of Montmartre of yesteryear: as usual, the terraces of the cafés are crowded with tourists and those portrait artists who practice their noble art leaning over canvases resting on easels, with brushes and palette in hand, reproducing for a few dozen francs the physiognomy, painted from life, of thousands of transients eager for an imperishable souvenir of the place: paying no attention to the machine-gun fire from the Japanese movie and still cameras, they outline profiles, sketch in features, fill out faces, capture expressions that cleverly reveal the soul and the character of the ephemeral, interchangeable, endlessly repeated models: next to you, a Flemish gentleman, whose name embroidered in red on the left-hand breast pocket of his jacket establishes a false, almost insulting, relation with that remote, visionary countryman of his who masterfully painted the devil expelling

wanton souls through the pupil of his abominable eye, will contemplate with satisfaction his image promoted to the rank of a Work of Art and will reward the skill of the portraitist with discreet munificence: as you walk off down the hill, the thought will occur to you that his face seems familiar, and as you saunter along the Boulevard de Rochechouart, you will wonder, for a fleeting moment, whether the two of you have not met somewhere before

Hence unafraid now, like someone with nothing to lose, like that person who now finds your company boring, like a poor traveler on foot who makes his way along without fear of brutal highwaymen, singing aloud.

—FERNANDO DE ROJAS, *La Celestina*

to eliminate from the corpus of the novelistic work the last vestiges of theatricality: to transform it into a discourse without a trace of a plot: to explode the inveterate notion of the character of flesh and blood: replacing the progressio dramatica of events with the conjuncture of textual clusters obeying a single centripetal force: the nucleus that determines writing itself, the genesic fountain pen that is the source of the textual process: improvising the architecture of the literary object, making of it not a tissue of logico-temporal relations, but rather an ars combinatoria of elements (oppositions, repetitions, variations, symmetrical diversions) on the whiteness of the rectangular page: rivaling painting and poetry on a purely spatial plane: indifferent to the threats, be they overt or covert, of the police commissioner–gendarme–customs officer disguised as a critic: deaf to the siren songs of mercenaries who tilt lances for content-in-the-service-of-a-cause, and to the petty criteria of social usefulness

▲▲▲▲▲▲▲▲▲▲▲ ▲

the paschal candle?: or the passion candle?: on the blank, immaculately virginal rectangle the double enticement (error, trap?) dizzyingly offers itself to your pen: the arbitrariness of the narrative, continually disguised by misleading sleight-of-hand tricks: seated on top of (underneath?) the play table, chilled by the feeble solar ray that penetrates the thick wall: a call signal (a presumable indication) of the rainy day which, with the dryness of a desert plain, sets the fertile antarctic landscape on fire: well-plowed streets and avenues, stone sycamores, gardens irrigated by taxis and streetcars: with your pen in your mouth, aiming bullets (words) in the many possible directions that you might take: a rigorous, restrictive causality, the miserly determinism of the sad bird in hand versus the intoxication of the hundred that are airborne: logical actions, coherent syntax, clear motivations!: a miserable succession of effects and causes, the tired, anemic invention of a careworn, sleepless Biblical Jehovah!: dreaming of the inordinate pleasure of the totally capricious and absolutely improbable: an infinite universe of the unlikely in which unreason would flourish and fascinating chaos scribble an enigmatic, liberating proliferation of signs all over the whiteness of the page

▲▲▲▲▲▲▲▲▲▲▲ ▲

the autonomy of the literary object: a verbal structure with its own unique relations of signs, a language perceived in and of itself and not as the transparent intercessor of an alien, outer world: through the act of delivering words from their subservience to a pragmatic order that turns them into mere vehicles of pure reason: of logical thought that scornfully uses them without taking into account their specific weight and value: fulfilling the functions of representation, expression, and summons inherent in an oral communication, whose components (sender, receiver, context, contact) also bring into play (albeit in a different manner) at the instant of reading a fourth function (an aesthetic one?) that will be focused exclusively on the linguistic sign: freeing language, thanks to this function, of its simoniac, ancillary entelechy: transmuting semantic anomaly into the generative nucleus of poetry and thereby uniting, in polysemic harmony, sexuality and writing: a general scorn for the useful, procreative series, thereby changing the abominable and sterile pleasure into a figure of speech, the crimine pessimo into an existential metaphor: finally resolving, at the end of this long journey, the secret equation lying behind your twofold deviation: unproductive (onanistic) manipulation of the written word, self-sufficient (poetic) enjoyment of illicit pleasure

▲▲▲▲▲▲▲▲▲▲▲▲ ▲

you will reproduce once more, in your fine handwriting, the letter of the aged slave women whose words, on being read, shed light on and give meaning to a life (yours?) organized (as a function of this letter) as an uninterrupted process of breaking off and breaking free, knowing that you possess the key that allows you to interpret its trajectory (that of the other) retrospectively, with the awareness of having reached the end of a cycle, following which, having undergone a change of skin, having paid a debt you owe, you may henceforth live in peace

my master

your lordship left me in the house of your children little mistress Fermina and little master Jorgito and I have done my very best to keep the promises I made to your lordship but when mistress Telesfora came to mistress Ferminita's house they made me leave and put me out on the street, so to speak, and that is where I am, still waiting for your lordship

I will also tell your lordship that mistress Telesfora sold Julian to Tomabella and Tomabella sold him to Montalvo and since summer your son Jorgito has refused to give him a single cent

may your lordship see fit to change this situation in some way since your humble servant has nothing to eat and would be much obliged if your lordship would help me

fond regards to Petra to Maria to mistress Flora to mistress Angeles to mistress Adelaida to mistress Josefita and to her ladyship

and your lordship's obedient slave seeks only to do
his bidding and asks his blessing

Casilda Mendiola

a cry of pain
the secret source of your pen's process of liberation
the hidden reason for your moral, artistic, social, religious,
sexual deviation

▲▲▲▲▲▲▲▲▲▲▲ ▲

ten years before, in the space of your own writing
the Zoco Grande spread out before you, vast, motley,
polychrome, with its awnings, its open air shops, its bazaars
with the sun beating down on them, and amid the incom-
prehensible gabble of the Arab merchants and the shrill
sound of the water vendors' bells, you heard the woman's
voice, or rather, her accent, the concentrated product, it
would seem, of long centuries of stable order, a hierarchical
sense of duty, the awareness of a lofty mission to take command of the destinies of other peoples, a blind faith in the
proper functioning of the laws that wisely govern the course
of the world
move away, Paco, he might brush against you!
you have turned around to see who has uttered these
words: a good-looking woman so typical of the sunnyspanish
peninsula that she turns your stomach, dressed to the hilt,
made up, dyed, painted, bathed in the aura of haute couture
costumes, perfumes, hair rinses, mascara, nail polish doubtless purchased in the elegant boutiques of the Faubourg
Saint-Honoré by the husband with a massive jawbone, a
Bourbon nose, a meticulously trimmed little hairline mustache whose tips resemble the sign over a Spanish ñ, eyes
hidden behind dark glasses, with heavy tortoise-shell frames
that conceal his temples like horse blinders
the fucking bastards, you thought

(in front of them, and in front of you too, an Arab beggar of an indeterminable age appeared to sum up in his person all the physical taints and defects of the human race
filth
misery
rags
sores dripping with pus)
I wish, you said to yourself, that I could inspire such horror, unite in my person the abjectness, the vileness, the hideous corruption capable of summoning forth the virtuous scorn of this stinking couple
and as the scraggly almond tree which in the icy heart of winter suddenly and miraculously bursts into flower, the beggar had turned into an enviable and precious symbol in your eyes, his former ugliness transmuted in an alchemical crucible, the very emblem and exemplar of an extraordinary beauty
you knew from that moment on that no morality, no philosophy, no aesthetic would prove to have any validity whatsoever when confronted with the flock of your ex-countrymen rendered utterly despicable by five centuries of conformism, unless they risked provoking the sort of disgusted comments forthcoming from this couple at the sight of the wretched beggar
deliberately laughable ones
willfully shocking ones
keeping you safe from the snares and traps of a loathsome respectability
a life of your own, on the margins of society
sooner or later, you thought
(and still think)
certain people, perhaps, would understand

▲▲▲▲▲▲▲▲▲▲▲▲ ▲

monotony or an accident?: reminding certain people of a

scratched phonograph record, the history of your ex-homeland is also reminiscent of Ravel's interminable bolero

in the reception room of the prefecture of Bayonne, in the former département des Basses-Pyrenées, the immortal pretenders to the throne are exhibiting their coats of arms and titles before a pompous Corsican with the heart of a corsair: the family pedigree is excellent and appeals, it would appear, to the snobbish pretensions of the ambitious maître de maison: the Cid naturally figures in this illustrious lineage, along with the wild and woolly Don Pelayo: one of the pretenders casually mentions his consanguinity with Tubal: another affirms that Wamba was his uncle, and his cousin, if you recall?, was Sancho el Bravo: the triumph of the royal peacocks is tinged a bright carmine red rivaling a commercial food coloring, chatterbox Sunnyspain mouths banalities, and Scotch plaid passes itself off as being Bourbon

chroniclers have commented for century after century on such heraldic tournaments, sowing confusion and doubt in the logical, cartesian mind of your ancient concierge of the rue Poissonnière

monsieur, par charité, où va l'Espagne?

à sa perte, j'espère

your body will not fertilize its soil: or will do so only if, possessed of a powerful toxic substance, its parasitic, perturbing activity gradually embraces the entire length and breadth of the peninsular space, little by little contaminating the national tree of letters until the latter dries up, like that accursed, tortured fig tree which the Bible severely chastens: but should reality not yield to your oneiric assaults, you must decide as of now what fate you consign this body to: its name will never grace schoolhouses statues public squares avenues parks: birds will not alight on its laurels, dogs will not stain its pedestal, merry, piping children's voices will not pronounce its syllables: past recovery, irredeemable, no one, absolutely no one, will claim its remains: and sparing them an obscene symbiosis with the land that you hate you will allow them to repose in the peace of a Moslem cemetery: amid the multitude of anonymous gravestones eroded by the breath of the insatiable wind: a circumspect geometry of overlapping scales and intersecting lines, crawling dunes that caress and smother in a sly, serpentine, voracious embrace: totally fused with the sterile sand: become a part, finally, of a barren landscape: unless, like the needy of your native land in the years that followed the terrible cataclysm, you sell it to a morgue or a teaching hospital for the instruction and practice of future Galens who may one day be capable of diagnosing the reasons for the collective ancestral case of constipation

▲▲▲▲▲▲▲▲▲▲▲ ▲

the cycle of biological evolution that converts the larva into an insect of sumptuous and splendid appearance, in no way resembling its obscure origins and turning its back on them, is now completed
like a batrachian whose successive, spectacular transmutation is neither accompanied nor followed by any moral apothegm
like Proteus, or a quick-change artist or a transvestite who stages his act in full view of an audience that is at once mocking and mocked
you have transformed yourself and transformed the instrument whereby you express yourself, leaving behind on each sheet of white paper rags and tatters of your former personality until you have at last reached your present state in which a blurred, nominal façade is all that identifies you
like that elusive, alienated, evasive old woman who, having put a sudden end to her previous life and ceased to recognize

her own family, retains only a veneer of courtesy that allows her the sort of impersonal interchange and dialogue with her anguished grandson that she might have with some stranger in a doctor's waiting room

so here you are now, after an arduous series of changes and metamorphoses, in an inevitable moment of melancholy, autumnal farewell

apostasies, transgressions, exile have forever estranged you from the native fauna, and the urbane commonplaces that you occasionally exchange with them are something as mechanical and empty as the faint smile of the grandmother on the memorable day when she failed to recognize him

him, but not you

that other whose changes of skin serve as signs, prudently strewn along the way, à la Tom Thumb, marking the adventures and misadventures of his proud, solitary treason

▲▲▲▲▲▲▲▲▲▲▲ ▲

if you write in the future, it will be in another language: not in the one that you have repudiated, the one you bid farewell to today after having turned it upside down, plunged it into chaos, desecrated it: an attempt at boring from within that goes to make up for the present, which, much against your will, you offer it: adding your modest artifact to its monument, but at the same time distilling the agent (caustic, corrosive, mordant) which corrupts and corrodes it: an artful gift (yours), curling back upon itself like the tail of a scorpion: an offering (its) with in cauda venenum: an ambiguous relation that has deprived you of sleep until you reach the logical conclusion of this diversion: the liberation of the instrument and vehicle of your (its) rupture: knowing that from this moment on you (it) may sleep in peace: with a clear conscience, knowing that the evil deed has been consummated: an infamous progeny, its (your) subversion (ideological, narrative, semantic) will continue on its own its labor of sapping and undermining till the end of time

▲▲▲▲▲▲▲▲▲▲▲▲ ▲

from this point on, break the habit of the language that was yours, begin by writing it in accordance with simple phonetic intuitions, without troubling yourself to ask the permission of Doña Hakademe, in order to foller from now on the trew speach patters of millyuns of spikers who youse it everie day without reelizing their vilating the penile code impozed by its mendarins, fergetting lil by lil everythin they taut you, in a deliverate and lusid effert to illiterate yerself that will lede you to renownse the wurds of yer naytive tung one by one and finaly replayce them by that lugha al arabya eli tebdá tadrús chuya b-chuya, lugha uára bissaf ualakini eli tjab bissaf, knowing verie well that from now on lassmék t-takalem mesyan ila tebghi tsáfar men al bildan mselma ua tebghi taáref ahsán r-rjal who enspired your tekst but wont rede it, rjal min Uxda Tenira Uahran Ghasauet El-Asnam Tanxa Dar-Bida whos wisdomme led you to the Perfict Nowledge of yerself and the posebility of ekspresing it by freeing yerself of yer preevius emposture and thanx to the practus of a bodie language, of a Wurd made trulie fleshe, of tebdá kif uáhed l-arbi al idu sghera ua min baád al idu Kbira bex temxi l-xamá ua tqrá al surat eli tjab

       qul ya ayuha al-kafirún
       la a budu ma ta budún
       ua-la antum abiduna ma a bud
       ua-la ana abidum ma abattúm
       ua-la antum abiduna ma a bud
       la-kum dinu-kum ua-li-ya din

الناس لي ماينصمونيش مايبقاوش يتبعوني

علاقتنا انتهت

أنا بدون شك في الجهة الأخرى

مع المساكين لي دائما

يوجدوا السكين